HOOD DRIVEN

A Crime Novel
By D Mack

Deep-Street Publications

Facebook: Hood Driven

Twitter: @HoodDriven

Instagram: @hooddrivenbook

Copyrights © 2004, 2009-Revised 2021

ISBN 978-0-615-28732-4
Cover Design: S. M./ W. C
Printed in the United States of America

PLEASE DO NOT ATTEMPT ANY OF THE
THINGS DEPICTED WITHIN THIS STORY.. THIS
IS FOR ENTERTAINMENT PURPOSES ONLY.

By no means do I glorify violence. I just touch on reality
the way it was revealed to me and so many others like me.
It is what it is.

This book is dedicated to everybody who jumped out on faith, or who will someday jump out on faith to turn their positive dreams into their reality.

And to my daughter Priya A. Mack, the best part of my world. You are my treasure.

Lovin you eternally,
Daddy.

As long as the sky is blue and the grass is green, negativity will at some point in time make its way into the mix of anything positive. There are no brakes on destiny; therefore, it can't be stopped.

As the cream Cutlass came to a screeching halt in front of the burgundy Benz, four oversized men quickly exited the Cutlass and aggressively snatched the two occupants out of the Benz. They forced them into the Cutlass, then two of the assailants eagerly jumped in the Benz and followed the Cutlass to their destination. When they pulled up to the two-family flat ten minutes later on Mack and Gray Street, they cruelly shoved the two men inside.

"Whuddup Bo-Bo? Whuddup Spade?" asked the older man they called Skin. Neither of the two answered as they stood there dressed in matching Celtics starter jackets, Lee jeans, and green and white Adidas top-tens. Skin took a pull off his Newport cigarette then casually replied,

"Yall sit down."

Bo-Bo and Spade complied.

"Now tell me what happened to my work, dawg?" He asked in a voice of unquestionable annoyance. Bo-Bo nervously began to speak."Man I think that bitch Teresa from St. Clair set us up, because she called me and told me that a nigga wanted to get some work, and soon as we got there the police came from everywhere. We had to throw the work and the heaters and get in the wind dawg, straight-up."

The dark-complected slim man took another pull from his Newport before casually responding.

"So you tellin' me that you had to just throw ten kilos away?" Spade and Bo-Bo stared nervously at Skin before Bo-Bo answered.

"Yeah man, that's what happened." Skin took another pull from the cigarette then mashed it out in the ashtray in a heated manner. He stood up from the table, walked over to the window, and signaled for the other two men who were sitting in the Benz watching the front door, to come inside.

The moment they entered, the first man knocked Spade out of the chair with a baseball bat. While one of the other men swiftly kicked Bo-Bo out of his chair. Bo-Bo quickly tried to get back up, but immediately got knocked back down. The four men didn't waste any time kicking, stomping, and violently beating them with baseball bats.

After a few moments of witnessing the assault, Skin gave the men a signal to stop, then casually walked over to them and grimaced,

"Now you lil bitches got thirty days to get my money."

Bo-Bo and Spade staggeringly stood to their feet. They both knew it could've been a lot worse, and that the only reason they were spared is to do just what the man said, 'Get his money.'

As they walked out the house pass their attackers, they all traded mean stares with one another. The moment they made it to the car, Bo-Bo instinctively toyed with the open cut on his bald head, while Spade looked in the mirror at his freshly missing front tooth. He suddenly stared at Bo-Bo for a few minutes without speaking. Then spoke up as his built-up thoughts could no longer be contained. He blurted out,

"Man look at this shit! Them bitch-ass niggas got off on us dawg." Bo-Bo nodded in agreement, then replied.

"We lucky we still breathin' nigga. And you da' one who got us into this shit in the first place, givin that soft-ass nigga Rodney five birds." Spade interrupted.

"Hold up dawg, the nigga told me he had a sale fo'em, and he usually come through on that tip and you know it. So don't start pointin' fingers-n-shit nigga. And if you really wanna get technical, let's talk about how much money yo' ass been spendin' lately on cars, clothes, and trickin wit 'dem nuthin-ass bitches. So get some balance in yo' conversation when you start talkin 'bout fuck ups, cause both of us definitely did our share of that. Now we gotta figure out how we gon' get up on this nigga's money, cause you know how that silly ass nigga play...Damn!" Spade slammed his fist against the dashboard before continuing.

"If that clown-ass lame wasn't so gottdamn guarded, I woulda' slumped his bitch-ass a long time ago. But it's all good. They say good things come to those who wait, so we gotta be patient dawg. In the meantime, I think I know a way we can get a nice piece of that money we owe, and then some."

Bo-Bo interrupted.

"Dawg, let's just sell the Benz and the Wrangler jeep." Spade looked at him sarcastically before responding.

"Man we don't got time for that shit, and I ain't sellin my shit noway. I told you I got something up, and if this don't work out, we might just have to go to war with that skinny ass nigga... Unless, we catch up with that hoe-ass nigga Rodney within thirty days and he still got our work or money with him, know what I'm sayin. I heard that his bitch-ass ran to North Carolina with our shit for a quick flip. And if that's true, we takin every dolla dat nigga got on'em when we catch that bitch. But we'a check into it after we see what's up with this other thang I'm focused on. So just chill dawg, I got this."

CHAPTER 2

"Ronald! You should know by now that I don't tolerate horse playing in my class." shouted the fourth grade teacher Ms. Smith. "Now both of you go stand in the corner and face the wall until the bell rings."

Ron and Sheila both walked to the corner and stood there facing the wall until the dismissal bell rung.

"She make me sick," said Sheila as her and Ron departed the classroom.

"I'll see you later," replied Ron when he saw one of his best friends coming his way.

"What's up Ray Ray?"

"Nothing man, what's up?"

"Man you know she like you, right."

"Who Sheila?"

"Yeah Ray. Sheila."

"She is kinda cute," confessed Ray Ray.

"Maybe I'll holla at her later, but let's go to the arcade and see if we see Pooh, Smoke and Bam."

They walked four blocks to the arcade, and when they entered, they saw their friend's playing the classic video games pacman and space invaders.

"What's up yall?" Ron spoke as they approached them. Pooh walked up and slapped five with them, then Smoke and Bam spoke as they continued to work the game controllers. They stayed in the arcade for the next hour eating candy and playing video games. And just as they were about to leave, Bo-Bo and Spade pulled up in the burgundy 300 series Benz with the gold rims.

As they walked in, they spoke to the youngsta's, then Bo-Bo handed each of them five dollars apiece to play the video games. They all accepted the money except lil Ray Ray. He was taught not to accept money from strangers. He had seen them drive through the hood from time to time, but he didn't know them. Although he did admire the way they dressed and the fancy cars they drove, his father had firmly planted the *"no money from strangers"* policy in his head.

Ray Ray assumed they were rich drug dealers because they always had money. He glanced at the tattoo on Bo-Bo's right hand that rested between his thumb and index finger that read *'G-Life,'* while Bo-Bo kept trying to hand him the money.

Finally, Bo-Bo was distracted by the owner of the arcade who yelled out.

"Bo-Bo, you and Spade come on back here and holla at me." Bo-Bo shook lil Ray Ray on the head and said,

"That's right lil man, stick to yo' guns." Then he walked off with the dark-skinned man with the braided hair and missing tooth known as Spade.

Everybody in the hood knew that the owner of the arcade known as big C was the biggest weed man in the hood, so Ray Ray figured that they were probably just passing through to cop some weed. After another 30 minutes had passed, Ray Ray and his friends agreed to meet back up with each other after they changed out of their school clothes. Ron, Smoke, Pooh and Bam showed up at Ray Ray's doorstep at the designated time, waiting for him to come out. As they waited, lil Ray's father pulled up in a new black 1985 Cherokee truck with the temporary license plate tag still in the window. His 6'5 frame emerged from the truck with the persona of a man who was sure of himself. He smiled at the boys and spoke to them as he walked up on his porch.

"Whuddup young hustlers?"

"Hey big Ray." The boys spoke and whispered to one another as he walked in the house. They admired his full-length leather jacket and his black alligator skin boots... Finally, Ray Ray emerged from the house with his shovel in hand.

"Bout time," said Bam. "Wit yo' slow butt."

"Shut up man and let's get 'dis money." said Ray Ray as they walked off the porch with shovels in hand into the December air, headed to the Gross-Point suburban side of town to make some pocket change.

Knock! Knock!

"Ray Ray knock a little harder and stop knockin like a sissy," Smoke joked.

"Man shut up and look through the window to see if you see anybody."

Just as Smoke peeped through the window, the door opened and the elderly white woman asked,

"May I help you young men?"

Ron was about to address her question, but Ray Ray shot him a look that said, *"shut up and let me handle this."*

"Yes mam, we would like to know if we can shovel the snow off of your sidewalk and driveway for a small fee?"

"Why of course you can." answered the woman, and the five of them began shoveling the snow. When they finished, the lady gave each of them five dollars. They thanked her then went to several more houses and made more money until they tired themselves out.

They all went back to Ray Ray's house for awhile before going home because they knew that big Ray would give them a bonus for today's work. He always told his son Ray Ray and his friends about the importance of a working man. And even though he was a hustler and had money, he didn't want to raise his son to depend on someone always giving him something out of love. He loved his son more than anything in this world and would give him his very last dollar, but the rest of this great big world wouldn't.

He wanted his son to know that the world didn't work like that, so he would always teach lil Ray Ray to be independent and realistic. And it always made him proud to see his only son taking heed to his words without always having to be reminded.

Big Ray would always meet Ray Ray and his friends more than half way whenever they took the initiative to show effort, so he ordered three large pizzas for the boys and promised to by each of them new winter coats the following day. They were excited as always and looked at big Ray as their hero.

After they were almost through with the pizza, Ray Ray's mother Cheryl walked out of the room and asked big Ray to go to the store and get her some Newport cigarettes. He agreed, then looked over at Ray Ray.

"Run to the store for me son to get ya' mama some squares."

"Okay dad, but first I gotta take a shi-, excuse me, I mean I gotta do number two." They all burst out laughin, then Ron stepped up and said,

"I'll go big Ray." Big Ray handed him a ten dollar bill.

"Get two packs and keep the change. And come right back 'cause it's dark outside."

Ron left and made it to the store in no time, but just before he walked in, he was stopped by the neighborhood wino that everybody called Sporty. The hood gave him that name because no matter how dirty or bummy he was, he would always wear his clothes as if he had on the most expensive attire in the city. He wore his bee-bop hat as if it was a Dobb or a Stetson. And his stride was that of a pimp straight out the late 1960's. Ron always laughed at the way he would sway his brown frail body and talk with a drag.

"Hey youngblood. What it is?"

"Ain't nothing Sporty, what's up?"

"Youngblood let me hold a little change so I can get up on me a sandwich, I ain't had nothing to eat in days."

"Sporty you lyin yo' butt off, you gon' use that money to get that Wild Irish Rose in ya' life." Sporty cracked a smile at how hip the youngsta was to his game, but he still stuck to the script.

"Naw youngblood, it's about hunger, straight up baby boy."

"Okay man, check this out, I'll buy you a submarine sandwich, a'ight."

"Aw youngblood that would be awfully generous of you but I don't eat meat baby boy, it's a habit I picked up back in the day when I was in the joint." Ron burst out laughin because he knew Sporty was runnin game.

"Sporty I ain't stupid and I know what's up, but I got you anyway when I come out the store, okay."

"Aw youngblood that's a beautiful thang baby, I'll be right here."

Ron shook his head and walked in the store smilin. He went straight to the potato-chip rack and got a couple bags of hot hots, then went to the coolers and got a red faygo pop.

As he walked up to the counter, he noticed the arab man who owned the store locking the front door, then turn around and face him with a strange look on his face. Suddenly he leaped forward grabbing Ron, knocking all the items out his hand. He slapped Ron across the face and yelled,

"I told you I would get you, I told you not to steel out of my store." Ron raised his hands up to block the constant blows, but the man continued to assault Ron despite his cries and the fresh blood that trickled from his lip. Suddenly, Sporty heard the screams from Ron, so he ran up to the door and attempted to snatch it open but it didn't budge. Then he looked through the window and grimmed at the drama that he saw taking place. He quickly started pounding on the plexi-glass door yelling.

"Whut the fuck is you doing to my nephew, open up this muthafuckin door!" At that very instance, Ron managed to break free from the man and run to the back of the store. He quickly grabbed one of the 12 ounce bottles of faygo cola, then hid behind one of the aisles. The man ignored Sporty's attempt to make him stop, and slowly walked from aisle to aisle breathing heavy in search of Ron.

"I told your leetle oss dat I was going to get you, didn't I?"

"Leave me alone!" screamed Ron. "I didn't steal nothing from you."

"You leetle bastard, you're a liar," replied the man as he inched his way closer to where Ron was hiding. Ron was terrified and he had no idea how he would make it out of the store.

His heart was racing fast, but he finally told himself

he would have to calm down and think if he didn't want to get annihilated by the man. He took a deep breath, then slowly peeped around the aisle that he was leaning against to see if the man was in view.

He wasn't, and being a blessing in disguise, he noticed the keys to the front door dangling from the key-hole. His mind started racing because he knew that he may only have one chance at making it to the door. Suddenly, he was gripped by fear as the arab man rammed him up against the back of the aisle by his neck. As Ron squirmed and fought to get a loose, the man applied more pressure to his neck with one hand, while repeatedly slapping him across the face with the other.

After a few moments of Ron trying to wiggle his ten year old body free from the man, he realized he still had the 12 ounce faygo cola in his hand. He knew it was now or never, so he gripped the bottle tight, and with all his might, he slammed it against his attackers skull then ran to the front door as fast as he could. He turned the key and opened the door, falling into the hands of Sporty.

Sporty quickly examined his face and asked him if he was alright. Ron shook his head yes, then Sporty ran toward the man. He reluctantly helped him off the floor and walked him behind the counter. He got on the man's store phone and called big Ray, then looked at the man square in his eyes and squawked,

"Whut the fuck is wrong with you desert muthafuckas! Huh? You think you can just come over to America and bully people that's been bullied all of their fuckin lives? You funny talkin muthafuckas are worse than the white man, and what I should be doing is making that gash on the side of your big ass head bigger. Cause that's fucked up how you did my lil nephew tonight. And I still haven't forgot about that shit you did last year to that poor little girl's father, so you just sit there and bleed you ornery muthafucka."

Big Ray pulled up a few moments later. He instructed lil Ray and the boys to stay in the truck, then walked over to Ron who was standing in front of the store. He briefly analyzed his wounds, and was relieved to see they weren't severe or life threatening. Afterwards, he stormed in the store where Sporty and the arab man was, and immediately collard the arab man up. Sporty swiftly pulled him off.

"Be cool big Ray, I don't like this piece of shit either, but I ain't trying to do no time for him, and neither are you."

Big Ray was furious, but he knew Sporty was right, so he attempted to take what was suppose to be a deep breath, but was more like a huffing bull ready to charge at any moment. He looked at the man angrily, then spoke as calmly as he could.

"Why in the fuck did you put your hands on him?" The arab man took a deep swallow of his own spit before answering.

"He steel out of mee store several times, but I could never catch he'm. Mee lose money dat way. Mee tryeeng to run business."

Big Ray called for Ron to come in the store. When he came in, big Ray looked at him sincerely and asked,

"Have you ever stole anything out of this man's store?"

Without hesitation, Ron answered no. Big Ray could always tell whenever one of the boys would lie to him, and he knew that Ron was telling the truth. And it was that very instant that he put two and two together. He figured he knew what happened.

He walked out the store and returned a few moments

later with his son Ray Ray, and soon as the owner saw him, his eyes widened and his mouth dropped to the floor.

"Oh me God! It eece two of them." Ron and Ray Ray were of no kin, but they looked like identical twins. And they had been going through these mistaken identity situations every since they met.

Big Ray looked at lil Ray disappointingly before questioning him.

"Son, have you ever stole anything out of this man's store?" Lil Ray gave a brief pause before answering, then confessed.

"Yeah dad, I stole from him." Big Ray was furious all over again because he had taught his son better than that. And besides that, he hated a thief. But despite his anger, he knew his son had a helluva motive behind his actions. He knew that lil Ray would stand firm on anything he did as long as he felt it was justified, so he simply asked him why.

"Why son, why did you steal?" Ray Ray looked directly at the arab man and angrily blurted,

"Because that punk right there beat that man to death last year with a tire-iron all because the man asked him to stop saying sexual things to his thirteen year old daughter."

Ray Ray began to cry as he continued.

"And he beat him to death in front of his daughter and he ain't do no time in prison. Fuck him daddy!!" He shouted as his tears continued to flow. Normally big Ray would've disciplined Ray Ray about his vulgar language, but in this case, he gave him a pass and let him get it off his chest because he knew his son was upset. He felt his pain, and on top of that, he didn't like the arab man either.

Sporty sat there staring at the man with disgust on his face because he was also there when the arab man beat the black man to death. He felt bad because he wasn't able to assist the dead man due to a prior debt that had caught up with him and landed him in a wheel chair with both legs broke. He was helpless at the time, and all he could do was watch. Big Ray strolled up to the arab man and slapped him viciously across the face.

"That's for putting your hands on a child that you thought was mines."

Another slap followed the first one.

"And that's for the man you killed in front of his baby. And I want you to keep this in mind muthafucka, just like the hood burned down your other store for that bullshit you pulled, this one can be burned down too. And Ray Ray, from now on, I don't want you or any of your friends to come to this store for nothin. Go around the corner to them other arabs, even though they don't give a fuck about a nigga either, at least they know how to act a little better."

The arab man sat there holding the side of his face as big Ray, Sporty and the boys walked out. Big Ray handed Sporty a twenty dollar bill and thanked him for helping out, then pulled off in his truck. The ride home was silent aside from a few coughs from Bam. Big Ray didn't have the radio on, and lil Ray was all too familiar with the scene. He knew his father was in deep thought whenever he rode like this, and he respected it and said nothing to break his solitude.

As they pulled up to the house, big Ray yelled out,

"What the fuck is this." as the barrel of a nine millimeter was pressed aggressively against his temple.

"Shut the fuck up and get out the car slow," demanded

the masked gunman.

"Damn!" Squawked big Ray as he looked at the boys. He turned toward the gunman and pleaded.

"Man I got babies in the car so be cool." The gunman pressed the gun up to his temple with more force then balked.

"First of all, you don't call no fuckin shots, so do what the fuck I tell you to do chump. And second of all, I give less than a fuck about these lil punk-ass kids. Now do yo'self a favor and get yo' ass out the truck."

They all stepped out and walked in tight formation up to the front door. Big Ray's mind was racing as he thought of what he could possibly do to turn this situation around in his favor. He had been in the streets for a long time and this wasn't new to him, but the only advantage to him then oppose to now, is that he didn't have a family. And for the first time in his life, he actually regretted the fact that he had a family. Because the perpetrator's could easily use his family as leverage against him, which is exactly what they planned to do. Big Ray Mack had planned on marrying Cheryl Thompson shortly after Ray Ray was born, but he ended up postponing it for years because of the conflict-of-interest that plagued his world. He was already entangled within the constraints of an unholy matrimony, he was ultimately married to the game. And despite how deeply Cheryl loved him, she stood firm on the fact that neither her, or her son Ray Ray would share his last name until he was ready to divorce the underworld completely and give her his heart in it's entirety.

Big Ray's thoughts were broken when he noticed another masked gunman answer his front door after the other one knocked. As they walked in the house, the first thing they noticed was his woman tied to a chair with a piece of grey duct tape across her lips. The flushed expression on her crimson face exposed her level of fear. She was petrified, and big Ray knew he had to do something fast.

Ray Ray's heart skipped a beat when he saw his mother in the life threatening predicament. He wanted to burst out in tears, he wanted to run up and save her, he wished the gunman would just leave and his life would return to normal. But he somehow knew it was all just wishful thinking, so he reflected back to something his father always told him about situations like this. *"Never show any emotions, just use your energy to think your way out of it and say as little as possible, but make sure everything you say is respectful to the perpetrators in hopes of not triggering their anger."*

Big Ray walked toward his wife to comfort her, but was immediately stopped by one of the men.

"Get yo' ass back over there guy, she a'ight, and if you wanna keep it that way, it's up to you. Now listen up cause I'ma keep it real simple. Open up yo' safe and let me get that change outta there and we outta here."

Big Ray felt relieved when he heard the man say they would leave as soon as they got the money, so he walked to the built-in wall-safe in the kitchen behind one of the cabinets and opened it for them. They pushed him aside as soon as it was open, then took the 45 caliber handgun and the fifteen thousand in cash that it contained.

"Man whut the fuck is this!" Yelled one of the men.

"Where is the rest of it?"

Big Ray looked at the man with a sincere facial expression before responding.

"Man that's all of it."

The two gunman looked at each other momentarily, then one of them spoke in a low tone.

"Man it suppose to be some more."

"Are you sure?" replied his accomplice.

"Hell yeah I'm sure."

The gunman closest to big Ray pushed the barrel of the gun under his chin.

"Muthafucka I'm gon" ask you one more time dawg, where is the rest of the money?"

Big Ray knew that his answer could trigger some serious problems depending on whether the two young punks were capable of cold blooded murder, or would they just slap him around and take no for an answer. He tried to read the situation as best as he could, but something just wasn't right. He heard something in their voices that told him they were sure there was more money in the house. His mind was going in circles and he knew it was a gamble. Finally he told himself everything would be okay, and the few knots that the young punks would put on his head was nothing compared to not having his connect's money that he owed. He slowly turned toward the man who asked the question, and spoke sincerely as he could.

"It ain't nomore money guy, you took all that I had, that's it."

The man looked at him with cold eyes piercing through the ski mask and grimaced,

"Alright muthafucka! Blame yo'self for this." Boh!! The sound from the 45 pistol echoed throughout the house as big Ray's common-law wife tumbled to the floor, leaving a hole in her head the size of a half of dollar. Everything seemed to be moving in slow motion as big Ray and the boys stood there screaming to the top of their lungs.

Suddenly, the mourning over her death was interrupted as the same gunman pulled Ron toward him placing the gun with the smoking barrel to his head.

"Snap out of it big Ray!" yelled the gunman sarcastically.

"Now do you want the same shit to happen to your son?" Big Ray didn't answer, he was visibly shaken.

"Okay dawg, have it your way." The gunman quickly positioned the gun perfectly on Ron's head.

"Okay, okay, okay, I'll give it to you." He removed the gun from Ron's head as big Ray and the trigger happy gunman headed toward his bedroom. Lil Ray couldn't believe this was happening. His mother was dead, his best friend was at gunpoint in place of him, and he'd never seen his father so helpless.

Smoke, Bam, and Pooh were also scared, and they all stood obediently close to each other as the gunman watched them at gunpoint. Ten minutes later, big Ray and Ron walked out of the bedroom with the other gunman behind them. He ordered them to stay put as he went back in the bedroom and grabbed the two pillow-cases full of money.

When he returned, he handed one of the sacks to his partner, then without warning, walked up to Ron and shot him point blank in the head... Then casually said,

"That's for bullshitten around and tryna' play us like sucka's, now you ain't got no wife or no son."

Big Ray screamed out, 'Noooooooooooooo!' To the top of his lungs as he ran toward the man at full speed, but was stopped in his tracks by the other gunman who squoze off seven quick rounds from the Barreta nine millimeter.

At that instance, lil Ray noticed the tattoo on his hand that read 'G-Life.' He instantly knew who it was, Bo-Bo and Spade. Ray Ray, Pooh, Bam and Smoke let out cries filled with fear as big Ray plummeted to the floor dying instantly. The gunman who killed Ron and Ray's mother, walked toward the boys with what now seemed to be a familiar look in his eyes. He aimed the gun at them, and just as he was about to squeeze the trigger, a knock on the door made him pause.

"Hello! Is anybody home?" said the male voice on the other side of the door.

"Damn!" whispered the gunman as he looked at his partner.

"Come on man, let it go, we gotta get up outta here. Let's go out the back door, come on!" said the man with the G-life tattoo.

The knocks became louder as Spade stood in front of the boys about to murder them at any moment. Suddenly, he lowered the gun to his side and whispered,

"Yall lil bitches lucky today." Then they left out the back door in a hurry.

Ray Ray quickly ran to the front door and opened it up as tears covered both his cheeks. The man at the door was the nosey neighbor's husband. She had noticed the strange activity at their house all night, and when she heard the gunshots, she called 911 and told her husband to go check it out 'til they arrived.

Lil Ray fell into his arms holding him tightly and crying hysterically. The man couldn't believe what he saw when he walked in. Three dead bodies and four scared children.

"Dear God!" said the elderly man as he looked at the horrific scene.

"Who in God's name would do something like this."

CHAPTER 3

"Hello Ray, my name is detective O'Neil, and I want you to look at these men in this line up very carefully. And if you recognize any of them or see anything that might jog your memory as to what happened at your parent's house that night, don't hesitate to tell me, alright."

Ray Ray answered with a simple nod of his head. The homicide detective pushed the speaker button on the wall and yelled,

"Okay Jake, send them out."

Five black males appeared behind the thick two-way glass.

"Don't worry Ray, they can't see you through the glass, so relax and watch closely."

"Number one step forward." said the detective. The tall light-skinned man with his hair corn-rowed to the back stepped forward.

"Turn to your left." The man complied.

"Now turn to your right." he complied again.

"Now face the glass." The detective looked at Ray Ray after the series of instructions were complete.

"Does he look familiar?"

"No." replied Ray Ray.

"Okay, step back against the wall number one. Number two step forward."

The heavyset brown-skinned man with the taper-fade

stepped forward. He went through the detective's routine, and lil Ray didn't recognize him either. But when number three stepped forward, Ray Ray began nervously fidgeting with his hands. He quickly looked away as if he'd seen a ghost.

"What's wrong Ray? Do you recognize him?"

Ray Ray didn't say a word as he stood there with his head down. The detective decided to use a little psychology on him, so he didn't press the issue.

"Number four step forward."

Ray Ray looked like himself again as he watched number four go through the motions of the procedure, but when number five stepped forward, he reacted the same as he did when he saw number three.

"Number three and number five step forward." yelled the detective. They both complied. The detective looked at Ray Ray and studied his behavior for a moment before speaking to him in a calm manner.

"Ray, I want you to take a good look at number three and tell me if you recognize him."

As Ray Ray slowly looked up at him, his heart was running a marathon. He stared at Bo-Bo with fear all over his face. He focused on the tattoo, then back to his face.

"What can you tell me about him Ray?" Ray Ray was about to put his head back down, but the detective interrupted by quickly asking another question.

"Well what can you tell me about number five?" Ray Ray focused his attention on Spade and suddenly seemed to be more irritated.

"What is it Ray? Do you know these punks?" Ray Ray didn't say a word, and the detective was becoming more impatient because he knew Ray Ray recognized them. He quickly decided to do a full press on Ray Ray to get him to say what he knew about them.

He rubbed the bald spot on his balding head, took a deep breath, then momentarily twirled the hair on his thick mustache before squatting his thin brown frame down beside Ray Ray.

"Look at me Ray." Ray Ray focused on the black detective with the look of fear still present in his eyes.

"I know you've been through a horrible, horrible ordeal." said the detective as sincerely as he could.

"And there's nothing we can do to bring your parents or your friend back. But there is a way we can get the proper justice they deserve, but you will have to put your fear aside and help me put those bastards where they belong. They can't hurt you anymore Ray. And the one thing we have to our advantage is the fact that they think you are already dead. Your father wasn't a saint, but he didn't deserve what happened to him. And the word on the street is, the men that killed him got away with eight hundred thousand dollars, which big Ray owed a half of million of it to some Mexicans that live on the southwest side for a heroin deal. At first we thought the Mexicans put a hit on big Ray from some kind of misunderstanding between them, but we found out that they had no beef. Your father was a drug dealer, and I don't condone any drug dealing activity, but I gotta say, he did business straight up with whoever he dealt with. He just got caught up in that vicious trap by some more drug dealing punks."

Ray Ray slowly began to look at Bo-Bo and Spade behind the thick glass as the detective continued to talk. He noticed Spade nonchalantly scratching his thick, nappy cornrows, and occasionally fiddling with his missing tooth as if he didn't have a care in the world. And Bo-Bo was responding the same way.

Ray Ray suddenly felt his fear transform into something similar to rage, only a thousand times worse. The detective's voice sounded very distant now as he stood there shifting his focus from Bo-Bo to Spade with only the movement of his eyes. He began to have momentary flashbacks of the terrible night he lost his love ones. Suddenly, the walls seemed to start closing in as the detective constantly repeated the words, "**ARE THESE THE MEN THAT MURDERED YOUR FAMILY RAY RAY?**" over and over.

Ray Ray noticed the detective's voice getting louder and louder, mixed with the loud screams from his parents. The room now seemed to be spinning, and the voices just wouldn't go away. Ray Ray continued to stare at them as his breathing became abnormal. He felt faint, angry, confused and hateful. And suddenly without warning, he yelled out,*"I HATE DRUG DEALERS! I HATE DRUG DEALERS! I HATE DRUG DEALERS!"*

He popped up quickly and screamed out, "I HATE DRUG DEALERS!" He gripped the bedsheets tightly as he sat there drenched in sweat and breathing heavily from the re-occurring nightmare.

"What's wrong baby, you dreamin' again?" asked his woman Sheila as she sat up beside him gently rubbing the back of his neck in an effort to comfort him. Ray Ray paused for a moment before answering.

"Yeah baby, I guess I was." Sheila looked at him sleepishly before she softly spoke.

"Baby it's been over ten years since you lost them, you've got to move on."

"I know baby, I know. But it's just that, I always find myself feeling guilty about the fact that I coulda' put those muthafuckas away when that detective questioned me about it. Now them lames are somewhere in the world enjoying life kickin it, when they should be dead or locked the fuck up somewhere."

He climbed out of bed stressfully and went to the bathroom, turning on the sink splashing his face with luke warm water as it ran in his prayer-formed hands. Afterwards, he grabbed a towel and dried off, then turned to the full body mirror, looking over his 5'9 medium built frame. He ran his hand over his low cut brush waves, then stared at his seemingly jet black eyeballs and wondered to himself just how much of his father did he have in him.

His father had those same eyes. And they both had the same caramel complexion, and were both fairly handsome men. When Ray Ray returned to the bed, Sheila concerningly moved closer to him.

"Baby, you were a little boy at the time, you were scared to tell that detective who they were. So don't keep blaming yourself, okay?"

Ray Ray turned his head looking off in the distance before responding.

"Naw baby, it wasn't fear that I was experiencing. Maybe at first, but it quickly turned into something else. Something that allows me to look in the mirror and live with myself. Something that gives me a reason to walk out the front door each day. And something that may someday do me more harm than good. I just don't know Sheila. I don't... But it's so ironic at times because I can clearly remember my father saying to me, *"We sometimes do things in life that we don't have the answers to, but just keep breathing and the answers will come."*

Sheila gently kissed Ray Ray on his lips, then gazed into his obscured eyes. He didn't say a word, he just stared back with mutual affection. Moments later, they embraced each other with deep passionate tongue-kissing that lead from her lips to her erect nipples.

He sucked and gently massaged her mounds of flesh simultaneously, then stroked her long wavy ponytail that fell down to the crack of her apple-bottom ass. Sheila moaned softly from the pleasure as he anxiously made his way to her inner-thighs. He teased her momentarily by licking close to her pussy, then without warning, her body was no longer hers as his tongue twirled and slashed across her clitoris. She gripped the bedsheets tightly and closed her eyes, moaning louder and louder from the pleasure his tongue caused. Ray Ray methodically slipped two fingers inside her and began massaging her G-spot, while he continued to lick and suck her protruding clit. Sheila instantly began to slide and squirm until she became violently out of control. Her petite lentil-complected body jerked and rocked from the multiple orgasms that flowed from her flesh, and Ray Ray grew more aggressive as the taste of her juices put his hormones in overdrive. He stopped momentarily to lay on his back, then directed her to sit on his face. She didn't waste any time climbin' on, gladly straddling him between her thick brown thighs. He fondled her erect nipples again as his tongue went back to work on her clit. She held on to the headboard and worked her shapely hips in a steady rhythm with her alluring owlish eyes closed. She loved how eager he always seemed to be for her during sex, because she would always be just as eager for him.

"Oh God!" she cried.

"Ray Ray, I- I-." Her speech was impaired and her body began to inch away from the overwhelming pleasure. Ray

Ray gripped her ass-cheeks to hold her steady as he licked, scraped, and sucked her open flesh with the skills of a porno star.

She bucked and cried as more of the thick white cream gushed from her pussy. Then moments later, she found herself sliding down Ray Ray's body as he guided her by her hips. He tongue-kissed her momentarily so she could taste herself from his mouth, then grabbed his erect dick and slid it in her aching pussy. He held her still by her waist to restrict her movement, then plunged inside her from underneath. He pumped her steadily for fifteen minutes, then rolled her over and locked both legs over his shoulders.

"Oh shit! Oh shit! Oow, Oow, Ray-Ray-Oow!"

Sheila chanted sex-talk and made fuck-faces as Ray Ray pounded her with deep long strokes. He often used sex with her as a tool to take his mind off of his parents, but sometimes even the sex wouldn't make the thoughts go away, like now. And the more he thought about it, the harder he would thrust. Sweat dripped from both of their bodies as he pounded her with brute force. Her tities bounced and her body rocked with every stroke. And even though she was enjoying the sex, she could tell where his mind was at because the sex wasn't only sex anymore, it was border line savage.

Ray Ray kept humpin as he tried to out-run his thoughts. And Sheila realized he could go on like this for hours, which would be too much punishment for her to take in that position. So she did what she always did whenever he was like this, she started contracting her pussy muscle's in sync with every thrust. Her being double-jointed at the top of her thighs provided her with the unique ability to make her pussy give phenomenal suction. And whenever she really put it to use, she knew it was just a matter of time before Ray Ray would bust-off. His blank expression suddenly disappeared as Sheila's pussy-contractions began to take effect on him. His rhythm suddenly changed, and his dick suddenly felt more sensitive than usual. He knew what Sheila was doing, and he didn't contest it as he kept grindin' inside her until his body finally submitted to the warm, wet sex that had a vacuum effect that could make the hardest man fold. His entire body tensed up as he released the thick globs of semen in her, then went limp when his nut-sack was emptied. Afterwards, they cuddled, kissed, talked, then did it all over again.

CHAPTER 4

As the black ZR-1 corvette made its way down Wilshire street, the Grand National turned off its trail, making way for the white Grand Prix that pulled in its place. After following the Vette for four more blocks, the voice on the walkie-talkie replied,

"We comin' yo way playa, so pick up the slack at the next check-point."

The white Grand Prix turned left as the blue Mustang pulled behind the Vette. After riding down several more blocks, the Vette finally pulled into the driveway of a red brick house on Rosemary street.

"1122 Rosemary" said the man on his walkie-talkie. A few moments later, the Grand National and Grand Prix pulled up at the address. And just as the man from the Corvette put the key in the door of the house, Ray Ray pressed the Desert-Eagle 44 to the side of his head.

"Nigga you know what time it is, so open the door and shut the fuck up 'til I ask my questions." Smoke and Pooh got out of the Grand Prix, and Bam got out of the blue Mustang, all with guns in hand. They quickly joined Ray Ray in the apprehension of the man, then they all walked him inside his girlfriend's house. Smoke and Bam quickly searched the house to see if anyone else was home, then came right back to where Ray Ray and Pooh held the man after realizing no-one else was there. Ray Ray grabbed the man by his collar, pulling him close to his bandana-covered face and grimaced,

"Okay bitch, here's the story. We've been watchin yo' punk-ass for a couple months now. And we know that you got a bitch name Ann, a dog name Lucky, and get twenty-five birds a month from a funny-lookin muthafucka name Hector. But I'm not interested in your drugs nigga, I'm interested in your Benjamins. Now where the fuck is all that money that yo' bitch been droppin' off over here for the last month? We know it's here because we never saw it leave. We figure you just wait until you collect a certain amount off the streets, then shoot it to yo' connect, so where is it guy?"

The dark-skinned man with the bald-fade started mumbling unclear words nervously. Ray Ray slapped him across the face with the Dessert-Eagle, then pulled him closer.

"Nigga open yo muthafuckin mouth before I fuck you over like the bitch you is. Now where is it?"

"Man I don't know what you talkin about!"

Suddenly, the 44 bullet ripped through the man's leg, removing a chunk of flesh the size of a grapefruit. The man screamed to the top of his lungs, nearly passing out from the pain. The cream-colored expensive carpet was instantly stained with splatters of blood, flesh and bone. Then Ray Ray gripped his shirt and yanked him closer and asked,

"Did that jog your memory muthafucka!" Then aggressively shoved him into the hands of Smoke.

Smoke punched him in the jaw, knocking a tooth out from the left side of his mouth. And the man begged and pleaded for them to stop, but Ray Ray was determined to make him talk. He pressed the gun on the man's groin and grimaced,

"This my last time askin you nigga, and if you don't come up with the right answers, you can walk around with a raggedy-ass pussy for the rest of yo' life, now where is it bitch!"

The man quickly pointed toward the kitchen while mumbling out barely audible words in agonizing pain.

"It's in da' freezer man, it's in da' freezer!" Pooh and Bam quickly made there way to the large deep-freezer... When they opened it, they both looked at each other with silly expressions and replied,

"Jack-pot."

There was no meat or any other food items in the freezer, only money and cocaine filled to the rim. The man begged Pooh to bring him some of the cocaine.

"Come on man, please let me get a hit to kill this pain dawg." He was sweating profusely as blood continued to pour out of his leg. The bullet did so much damage that it would surely have to be amputated. Pooh looked at Ray Ray before reacting to dude's request, then a few moments later, Ray Ray nodded his head yes. Pooh walked to the mark with a taped-up kilo of cocaine. He stared at the man for a few long seconds as he sat there bleeding, crying, and reaching for the coke. Pooh smiled, then suddenly stabbed the center of the kilo with the pocket knife, leaving the knife stuck in it. Then handed dude the cocaine.

The man quickly snatched the knife from the coke, scooping up small mountains of the powder with it. He made it disappear in record time.

And before the narcotic could take effect, he hastily snorted another small mountain off the knife. Ray Ray suddenly looked at the man with disgust on his face and yelled,

"Snort it all muthafucka!" the man didn't respond, so Ray Ray quickly pushed his face back down in the coke.

"Didn't you hear what the fuck I just said nigga!" The man looked up at Ray Ray with tears in his eyes then responded.

"Why are you doin this to another brother man?"

"Muthafucka you ain't my brother! Now keep snortin and shut the fuck up!!"

The man continued to snort until he was so high that he felt nothing. Ray Ray kept making him sniff mountains of the white powder, and he could tell by the marks condition that the cocaine was high quality. Then after almost three ounces of the coke was gone, the man started going into wild convulsions. He kicked, jerked, and foamed at the mouth violently. While Ray Ray and his friends watched with lack of remorse... A few seconds later, the urine and fecies that soiled his pants, was the clue that said his fate was sealed. He died with his eyes open, and Ray Ray continued to display no sign of empathy.

"Yall grab that money and let's get the fuck up outta here." ordered Ray Ray in a calm voice.

"What about this," asked Pooh while pointing at the cocaine. Ray Ray looked at Pooh dumbfoundedly before replying,

"Whut about it? You know we don't never fuck wit dat shit! So leave it where the fuck it's at and let's ride."

"But Ray it's over a hundred birds up in this bitch, dawg we could get straight with that."

"Man we already straight, now grab that change like I said and let's bounce."

Pooh and the fellas loaded up the 1.2 million dollars

in cash and left the scene quietly. Pooh didn't like the idea of leaving all of that profit behind. He felt that it was defeating the purpose, and out of each one of the fifteen to twenty dealers they had already hit licks on, Ray Ray never allowed any of them to touch the drugs. Even on the two occasions when there was only drugs and no money in the house, he still wouldn't take it. That's why 'til this day, Ray Ray believed in doing thorough investigations on whoever his target was. So that nine times out of ten there would definitely be money, even if there were drugs....

****

Bam and Smoke pulled up in front of Bam's mother house in a candy red Hummer. Bam took the last drag of the blunt they were smoking, then they walked in the fly colonial-style house that he had purchased for her a few years ago.

"Hey ma!" he spoke as he gave his short plump mother a warm hug. He looked more like his mother than his father. They contained the same brown complexion with the same series of freckles on their faces.

"Where's pop at ma?" She looked at him carefully with her eyes slightly squinched before responding.

"Where is your father always at Bam? He's in the dining room sitting in his favorite chair."

Bam suddenly realized the marijuana had taken effect on him because he'd just asked his mother a stupid question. He knew that he could find his father sitting in his favorite chair at any given time. He suffered a massive stroke three years prior, and it left him speechless with the entire right side of his body paralyzed. And every since they moved in that house, he's occupied that chair consistently. He would sit there and stare at the television expressionless until he nodded off to sleep.

"Hey pops," said Bam after giving him a light kiss on his forehead.

"What's goin on?" The elderly man didn't move or respond to Bam. It was as if he really didn't know him, yet he's been in Bam's life since the day he was born.

Bam really hated to see his father in this condition, although he was use to it by now, it was still hard to believe a man with so much energy can just fade away to a person so helpless. But in spite of it all, he still loved his father dearly. And respected him for sticking by his mother's side for so many years.

"Pop, do you know what today is?" asked Bam not really expecting a response.

"Today is Father's day, and I got you a little sumthin." Bam pulled out the diamond encrusted Movado watch and placed it on his father's wrist.

"Pop, one day you are gonna get up out of this chair and take me to the gym to punch the bag and spar like we use too. I miss those days pop. But don't fret old-timer, our time will come again. Until then, I'll be waiting patiently."

Bam planted one more kiss on the man's forehead, followed by a

"Happy Father's day pop," then he strolled back in the living room with his mother and Smoke.

"Bam you and Smoke come and get some of this apple pie that I made, I have plenty." They all went to the kitchen and ate his mother's delicious pie then left...

****

"Dad for the longest time I've been waiting on you to

come wake me up and tell me this shit is all a bad dream, but you never come," said Ray Ray as he sat down on a blanket beside his father's grave.

"I've been doing some things that I know you wouldn't be proud of, but hopefully you will forgive me someday dad. Tell mama and Ron I send my love, and that they are always in my heart."

Ray Ray took another swallow from the fifth of Hennessey he held, then poured the rest of it out on the surface of grass above his father's grave. He stood up, lit a Cuban cigar, puffed it a couple times, then gently placed it on top of the tombstone still lit.

"Happy Father's day dad, I'll see you later."

CHAPTER 5

"Hey handsome!" yelled Rashia over the loud music in the club Double O Seven.

"Whuddup baby, long time no see." replied Pooh. 'Where you been hidin' at girl? You know a guy gon'miss it whenever it talk back like yours do?"

"Is that so? Well how bad have you been missin this kitty?"

Pooh swallowed the last two gulps of the liquor in his cup before replying,

"Bad enough to let you spend the night with me tonight."

Rashia stepped a little closer to Pooh seductively.

"Well what's takin' you so long, let's bounce." Pooh stood up and followed her through the crowded club to the front door.

He admired how the short, white, Christian Dior dress hugged every curve on her beautiful brown body. He could tell she wore thongs under her dress, and he watched her voluptuous ass bounce and wiggle with every step that she took. Her white stiletto pumps slightly made her calfs stand at attention, and every man that she passed, made it his business to check her out from head to toe. Her shoulder length hair was in a Chinese wrap, and it highlighted the gold heart-shaped earrings she wore.

It was a fairly short drive to Rashia's house from the club. Pooh followed her there in his black Nissan 330 ZX. As he pulled in front of her house, she pulled her Honda Civic in her driveway. Pooh scoped out the area, making a mental note of anything that looked suspicious. It became a habit due to his line of work.

When they made it on the porch and walked through the front door, they were immediately hit in the face by a thick cloud of marijuana smoke. Her brother Buzz was sitting on the couch with one of his boys and two females. Buzz stood up from the couch and yelled.

"Pooh! Is that you nigga!"

"Yeah it's me lil nigga, whut up witcha?"

Buzz ran over to Pooh and slapped five with him.

"Man I haven't seen you in a minute, whut you been into Pooh?"

"Aw man you know me, I ain't been into nothing special. I just been doing me and tryin to stay sucka free, know whut I'm saying."

"Yeah dawg, I feel you, but check this out dawg, I need to holla at you about something in private."

"Not now boy!" yelled Rashia.

"You can holla at him later, but he is goin' to my room with me right now, so we'a holla back."

Buzz frowned at his sister before grumbling.

"Shut up girl, ain't nobody even talkin to you. And yo' hot ass just want some dick."

"You must be a psychic nigga." said Rashia with a sarcastic smile. Then she grabbed Pooh by the hand and led him up the stairs to her room.

She quickly slid out of the tight body dress down to her thongs.

She didn't have on a bra, and just as Pooh began to

admire her curvaceous body, it was interrupted because
her tongue was deep down his throat in a flash. As she
kissed and helped undress him, he thought to himself,
'This why I like this bitch, she don't give a fuck about
foreplay. She gets straight to the point.'

After Pooh was fully undressed, Rashia waisted no time
kissing down his body 'til she reached his already hard
dick. She placed the head of it in her mouth and rolled
her tongue around it. Pooh was light-skinned and stood
about six feet two inches in height. His face immediately
turned red as Rashia inched her warm mouth deeper and
deeper over his manhood. She worked her jaws until the
entire length of him was in her mouth, and Pooh loved
the way she would suck him like a pro. She played with
his balls with her free hand, and made little 'umm' noises
as she covered his dick with warm, wet saliva. Pooh knew
that if she kept this up, he would be cumin soon.

Rashia rocked her head in a constant up and down
movement. Swallowing him partially at times, then
entirely at others. Pooh felt himself about to bust off, and
his body tensed up as Rashia continued to suck, stroke
and massage his balls.

"Aw shit bitch! I'm 'bout to bust." He knew that she
loved when he talked to her like that, so he continued.

"That's right bitch, eat dat dick up, eat it up." Rashia got
excited and began suckin him like she was on death-row
and it was her last sex-session. Suddenly, Pooh started
jerking and rocking as the cum shot to the back of her
throat. Rashia was such a freak that she swallowed some,
then pulled his joint out of her mouth and let the rest
skeet all over her tities. She pumped his pipe until his nut
came out in small trickles of fluid… To her delight, his
dick was still hard. And it only reminded her of why she

enjoyed fuckin him in the first place. She stood up and was about to pull her thongs off, but Pooh quickly told her to leave them on. He put on a condom, then ordered her to get on all fours. He slapped her across her juicy ass, making it shake like jelly.

"Oow." moaned Rashia as he slapped her across her ass again while grabbing the string from her thong. He moved it to the side, then pushed himself deep inside her soaking wet hole.

"Oow baby that feels so good," she moaned as he went inside her. Pooh gripped the thong tighter as he started pounding her harder and harder. Sometimes he liked when a female would keep her panties or thongs on, because whenever he would pull them to the side and slide up in it, it just seemed more taboo that way. The harder he pumped her pussy, the louder she moaned.

Rashia had only had sex with two other boys by the time her and Pooh had started sexing. She was twelve years old at the time, and Pooh was eleven. They never made any serious commitment to each other, but she never stopped letting Pooh fuck her because he made her feel exactly like she wanted to feel during sex. Pooh kept stroking her wetness, and Rashia gripped the bed sheets tightly as she felt herself about to cum.

"Oh Pooh, that's it baby, that's –ooh shit!" She put her face down on the bed as both of their bodies twitched and jerked, releasing their cum at the same time. Her body went limp as she laid there breathing heavy from the intense session.

"Damn nigga, I see you still got it like dat." Pooh smiled at her compliment before responding.

"And I plan to keep it like dat so I can get this pussy rain sleet or snow." They both laughed, then cleaned up and went downstairs to prepare something to eat.

"Yo hot ass happy now aint'cha," yelled her younger brother Buzz.

"You damn right you lil nosey muthafucka, now get you some bidness nigga and stay the fuck outta mine." Rashia grimaced as she made her way to the kitchen.

"Ay Pooh, let me holla atchu' about what I wanted to holla atchu' about earlier."

Pooh stepped off to the side with Buzz to listen to his issue.

"Man, I been doin' dirt-ball bad lately. I ain't been able to get no work from nobody, and shit is just flat out hectic. So I desperately need you to front a nigga some work dawg. You know I'm straight up and yo' ends gonna come back right, so what can you do for a dog needin a bone?"

"Man you know I don't fuck around like that, so what makes you think I'm holdin work?" Buzz hesitated before he spoke.

"Man don't say nothing, but that lil nigga Pee-Wee told me that you looked out for him on sumthin, so I figured I'd cut into you about gettin straight."

Pooh instantly got angry because he specifically told his lil cousin Pee-Wee not to tell anybody about him having cocaine on the streets. He knew that Pee-Wee and Buzz were good friends, and that Pee-Wee didn't mean any harm by telling Buzz, but he still didn't like it and would let Pee-Wee know about it later.

"I'll tell you what Buzz, I'll get back with you in a few days on something young dawg. Until then, here go a lil pocket-change to keep you straight until better days, a'ight." Pooh handed him five one-hundred dollar bills.

"Good lookin Pooh, I really appreciate it. And I'll be lookin forward to seein you in a few days, holla."......

CHAPTER 6

Pooh pulled up at Smoke's house at the designated time for that particular day, which was 6pm. He knocked on the door and admired the fine teenage girl across the street while he waited for Smoke to answer. Her tight guess shorts constantly slid in and out the crack of her ass while she drank cherry cola and demonstrated a Jamaican-style dance for her girlfriends. Her thick legs opened and closed in a smooth rhythm as she moved her body to the outdated song *"Mr. Loverman"* by Shaba Ranks. Smoke finally opened the door.

"Come on in dawg, I'll be ready in a minute."   "Man who is that lil hot thang right there?" Smoke looked out the window.

"Who her? Man that's Tammy lil hot ass."

"Dawg did you hit it yet?"

"Man I hit it all the time."

"Well when you gon' let yo' dawg get some dude. You know Snoop told you that it ain't no fun if the homies can't get none." Smoke smirked before replying,

"Yeah I feel you homie, but she ain't gon' give you none."

"Why?"

"Because she don't like light-skinned niggas homie. She like'em 5'8, 170 pounds, black as these boots I got on, with brush-waves nigga, like me!"

"Yeah right dawg, I'll betcha' she like green better."

They both laughed.

"Anyway, hurry up Smoke, you know dat nigga Ray Ray will have a fit if we be late."

"Aight man, just let me throw my vest on and we can bounce." When Smoke finished strapping on his Kevlar bullet-proof vest and headed for the door, a news bulletin that appeared on his television made him pause momentarily.

"Police are searching and urging citizens to call if you have any information concerning the disappearance of nine year old Iyonna Brown. Iyonna disappeared four days ago while she was on her way home from school, and she's the fifth child that's been abducted within the last three months. Police have questioned at least two men from her neighborhood who served time in prison for pedophile convictions. Both men claim that their civil and privacy-rights act have been violated and tend to follow up the matter with legal representation. More news at seven."

Smoke stood there shook up for a moment as the news report made him think about how his little sister was a victim of a pedophile piece of shit. His mother's boyfriend had repeatedly raped his eight year old sister, then strangled her to death. Smoke was left without a mother or a sister, and had to be raised by his aunt Mattie while his mother served a 30 year sentence for murder. Her original sentence was 7 years for attempt murder because the six 38 bullets that she put in her pedophile boyfriend left him paralyzed from the neck down. But when he suddenly died four years later of complications from those wounds, the state of Michigan took her original sentence back, then tried and convicted her of first-degree murder. She's been incarcerated for twelve years, and Smoke loved his deceased aunt Mattie dearly for never letting him lose touch with his mother. He knows the prison visiting room well from being in it so much with his mother over the years. And soon as he became old enough to help his mother fight her legal battle, he's been there a hundred percent, paying for all of her legal fees and keeping money on her books for commissary.

"Yo Smoke!" yelled Pooh.

"Let's bounce dawg."

Smoke snapped out of his trance.

"A'ight dawg I'm ready, but I gotta swing by a mailbox to drop this money-order off for my moms."

Pooh and the rest of the crew had much respect for Smoke's mom, so Pooh displayed a serious expression before responding.

"I can dig it dawg, and make sure you tell Yvonne I said hi wheneva you holla at her again." Smoke agreed, then followed Pooh out the door.........

As the grey Monte Carlo turned left, leaving the white Explorer's trail, Pooh and Smoke pulled behind the white Explorer in a black Chevy Trailblazer. They followed the Explorer til it came to a stop in front of a house in the 1400 block of Promenade. A man known as Zoe got out and made his way toward the front door.

"Roger Rabbit, we posted in front of 1420 Promenade and dude is on the move." Pooh spoke eagerly into his walkie-talkie to Ray Ray and Bam.

"We 'bout to approach."

"Hold up a minute dawg, look!" said Smoke as he noticed the two twin girls about the ages of six, run out the house up to Zoe playfully screaming, "daddy! daddy!"

followed by a female who appeared to be about eight months pregnant.

"Roger Rabbit, two kids and a pregnant bitch is at the house wit'em, but we still 'bout to proceed" replied Pooh.

"Wait a minute dawg!" yelled Ray Ray.

"Give it a minute to see what they do."

Zoe picked up both of the girls, then placed a kiss on the pregnant woman's lips as they all walked in the house oblivious to the present danger that awaited them... When Pooh saw that, he anxiously spoke into the walkie-talkie to Ray Ray again.

"Double R, they just went in and it looks like they campin' out, so we goin at'em dawg."

"Naw dawg!" yelled Ray Ray.

"Fall back, we'a get dude another day, bounce."

"Man what you mean fall back!" Pooh snarled.

"Man fuck dat bitch and them kids, this ain't no muthafuckin Scarface movie! We 'bout to get that lame."

"Nigga chill!" demanded Ray Ray,

"And meet me at the neutral zone now!!"

"Damn!" yelled Pooh as he threw the walkie-talkie on the floor irately and slammed the blazer in drive. He raised the smell of burnt rubber and smoke as he skidded away wildly from the mark's house.

Fifteen minutes later, the grey Monte Carlo and the blazer pulled up five minutes apart at the single-flat house on Theodore and Moran. Ray Ray immediately ran up to Pooh and jumped in his face aggressively.

"Nigga what the fuck is yo' problem! Huh!"

Pooh stepped closer and matched his aggression.

"What da' fuck you mean what the fuck is my problem! What the fuck is yo' problem Ray Ray! Huh? You the one who been on this lil killa slash moral shit a lil to long, don't you think? Man I know it was fucked up what happened to yo' parents in that house, but dawg you gotta realize the fact that we was in the muthafuckin house too! And yo' parents was like our parents too! And Ron was our ace too! That shit effected all of us nigga, and it made us who the fuck we are today. All the blood we spillin in these streets don't come from Hollywood, this shit is real-life 24/7 three-sixty-five. So it's like this dawg, if this shit is getting to be a little too much for you to handle, just fall the fuck back and get the fuck out the way dawg.

Pooh and Ray Ray stared each other down with eyes locked on one another for the next 30 seconds until smoke walked up and intervened.

"Man, both of yall fools got issues, but I know in my heart that it ain't nothin' we can't work out, 'cause we family yall, and we gon' stay family. Now we still got enough time to get that other lame we had on the list, so yall kiss and make up and let's get this paper."

Pooh and Ray Ray both walked away without saying a word to each other... They got in their cars and headed to the next mark.....

CHAPTER 7

"Ray Ray!" yelled Sheila.

"Cumeer baby, hurry up!" Ray Ray ran to the living room with a couple spoons in his hand as Sheila pointed at the television.

"Today our top story comes from the 1200 block of Rochelle and Gratiot. A well known drug dealer by the name of Raymond Bell was found shot in the head execution style alongside his male Rottweiler. Law officials are saying this is the work of a group of men still at large known as the 'Get Flat Crew.'" We are standing by with Detective Nolan Sykes of Detroit's ninth precinct for a live update. Detective, approximately how many of these cases are these people responsible for?" The attractive black female reporter placed the microphone a few inches away from the detective's mouth after her question.

"Well, from our investigation, we can solidly penpoint twenty invasions that these people are responsible for. They are cold-blooded killers, and they are very professional at what they do."

"Well exactly how many individuals are in their organization, and has any of them been identified by name?"

"We don't know exactly how many individuals are involved at this time, and we have no knowledge of their identities. But if we did, all of that information would be turned over to the FBI, because as of three days ago, this case has officially been picked up by the feds."

"Dayum." mumbled Sheila as she took in the information from the news report.

"Baby whoever them dudes is, they're in way over their heads."

Ray Ray paused briefly before responding to her comment.

"Yeah baby I agree. They are in a little too deep." He broke their train of thought within seconds after his response by playfully diving on her, wrestling her to the floor on the thick carpet.

"Stop Ray Ray." Sheila yelled as she laughed and curled up in the fetal position from him constantly tickling her stomach.

"Ray Ray sto—pit, ha ha ha, boy you is crazy!"

He finally stopped, then went to the kitchen and returned with two separate pints of strawberry shortcake Hagen Daz ice-cream. They sat in the living room on the floor eating ice cream and enjoying each others company. Sheila was home on her summer break from Michigan State college, and Ray Ray loved having her around. They had been a couple every since Ron introduced them in grade school, and they loved each other dearly.

Ray Ray always wanted the best for Sheila, so he paid for her to go to college and take up Business Management and Accounting. She was in her third year and would surely have her Bachelor's degree in her fourth. Ray Ray never allowed Sheila to know about his street activities. This practice went all the way back to his father telling him, *"Son, don't ever tell a woman all of your business nomatter how much you love her. You share information with her on a need-to-know basis. So if there's truly something that she don't need to know, then you truly don't need to tell her."*

Ray Ray knew Sheila would have a fit if she ever found out he was a major role-player in the organized robberies and homicides that had the city in an uproar. She always thought his money came from his father's will, but little did she know, his father never got the chance to build the legacy and riches that he wanted to leave his only son. So Ray Ray took it upon himself to build that legacy on his own.........

The stripper with the thin waist, big butt, and wide hips worked her body in an erotic and seductive manner in the VIP section of the club to Vanity six's *"Nasty Girl."*

Bam constantly threw balled-up five dollar bills at the woman. She winked at Bam then turned away from him facing the opposite direction and made her phat ass hop like a 64 chevy on hydraulics. Bam stood up clapping and cheering his staggering body to her impressive performance. Suddenly, the DJ scratched the record two or three times then let the song from Outkast *"Player's Ball"* flow out the speakers. The dark-skinned female switched her routine and slid down to the floor with her legs spread eagle. She put her hands flat on the floor and pressed down hard until she lifted herself a few inches in the air.

The DJ mixed the old with the new as she put on a helluva show for her five-person VIP audience. The last song she danced to was *"Vibrant Thang"* by Q-Tip, then the DJ slowed it down.

"You may be young but you're readaay" Keith Sweat was the perfect voice to set the stage for the young stallion that suddenly appeared on stage with her co-worker.

She had on white silk panties, with everything matching from the garter-belt and stockings, to the camisole and high-heels. She was a redbone with deep dimples that pierced her cheeks, jet black hair with jumbo Shirley Temple curls that fell just past her shoulders, and a body that came straight off the front pages of the Blackmen Swimsuit issue. Bam had paid to be the only man in the VIP section at the time, so at that point, the world was his. The other four people that were in company were women that were just as beautiful as the ones on stage. Bam's mouth dropped open when the bombshell of a woman began her routine to the slow R&B music. She stared directly at Bam while she moved her body seductively all over the stage. Suddenly, the other woman on the stage approached the young stallion. She slowly helped her slide out of her camisole, then stood behind her and covered the girl's nipples with her hands. The somewhat exposed woman had a tattoo close to the inside of her left thigh of a tongue licking a lollipop along with the words *"How Many Licks!"* Bam continued to pour himself shots of the expensive Louis the Thirteenth Cognac. He was drunk and he staggered toward the stage with the newcomer on his radar.

"Cumeer baby!" He slurred the words out as the other four women sat patiently in the booth. The redbone continued to dance seductively then got on her knees and crawled toward Bam like a lioness stalking her prey. When she reached him, she whispered in his ear,

"How long have you been wanting me?"

Bam drunkenly answered.

"All my life baby, and by the way, what is your name?"

She didn't bother to answer him, she just turned around while still on her knees, then put her ass about three inches away from his face so he could see the other tattoo that rested on her right ass-cheek that read *"Syann, Handle with Caution."* Bam leaned forward and kissed her tattoo and stated,

"Baby I can't make that promise," then pulled out a thick roll of money and walked around the room and gave each woman a thousand dollars. He saved Syann for last and gave her two-thousand dollars. Then without another word, he slid off his black Armani suit-jacket, then slid out of his slacks down to his boxers. He shot the women in the booth a look as if to say, *"take off yall shit!"*

They all got the message and began undressing, all except one. The short brown-skinned girl with short blonde hair, small tities and a big ass. She stood up before expressing herself.

"Bam, baby I'll make it up to you another day because I got something really important that I gotta do, okay." Then she headed for the door leading to the regular customer section of the bar.

Bam quickly responded.

"Okay, well drop that money I gave you on the table on ya' way out." She looked at Bam with puppy-dog eyes and replied,

"Bam, let me hold on to it baby. I told you I would make it up to you."

"Bitch! I will put these 10-and-half lizard skins so deep up yo' funky ass if you don't put my money down and get the fuck up outta here."

The short woman known as Dot quickly changed her mind. She seductively walked over to Bam apologetically.

"Baby I'm sorry. I don't know what I was thinkin. I wanna stay and play. Can I stay and play daddy?"

Bam liked the fact that she submitted, and he felt that

her submission was the perfect element to let the games begin. So he pulled out his dick and addressed her with a proposal.

"Let me see how well you can play with that, and I'll think about letting you stay bitch."

Dot took off her clothes and began sucking his dick. Every other woman in the room was instantly turned on at the sight of watching his dick grow in her mouth. This wasn't new to them when it came to Bam. He was one of the biggest tricks in the city of Detroit. And mostly every stripper knew that when he came around, he would surely be providing 'Down-payments' on car notes, due rent, college tuition, and whatever other purpose the money could be used for. Dot had a quarter-of-an ounce a day cocaine habit. That's why she tried to cut out so fast. All she needed was a good line or two and she would freak however whenever. She wanted some coke bad, but she knew she couldn't afford to walk away from a thousand dollars, so her score would just have to wait until Bam's usual freak-session was over.

Syann laid back on the stage with her legs open while her co-worker began licking and sucking her pussy. At this point everybody in the room was naked and committing some kind of sexual act. The three women in the booth formed a three-way sex chain. While one was eating the other one out, the third one was behind her fucking her with a dildo. Dot continued to suck Bam's joint until he told her to stop, then instructed her to go cut in and eat Syann's pussy. She did as she was told, then Bam started fuckin Syann's chocolate co-worker. He penetrated her from the back, and enjoyed watching his dick slide in and out of her wetness. Her tities bounced with every thrust, and she was enjoying every minute of it. It was one big orgy in the room, and Bam constantly pulled condoms off to put fresh ones on. And within a three-hour period, Bam had fucked every woman in the room, but he saved Syann for last. He laid down on his back and let Syann climb on top of him and ride his still hard organ. As she grinded her juicy yellow ass all over him, he thought to himself, *"Thank God for Viagra."* He knew he would sex Syann 'til her pussy was dry. He wanted his money's worth, so he bent her over and penetrated her asshole. As he grinded, his thoughts ran wild, *"Look at this fine bitch wth this voluptuous yellow ass."* He pounded it for thirty minutes straight while she screamed, moaned, and dealt with the pain. It suddenly seemed as if an orgasm came out through Syann's ass, and Bam loved it because he had heard about this phenomenon before, but this was his first time experiencing it. His pole suddenly slid in and out of her more freely as her ass constantly seemed to lubricate itself. Syann took advantage of the relief and started backin herself into him aggressively. Her ass-cheeks shook with every thrust, and Bam continued to grip her by her tiny waist and slam all ten inches of his manhood inside her. He liked the way she countered his every stroke, and he felt his cum rising to the surface fast. He suddenly started pumpin her with stiff, hard strokes.

"Unnnngg, unng. Aah, aah Bam." Syann groaned as Bam pumped his way too bustin a nut. His face suddenly contorted as if he was in pain as he shot his load in Syann's lubricated asshole. After the session was finally over, Bam stood in the center of the stage naked and replied,

"Thank you ladies, we've got to get together again sometime soon, holla."

CHAPTER 8

The room full of federal agents all listened attentively as Special Agent E.Burns began his debriefing process on case no.14344GFC.

"Okay ladies and gentlemen, we are gonna get straight to the point this morning, so listen up. We have recently developed new information on the individuals that are known to us as the 'Get Flat Crew.' And we feel that this new discovery is key in affording us the opportunity to get them off the streets. We've been closely monitoring the patterns of these people from when they first started this spree of terror. And what we've noticed is they've always been the same in their approach until recently. These guys or girls never take any of the drugs whenever they invade a home, but now all of a sudden, we are getting the same dead body or bodies, the retrieval of the money, and guess what?... The retrieval of the drugs, which leads us to believe there's betrayal somewhere in their organization. I got a big hunch that we are right on this one, because whoever the head of the organization is, judging by the consistency and discipline to leaving the drugs behind, this person doesn't strike me as the kind of figure that would just have a change of heart all of a sudden and do otherwise. It almost seems personal with this person, so I'm gonna ride with my gut on this one and put the proper elements in place to see if we can shed a little more light on these people, which is where you will come in at Special Agent Lawson." The Chubby black agent walked up to the front of the room and stood beside the white agent conducting the debriefing.

"Okay people, this is Special Agent Nathaniel Lawson, and he will soon be placed on the streets under cover. He will be known as Boon, a heavy-hitting drug dealer with clout. He will dress the part and look the part on a daily basis, and hopefully these guys will take the bait. We will put a chemical-agent into our sums of cocaine so that we can identify it when it's in the proper hands. The chemical that we will be using is odorless and harmless to the human body and has no known side-effects when used. All it does is turn red whenever we mix it with our testing solution, which let's us know it's ours. Otherwise, the solution would turn the coke blue. People, I want all of you to keep in mind the fact that these individuals are considered extremely dangerous. They sort'of remind us of a group of individuals that we took down not long ago called the Home-Invaders, only these guys are much more proficient. So, with that being said, does anybody have any questions?" The room full of male and female agents mumbled and nodded lazy no's.

"Well I think we've covered everything that we need to cover today, so that'll be all for now people, you're dismissed."

The black 740 Beemer with twenty inch Giovoni rims pulled up to a slow cruise at the casino's valet parking in downtown Detroit. Special Agent Lawson, a-k-a Boon, got out and walked up in the MGM Grand dressed in a grey tailor-made Versace suit with matching gators and a fresh low haircut lookin like new money. He was a little overweight for his 5'8 frame, but who cares when ya' look like money. He went straight to the crap table and immediately started betting big. He lost fifty-thousand dollars within an hour then left, only to return the next day to lose fifty-thousand more. He stayed in the casino enough to start a buzz about himself in the streets, which he did within a two month period. He was known for having good quality coke, and could produce as much weight as the average hood dealer could cop. He befriended a few local pusher's that he knew would help his credibility spread quicker, which it did. And just as he'd planned, it wasn't long before Ray Ray got on his trail. Ray Ray started watching Boon's every move until he was convinced that Boon was major enough for him to hit. When it would happen, was just a matter of time.

CHAPTER 9

After the intense sex session between Ray Ray and Sheila, they laid in bed cuddled up next to each other.

"Ray," whispered Sheila in a low tone as she rested her head on his chest.

"Whussup baby." Answered Ray Ray.

"I seriously think we should start planning for the future."

"Sheila we always plan for the future baby."

"No Ray, I'm not talkin about planning a trip to the Bahamas or planning for some kind of musical event, I'm talkin about marriage, children, financial stability, and seventy-fifth year anniversaries. Know what I'm sayin baby?"

"Yeah baby I know what you sayin, and those are things that I think about all the time for us. I just wanted to wait until you finished college before we start a family."

"Ray Ray I only got one more year 'til I'm finished, so we should start making preparations now. And first of all, I feel that you spend a lot of unnecessary money. We should start a lucrative business of somekind, and incorporate most of our finances into the business in the form of what is called a stock-holder's equity, that way it limits the security risks."

Sheila sat up in bed, now facing Ray Ray as she anxiously revealed her ideas to him.

"Ray Ray, you always said you wanted to own a chain of fitness centers someday, so why not start now with one, then gradually expand in time. We've got enough capital to put up now, and you know I will handle the business transactions to make sure we don't get fucked, it's what I go to school for baby."

As Sheila rambled on, Ray Ray just sat their taking in all of the information. And it just reminded him of one of the reasons he was so crazy about his woman. Aside from her schooling, she's always been a thinker. And the combination of her schooling and thinking ability had created a monster. Sheila kept on talking, and Ray Ray cut her off when she said something about an accounting equation.

"Hold up a minute Sheila, what da' fuck is that?"

"Baby it's an equation that shows the relationship among assets, liabilities and capital. Sometimes you will hear it stated as assets=equities, but it's more commonly stated as assets=liabilities+capital. And keep in mind that we will have to keep four journals when it comes to this game. There will be a Purchase Journal for all purchases on account, a Cash Payments Journal for all cash payments. A Sales Journal for all sales on account, and a Cash Receipts Journal, for all cash receipts. That's how the white folks do it, and that's how they keep them folks off they back.

Ray Ray's mind was blown with everything his woman had just laid on him, and he knew it was time for him to jump head first into the picture she'd just painted for him. He always knew that Sheila would be the woman he married, but he wasn't in any rush because he already felt like she was his wife. But he realized she was right, it was definitely time to make some major decisions because

Sheila would be out of school in another year. And besides that, how long would his lifestyle be able to go undetected with a full time woman at his side. Something had to give, and time was running out...........

As Smoke sat in the sports bar with one of his Puerto Rican girlfriends on the southwest side of Detroit, he couldn't help noticing the already familiar face that kept showing up on every news channel.

"This is a channel 7 action news report. Today we spoke with the mother and family of nine year old Iyonna Brown, who's been missing for two months along with several other children. Police have found the bodies of three of the other missing children who were brutally molested then strangled to death. Iyonna was not among those bodies found. Police believe the series of abductions all came from the same man, the man that we've been showing you for the past week known to us as William Smith, a-k-a, Will. Police received a photo of Smith after a composite sketch was created through a witness who said she saw Smith in the area on the day of Iyonna's disappearance. And since police have been airing his photo, several more people have come forward with information that is helpful in this investigation. Iyonna's family is devastated about the abduction of their child, and here's what her mother had to say.'

"Iyonna, baby it's me, mama. And I want you to know that mama loves and misses you so much." The welled up tears in her eyes began to fall down her dark, attractive, middle-aged face as she continued.

"And to the man that's holding you against your will, I just wanna say please! By the good grace of God don't hurt my baby. She is such a sweet little girl and I desperately need her home."

The woman broke down after her last statement and was immediately comforted by her husband and loved ones.

"More news at eleven." Stated the female reporter as she concluded the broadcast.

"Smoke!" yelled the Puerto Rican female name Valencia, breaking his thoughts and bringing his attention back to her.

"Whussup baby? What's wrong?" Smoke asked in a concerned tone because of her yelling.

"I'm ready to go get prepared for our dinner-date tonight like you promised.' She squawked.

She didn't like that strange look on his face, so she asked skeptically,

"We are still going, aren't we?"

"Of course we are sweetheart."

"Well why is that strange look on your face?"

Smoke took about thirty seconds to answer her question.

"I just hate muthafuckas who pick on little girls, that's all baby."

Valencia slid her tight body and beautiful face close to him displaying a serious facial expression and replied,

"Me too poppi, me too."

CHAPTER 10

When Bam's cell-phone rung, Syann, the girl from the strip club answered it. After briefly speaking to the caller, she handed it to Bam. "Here, it's for you."

"Well who is it?" Asked Bam as he inhaled the Smoke from the blunt he'd just lit up.

"He say it's your older brother."

"Whut!" yelled Bam. He snatched the phone from her, and as he spoke to the person on the other end, he had a look on his face like something was really bothering him.

"I don't know if that's a good idea dawg." Bam squawked as he continued to talk, then suddenly he yelled out,

"But that was some fucked up shit and you know it man!"

There was a momentary pause before he continued.

"A'ight, but after you see moms and pop you gotta bounce, I'll holla!" Bam hung up the phone and took a couple more pulls off the blunt. He passed it to Syann, then laid back across the bed thinkin about how much he didn't want his older brother coming around anymore. But unfortunately, having the same parents made that option obsolete............

Pooh and Bam sat in the parked car as they watched a well-known drug dealer name Keith emerge from his cocaine-white Q-45 Infinity alone. The night skies were unusually quiet, and Ray Ray and Smoke sat in the shadows only a few meters away. They usually hit their victims in broad daylight, but they would have to improvise from time to time like tonight....

Bam casually adjusted the volume on the song that he would always listen to whenever he was about to put in work. *"Natural Born Killa"* by Ice-Cube and Dr. Dre. He rocked to the track as the words put him in killa mode. *"Should I kill'em, should I kill'em am I illa, than a natural born killa."* The song made him feel like he could take on the whole world if he had too, but he had to keep the volume low because he knew how Ray Ray felt about it. Ray Ray never wanted any distractions during their capers, so he would always remind his crew of how much he respected the quiet approach.

They waited 'til Keith went in his front door, then Ray Ray's voice came across the walkie talkie.

"Okay yall, let's try to get this nigga quickly as possible because we usin' a little extra force tonight, and yall know this area is hot, so we ain't got time for no games, let's do it."

They all exited the two cars and rushed up to the front door in a hurry. And once they were in position, Ray Ray and Smoke swung the heavy police batta-ram one good time, knocking the front door off the hinges. Keith tried to run toward the back door, but Pooh caught him and dragged him back in the front room. They roamed the house and interrogated Keith for about five minutes before Bam noticed the balled-up figure on the couch under the cover. He walked over to the couch and snatched the cover off the man's body.

"Please don't hurt me," pleaded the man when he saw the invaders.

"Who in the fuck is you?" Asked Bam as he stood there pointing the ten millimeter glock at the man's face.

"I'm his brother man, please don't shoot! I ain't got nothing to do with his business, and I was just leavin."

As the middle-aged black man with the receding hairline babbled on and on, Smoke focused on him momentarily from where he was standing...Then suddenly began walking toward him with the expression of a male lion spotting a hyena. When he finally reached him, he punched the man in his mouth, sending him flying off the couch. Then he pulled the man close to him and started viciously slapping him across the face with his nine-millimeter.

"Where is she? Huh! Where is she muthafucka!" yelled Smoke everytime he slapped blood from the man's face.

"Where is she?"

Bam grabbed Smoke and yelled,

"What's wrong with you man, where is who?"

Smoke snatched away from Bam and proceeded to swing and ask the same question until the man suddenly started mumbling something. Smoke pulled the barely conscious man closer to him and grimaced,

"What did you say?"

The man tried to say something again, but Smoke still couldn't understand him. Smoke slapped him viciously again and screamed to the top of his lungs like a madman.

"Where is she muthafucka!"

The man spoke a little clearer this time. Clear enough for Smoke to understand him.

"The basement man, she's in the basement."

Smoke looked at Ray Ray and demanded,

"Don't let this bitch out your sight dawg," then he immediately ran to the basement. When he finally reached the bottom of the stairs, his heart felt as if it had stopped. He felt a million tons of anger, with a sense of relief at the same time the moment he saw nine-year old Iyonna Brown still alive, but barely. He gently untied the rope that bound her tiny brown legs and arms together, then examined her face and got sick to his stomach when he focused on her bruises and her malnourished body. She had been repeatedly raped, and Smoke could only imagine what a horrible ordeal she must have went through. All he could think about was his little sister. A single tear fell from his eyes as he gently wrapped her in a blanket and carried her up the stairs. The molester's brother Keith was more shocked to see the little girl in Smoke's arms than Ray Ray and the rest of the crew. He had no idea that his brother was into that type of shit, and he instantly knew that this could cost him his life. Suddenly, without hesitation, he jumped up off the floor running full speed and dove through the living room window sending broken glass in several directions. But Pooh was on him like a hawk on a small animal. Pooh slapped him around a little, then attempted to drag him back in the house to finish what they started, but the resistant Keith wouldn't let go of the banister. Then after several times of trying to make him release his vice-like grip, Pooh got furious and decided that play-time was over. He snatched his nine from his waist and shot Keith point-blank in the head right there on the porch.

Smoke swiftly carried the little girl to the car, while Ray Ray and Bam dragged the duct-taped molester to the trunk of Smoke's car then jumped in their rides and sped off. Ray Ray and Smoke rode in a blue Maxima, and Pooh and Bam rode in a black SS Impala. The first thing Smoke did was make it to the hospital in a hurry, and when he pulled up at the entrance, he jumped out with Iyonna in his arms yelling help to a nearby nurse. The nurse came running toward him the moment she saw the condition of the little girl. She was in her early thirties but looked ten years younger. Her peanut-butter skin blended well with her sandy brown eyes. Smoke handed Iyonna to the nurse and pleaded.

"Help her, she's in bad shape."

"Who are you?" Asked the nurse. "Are you her father?"

"I gotta go!" yelled Smoke

"But sir, what is your name?" The nurse asked again as the car sped off leaving her baffled.

Smoke and Ray Ray agreed to meet up with Bam and Pooh at one of their safe-houses, and Ray Ray knew exactly what Smoke had in mind for the man in the trunk.

As Ray Ray turned down Gratiot heading toward 7 mile, the night traffic was average. They rode in silence for the majority of the ride, and when they reached 7 mile, Ray Ray made a left.

"Aw shit!" he cursed when he noticed the police car in his rearview mirror.

"Man I hope them bitches don't pull us over."

They rode for several more blocks with the police-cruiser still on their tail. Ray Ray was all too familiar with this scene, so he started chatting the procedure out loud.

"Dawg, they runnin our plates." He paused for a moment then continued.

"Now they is waiting for them to come back." He paused again, then a few seconds later he completed his theory.

"And they should be comin back right-a-bout now."

The police lights immediately popped on, and Ray Ray instantly pushed the gas-pedal to the floor.

"Sonuvabitch!" Yelled the white police officer as the Maxima shot away from them.

Ray Ray ran several red lights and swerved through the night-time traffic with grace. He ran over a pedestrian's foot as the man and woman stepped into the street holding hands, not paying attention to the approaching vehicle that was running at top speed. He was left laying in the street crouched over in pain, clutching his disfigured foot. Dude was lucky it was only his foot that got smashed at the speed Ray Ray was going. And his girl was a little luckier because she'd just barely made it out of the way.

The police continued to give chase as Ray Ray swerved through traffic side-swiping cars and nearly causing major accidents with others. Within minutes of the chase, several more police cruisers joined in, which only made Ray Ray drive harder. He continued to slightly hit the brake and accelerate down narrow streets and alleys until he got the break he was prayin for. A city bus committed a traffic violation by making a wide right turn in Ray Ray's direction and not yielding for the yield sign that sat at the corner. Ray Ray used the bus driver's negligence to his advantage. He instantly sped up toward the front of the bus, then quickly hit the brakes with his foot still on the gas, causing the car to slide toward the bus barely missing it by inches, then accelerated around it until he was back on open road. The police cruiser that was directly behind him was forced to make an unusually sharp turn to his right, which caused him to skid out of control knocking down a nearby stop sign. The other cruisers were also forced to stop momentarily before pursuing the car that was now completely out of their sight. After Smoke realized they were in the clear, he suddenly stated,

"Pull over Ray Ray! If them filthy pigs want'em, we gon' give'em to'em."

Ray Ray drove until he found a secluded side street, then pulled over.

"Pop the trunk," snarled Smoke as he angrily emerged from the car headed toward the rear.

The man appeared to be a little banged up from the high speed chase but he was still conscious. His eyes was suddenly enlarged when he noticed Smoke pull out a hunting knife while standing over him. And without hesitation, Smoke began poking and slicing at the man's flesh savagely. The sounds of the molester's screams were muffled from the thick layer of duct tape on his mouth. Smoke continued to work on the man for about fifteen more minutes, then slammed the trunk shut and got back in the passenger seat breathing heavily with fresh blood all over his clothes. He instructed Ray Ray to drive to the nearest precinct. Once they arrived, they both removed the dead corpse from the trunk and tossed it on the lawn of the police station, then drove off in a hurry. A few police officers came out moments later and went berserk when they saw the dead black male in front of their station with his penis cut off and stuffed in his mouth, and a half of a baseball bat hanging from is rectum.

CHAPTER 11

One week later, a composite sketch of Smoke showed up on the news. The description was given to authorities by the nurse at the hospital. The police told the public that Smoke and the molester were partners, and that Smoke had killed his partner in an effort to make himself look innocent because the pressure from the police department was extremely intense. They went on to say that Smoke knew that it was just a matter of time before they were caught, so he acted fast to mask his guilt.

"If you have any information that would help authorities with the whereabouts of this individual, please contact us at 888-555-5545. We'd really appreciate your assistance and all calls will be confidential," said the middle-aged chief of police as he concluded the live report.

"Dawg! You see how them bitches gon' play me. Man I should go find the chief of police and empty a clip in his bitch ass."

Ray Ray took a sip of the Hawaiian punch fruit drink before responding.

"Dawg, you know how them bitches play. They just sayin that to get public support in large numbers in hopes of catchin you quicker. But you best believe this, the longer it takes for them to catch you, the more they gonna believe that bullshit they self. But don't sweat it dawg, all they got is that weak ass sketch of you and nothing else.'

Smoke looked at Ray Ray sarcastically, then responded.

"But dawg, let's be real. That damn sketch do look a little like me.'

Ray Ray took a few moments to respond, then suddenly through his trembling lips and suppressed smile, he blurted out.

"It look just like you man!" They both exploded in laughter at the same time, and Ray Ray playfully used the moment to create more laughter.

"All I can tell you is lay low nigga!" They both exploded in laughter again as they finished the last of a blunt and headed out the front door...

Twenty minutes later, they pulled up at Bam's parent's house.

"Is Bam here Mrs. Williams?" asked Ray Ray as she opened the door.

"Nah baby, but I'm gonna be awfully upset if you and Smoke don't come in here and help me eat some of this pecan pie that I made."

They immediately agreed because they knew how skillful she was with anything dealing with cooking, especially pastries. She could probably take a biscuit and a few other minor ingredients and turn it into something that taste better than any hostess cupcake or twinky on the market, like most black mothers could.

They wolfed down the delicious pie, then washed it down with a warm cup of cappuccino. Ray Ray went to the bathroom to wash his hands again, and on his way back, he noticed a picture on the fire place of a young boy about nine years old, holding a baby about a year old. The two boys resembled each other a lot, so Ray Ray's curiosity made him ask Mrs. Williams who they were.

"Child that's Bam and his older brother Tyrone, my oldest son."

Ray Ray displayed a puzzled expression before responding.

"Mrs. Williams, I didn't know you had another son, where he been?"

"Baby, that boy has been in and out of trouble every since he started walkin. And when he turned eleven, he stabbed a boy in school and went to the youth home for about 3 years, then got out and went right back for 2 years for some kind of violation from the first case. And when he got out that time, I realized he wasn't gonna listen to me so I let him live his life the way he wanted to, only not in my house. He use to come by from time to time to see us and give Bam money. Other than that, he's on his own. Let me show you some more pictures."

Mrs. Williams went to her bedroom and came back with a photo album. As she flipped through the pages, Ray Ray thought about how funny life could be sometimes. He's known Bam his whole life, and never knew he had an older brother. Ray Ray wished he had an older brother sometimes because he felt that it was good for a young man's upbringing. Mrs. Williams steadily talked and flipped the pages that showed her sons from their adolescent years to several years later. As Ray Ray looked on, his heart suddenly tried to beat its way through his chest. And he broke out into a cold sweat when he looked closely at the face of Bam's oldest brother.

"This can't be right, it can't be him." He mumbled to himself.

He suddenly started having flashbacks to the night that his life changed forever. *"Where's the rest of the money!"* yelled one of the gunmen. *"That's all there is man, you cleaned me out." Big Ray pleaded. "Hello Ray Ray, my name is detective O'Neil. We believe there was inside assistance because you said the gunmen acted as if they knew there was more money in the house. Was your mother having an affair of some kind that your father wasn't aware of? Maybe she set it up and her lover turned on her. Do any of your friends have older brothers that you know of? We believe their was inside assistance, inside assistance,"*

"Ray Ray!" yelled Smoke, snapping him out of his trance. "You a'ight man?"

Ray Ray didn't answer right away, then after a few lingered seconds he answered calmly.

"Yeah man, um a'ight."

He still couldn't believe the man in the photo was Spade. His mind was going in circles as he unlocked the secrets to so many unanswered questions. The revelations that appeared in his mind brought one of his greatest fears to life, 'Betrayal from a best friend. Someone who he'd fought for, bled for, ate with, gave his last too, and even slept in the same bed with as children. Bam was the reason the gunmen knew there was more money than what big Ray had initially given them. Bam helped his older brother Spade rob and murder Ray Ray's parents as well as lil Ron. Bam was the reason Ray Ray was the man he'd become. Bam was now public enemy number one.

Big Ray always told Ray Ray that inside betrayal would someday come, but he didn't realize it would come at the age of eleven in such a heavy magnitude. Mrs. Williams continued to flip the pages and reminisce on the past memories of her children until Ray Ray interrupted.

"When was the last time you saw your oldest son Mrs. Williams?"

"Baby he came by here this morning and picked up Bam, so I think they are still together somewhere."

Ray Ray could hardly control himself after learning that Spade was in the vicinity. He smelled blood, and he desperately wanted to quench his thirst. He managed to pull himself together before speaking so she wouldn't detect any annoyance in his voice.

"Mrs. Williams will you beep Bam or call him on his cell-phone and find out where he's at. I have a surprise for him that I want to take to him, so don't mention me when he calls back, okay."

Mrs. Williams smiled and dialed his cell number but got no answer. Then she paged him and served Ray Ray and Smoke more pecan pie until Bam called back. As soon as she told Ray Ray that Bam was at Chandler Park, him and Smoke said there goodbye's... Ray Ray explained his discovery to Smoke on the way........

"Man you used me to set up my best friend for some punk-ass money!" Tears welled up in Bam's eyes as he continued.

"Man if I woulda' ever imagined that you and Bo-Bo would do some shit like that, I never woulda' told you about the money that I saw big Ray put in his bedroom. I looked up to you Spade. I was proud to have a big brother like you until I finally got a chance to see how cold your heart really is."

"Nigga look who's talkin!" shouted Spade.

"I heard about what you and Ray Ray been puttin' down, so what makes you more righteous than me?" Bam stepped a little closer with a grimacing expression before responding.

"Nigga who in the fuck do you think put people like us on paths like the one we on? Nuthin-ass niggas like you!

I'm livin with demons and guilt every second I breathe. And everytime I look at Ray Ray I get sick to my stomach just knowin I helped create the monster that he's become. So everytime I stick a gun in some sucka's face and take his ends, I do it for several reasons. The first reason is the fact that I'm doin it for Ray Ray because I know what he's goin thru in his head, and I feel obligated to him 4-life in a guardian kind of way. And another reason is the fact that everytime I do it, I see your face on whoever the mark is, and it gives me a sense of making a wrong right, you dig?"

At that moment, it was the first time in Spade's life that he realized he put a serious mental-impairment on his younger brother. And he couldn't blame him for feeling the way he felt. He never thought about the mental trips that a child would go through from seeing so much death and bloodshed. And some of the most violent people in the hood would never stop to think about things like that. Now Spade found himself face to face with the aftermath of his heartless contribution to the hood. He loved his baby brother dearly and wished that he could change the way Bam felt about him, but he couldn't, the damage was done. But he figured he'd just keep trying until Bam would eventually forgive him, it was just a matter of time is what he told himself.

Bam looked at Spade sarcastically and asked,

"What ever happened to that nigga Skin that yall owed that money to?"

"Man that nigga caught a fed case and got thirty years right after we paid him. We shouldna' gave dat nigga shit, but it's all good because now the nigga ain't got no reason to be muggin a nigga if we ever cross paths again."

"So how L.A. been treatin you and Bo-Bo?"

"Man its sweet out there. And it's just as live as Detroit,

Bo-Bo luv it."

Bam smirked a little at his comment, then decided it was time to leave the park. And just as they pulled off, Ray Ray and Smoke pulled up, missing them by less than twenty seconds.

After riding through the park several times searching for them, Ray Ray suddenly yelled

"Damn!" then ordered Smoke to drive back to Bam's mother house. Smoke didn't say a word as he headed in that direction. Neither one of them said anything during the fifteen minute trip. Once they arrived, Ray Ray swiftly got out the car and headed toward the front door. At first, Smoke thought Ray Ray would just wait them out, until he saw him brandish the Ruger nine-millimeter from his waist as he approached the porch. Smoke jumped out the car as fast as he could, while Ray Ray stood there waiting on someone to answer his knocks. Suddenly, the door swung open and Bam's bright-eyed cheery-faced mother welcomed Ray Ray again with a warm smile.

"Hey Ray baby, did you see Bam?"

Her words seemed to be playing in slow motion as Ray Ray's blank stare and right arm slowly raised the gun with intentions to pump several rounds of ammunition in her body until it was lifeless. But just before the act could be carried out, Smoke wrapped his arms around Ray Ray from behind and leaned around him facing Bam's mother in one smooth motion. He smiled at her and said,

"Mrs. Williams, we liked that pecan pie so much that we decided to come get another piece to take with us." She smiled and summoned them to come in. She never noticed the gun in Ray Ray's hand, but she did notice the strange look on his face.

"Ray Ray, are you alright baby?"

"Yeah, he's alright Mrs. Williams, he just been feeling a little under the weather lately."

"Well come on in baby and I'll fix you something that will make you feel better."

"Mrs. Williams, we just realized we have something very important to do, so we will take a raincheck on that pie, and we will see you later." Smoke explained nervously as he shoved a seemingly intoxicated Ray Ray to the car.

After they finally arrived in front of one of their safe houses, Ray Ray slowly began to speak his mind as he gazed off in the distance.

"Man, I was actually gonna kill that sweet lil lady and I've been knowin her all my life."

"I know man," answered Smoke with sympathy in his tone.

"And you don't have to explain why to me because I already know. I know how you feel dawg, trust me. Them low-life niggas took your family from you. But I couldn't let you take Mrs. Williams out dawg. Just relax my nigg, and we gon' make something happen. It's just too late in the game to get side-tracked. And besides, Mrs. Williams has been like a mother to you every since your family passed away, so don't forget who you are, or where you came from." Smoke kept on.

"Dawg, we gangsta's, and my uncle always told me that a gangsta without principles is a foolish gangsta. And foolish gangsta's make foolish mistakes. Mistakes that can end a good thang prematurely, know what I'm sayin dawg. So kick back and re-focus, we got this, just chill."

Ray Ray sat there and absorbed everything in that Smoke had just ran down to him. And he without a doubt knew that Smoke was right, but he also knew he had become something that was sometimes frightening to himself. And what bothered him the most was the fact that he found comfort in this inner demon, and truly had no desire to change. But despite all, he knew that change would eventually have to come if he were to ever become the family-man his woman desperately needed him to be. Otherwise, his family was doomed before it began... And at this point in Ray Ray's life, that was the unthinkable.

CHAPTER 12

In the maximum security female penitentiary in Cold Water Michigan, a group of female inmates sat cramped up in one of the prison tv rooms watching the local news. Inmate Brenda Jackson suddenly became alert when she saw a sketch of Smoke on the news as a fugitive. And as she listened to the allegations against him, she became stirred up and anxious to go tell his mother Yvonne, whom she shared a cell with, because she doubted that Yvonne knew anything about it......

Three days later.

"Inmate Yvonne Broxton, report to the wardens office." The message blared over the intercom for the second time, so Yvonne quickly woke up her cellmate.

Brenda sat up in the top bunk sleepishly.

"What's up girl?"

"Brenda these people just called me to the wardens office and I don't know what it's about, but I want you to get my clothes out the dryer for me just in case I don't come back."

Brenda yawned before giving a reply.

"Girl you know I got you, now go see what them muthafuckas want."

"Thanks girl, hopefully I'll see you later 'cause you know how they is." Yvonne mustard up a half-hearted smile as she exited the cell.

A few moments later, Yvonne lightly tapped on the warden's office door. The middle-aged slender built white man with a receding hairline known as the Warden opened the door with a smile.

"Come on in Ms. Broxton and have a seat."

As she walked in, she noticed two more white men with suits sitting down.

"Hello Ms. Broxton, my name is Detective Edward Jenkins, and this is my associate Detective Wayne Gunter. We are both with the homicide division and we'd like to ask you a few questions. So first of all, when was the last time you spoke with your son?"

Yvonne immediately showed an expression of a distressed mother.

"What's goin on?" She asked in a confused tone.

"Ms. Broxton we will explain all of that to you shortly, but first you need to just answer the questions as we ask them. Now when was the last time you heard from your son?"

Yvonne thought carefully before answering the question because she didn't want to say anything that might make things worse for her son. So after pausing momentarily, she answered.

"I haven't heard from my son in a couple weeks."

"Well do you know how to contact him Ms. Broxton?"

"No, because he moved to a new house and I haven't received the address yet."

The detectives glanced at each other as mutual recognition of the lie she'd just told, then they proceeded with the interrogation.

"Ms. Broxton, is this your son?" They produced a picture of Smoke that came from her photo album.

Yvonne immediately became furious.

"How in the hell did you get that photo out of my personal belongings? You sonuvabitches had no right!"

One of the detectives quickly jumped out of his seat and yelled.

"You just calm yourself down right now Ms.because we are not gonna tolerate your aggression towards us."

"Fuck you!" yelled Yvonne.

"And you still haven't told me what my son is accused of."

The standing detective became angry at her behavior, so he moved a little closer to her and spoke in a stern voice.

"Okay Miss, you really wanna know what your son is accused of? Well listen carefully because it hits closer to home than you can imagine. Your son is accused of conspiracy to child molestation, and the murder of his accomplice in that conspiracy."

"What!" yelled Yvonne in disbelief.

"Are you people serious? My son would never do no shit like that, so you might as well look for somebody else because you got the wrong guy."

"Ms. Broxton, that just might be true, that's why we need to find him so we can help him prove his innocence."

"Yeah right," blurted Yvonne. And just as she made the sarcastic remark, she noticed one of her letters from Smoke in one of the detective's hand.

This enraged her even more because she knew they already had his address, and had already kicked in his front door. But obviously he wasn't there, which is why they came to see her. She sat quiet for a moment and tried to figure out exactly when the correctional officer came in her cell and retrieved the letter and picture from her locker. She couldn't pin-point it but she knew that they would get on some James Bond type of shit when it came to getting what they wanted, yet it still had her puzzled. The detective that was standing up began pacing the floor from one direction to the other with his hands rested behind his back. Then a few moments later, he stopped directly in front of her, staring at her deeply without speaking, which was a common psychological tactic they often used during interrogations, then he let out a exhausted sigh before continuing.

"Ms. Broxton you are doing a 30 year sentence for the murder of your boyfriend, and that's a very long time. But if you help us find your son, we can possibly help you come home before you complete a sentence like that. So what's it gonna be Ms. Broxton?"

Yvonne looked at the detective coldly in his eyes and yelled, "You piece of shit! Do you think I would give you muthafuckas my son. Take me back to my cell goddamit!!"

The detectives looked at each other with a disgruntled expression, then the taller of the two responded.

"Well if that's the way you want it, that's the way it is. But it really makes no difference whether you help us or not because we're going to catch him regardless."

"Or maybe you won't detective!" said Yvonne sarcastically as she walked out the door.

Five minutes later, she walked in her cell crying profusely. She sat on the side of her bed and tried to gain control of herself. She wondered how Smoke could get himself caught-up in something so hideous. She knew her son was capable of murder, but child-molestation was out of the question. She closed her eyes tightly and placed her hands together in prayer, then silently asked God to watch over her son and spare his life from those that would easily hunt him down and kill him just as easily as they would hunt and kill deer. Smoke was all she had left in the world, and she knew her world would surely crumble without him. Smoke had paid for his mother's new legal-defense attorney's, and there was a good possibility that she could get her conviction reversed back to manslaughter... Which would knock a lot of time off of her sentence, so she knew that she had to remain strong with such a heavy case pending. And definitely keep her focus for the freedom-fight that was soon to come.

Yvonne looked down beside her and noticed her laundry folded neatly on her bed. She silently thought about how grateful she was to have a cellmate and friend like Brenda. They had been cellmates for two years and had grown very close within that time.

Brenda wasn't as fortunate to have someone from the outside world send her money like Smoke sent Yvonne money, so Yvonne made sure she shared everything with Brenda because she knew how much harder incarceration could be without outside support. Brenda was only 24 years old, and she was serving a eight-year sentence for assisting her boyfriend in a string of armed robberies. He received fifteen years,

Yvonne glanced around the cell and noticed something strange about the view. Then suddenly it dawned on her what it was. Brenda's bed was stripped of its linen, and her locker was empty of all her belongings. Yvonne quickly jumped up and scanned the cell closer, then ran to the cell next door to converse with her neighbor.

"Monique, have you seen Brenda?" Monique held up a finger as a gesture to hold up a minute while she read a couple more sentences from the book entitled 'I Know Why the Caged Bird Sings' by Maya Angelou, then answered.

"Yeah girl, Brenda left shortly after you. She had all of her stuff with her and she told me to tell you she's sorry."

Yvonne didn't quite understand what was going on.

"Sorry. Sorry for what?" she thought to herself.

"Girl, you know where she went, right?' asked Monique.

"Naw, where did she go?"

"Girl she went home."

"Home!!" shouted Yvonne excitedly.

"That's great girl, damn. She must've got some play on her case. Did she leave her address for me?"

"Nope, all she said was tell Yvonne I'm sorry."

Yvonne scratched her head curiously.

"Okay, thanks Monique. I'll see you later."

She went back to her cell and sat back down for a moment, thinking to herself, *"What could Brenda possibly be sorry about. She took my clothes out of the dryer like I asked her too, so it couldn't be that."*

"Maybe she had to borrow something from me that she wouldn't be able to return, maybe some cosmetics or something. Let me see..."

Yvonne began rambling through her belongings and she didn't notice anything out of the ordinary missing. But when she got to her photo album, an unpleasant thought suddenly crept into her mind. She thought about every strange thing that took place within the last 24 hours, and the wicked truth that suddenly dawned on her gave her body the reaction of an asthmatic patient having an asthma attack. She could barely breathe and her legs instantly became weak. She suddenly yelled out, "NO BRENDA!" as streams of tears covered her face.

Yvonne reflected back to the other night when Brenda asked her about Smoke an unusual amount of times...

Inmate Brenda Jackson suddenly became alert when she saw a sketch of Smoke on the news as a fugitive.

"Girl yall be quite, I'm trying to hear this."

As she listened to the allegations against him, she became stirred up and anxious to go tell her cellmate Yvonne, because Yvonne was his mother and she doubted that Yvonne knew anything about it. Then suddenly, her dutiful thoughts of friendship was replaced with thoughts of deception. So she slowly sat back down in the metal chair and thought of how this discovery could benefit her. Especially since the authorities only had a sketch without a real photo or even a name. Her thoughts raced for the remainder of the night until she finally pieced it all together....

Yvonne continued to weep as she thought about how Brenda violated their friendship and turned against her. Yvonne became even more disgusted when she thought of how Brenda went in her locker and stole the photo and letter the detectives had. She prayed for her son again, then cried herself to sleep. Brenda was given an immediate release for the information she provided. And even though she was in a state facility, the feds involvement in the case made the deal possible.

CHAPTER 13

Just as Pooh was releasing into the condom for the second time that day, his cell-phone rung. He ignored it momentarily and continued to grind between Rashia's legs until he emptied his nut-sack, then sat up and answered the phone. He spoke into the receiver briefly then hung up.

"I gotta go Rashia, I gotta handle something so I'll get back with you later, a'ight baby."

Rashia wanted to ask him questions like

"When will you be back? Where are you going? And will you take long? But she knew that she would be totally out of line because her and Pooh never really played that game with one another. That's why he could come and go as he pleased. They agreed to just remain sex partners to make things less complicated, but Rashia found herself falling deeply in love with him again. And she knew her feelings would only get stronger.

Ten minutes later, Pooh pulled up at an undisclosed area where Ray Ray, Smoke, and Bam were waiting. And for the first time in Ray Ray's robbery career, he felt a little uncomfortable with his crew. Mainly because of all the recent events that took place. Things like, him being on bad terms with Pooh, Smoke being the top story on every news channel because the law now had his real name and a real photo of him. And the fact that Ray

Ray and Smoke had decided to confront Bam about his betrayal once they got inside Boon's house. It seemed like their problems were beginning to come in numbers, and it was all taking a toll on him. The mission was to execute Boon first, then make Bam tell where his brother Spade was at, then execute him as well. The situation nagged at Ray Ray because it didn't feel right to have to execute your childhood friend, but he knew it had to be done because Bam had crossed a line that had no statue of limitation.

After 45 minutes of watching Boon's every move closely, they began to realize the fact that the engagement would be a lot different as planned. Because after Boon and a few of his partners dropped off the four heavy duffle-bags they had, they left. And it was taking a little to long for him to return.

Ray Ray really wanted to wait for him so he could follow the original plan and rid the world of one more drug dealer, but he decided to go ahead and run up in Boon's house anyway because opportunities don't always come so effortlessly. So without further delay, they all exited their vehicles and made their way to the front door.

The June heat beamed on their heads making the black skull-caps they wore feel like microwave hats. They used a conventional method of entry on this house because of the type of wood and bolts that held it together. They simply kicked it open.

They searched the house to make sure they didn't get any surprise guests, then opened up the four duffle bags that they saw Boon bring in earlier. Two of the bags contained two-hundred and fifty-thousand dollars apiece, while the other two bags held fifty kilos of cocaine apiece. Ray Ray walked over to the window and glanced out the curtain briefly. Then suddenly balked,

"Ay Bam, where you been for the last coupla' days dawg?"

Bam hesitated before answering the question.

"Dawg, do you remember that bad bitch from the strip club *'Pretty Woman'* name Syann?"

"Yeah, I remember her."

"Well I've been spendin' a little extra time wit dat bitch lately. Her head is something serious dawg."

Pooh wasn't aware of the situation, but he silently thought to himself,

"That bitch head ain't shit." He knew because he had dealt with her on a few occasions.

"She is so fine that she try to look to cute while she suckin the dick, that's her downfall in that department." thought Pooh as he concluded his reflection of her.

Ray Ray smirked a little because of the lie he'd just heard, then responded.

"Dawg, you know you missed my family reunion this weekend."

Bam looked surprised before replying.

"Fa'real dawg? My bad homie. You know I woulda' been there if I woulda' known about it, straight-up."

"Well you woulda' knew about it if you wouldna' been fuckin around wit dat bitch!" barked Ray Ray.

Smoke knew where this was about to go, but he couldn't let it go down because this wasn't the initial plan. They specifically agreed to only do it if Boon was there too, or they would wait until another day. And now that he realized Ray Ray decided to do it anyway, he had to defuse the situation while Bam was still naïve to what they really knew.

Smoke hastily interrupted.

"Ay Ray Ray, man we will discuss that shit later, let's get the fuck up outta here dawg."

Ray Ray had a look of disagreement in his eyes as he stared at Smoke. Then after several moments with no response, he suddenly spoke up irately.

"Yall grab those bags and let's get the fuck up outta here."

Smoke and Bam grabbed the two bags with the money, then they all walked out, leaving the other two bags where they were.

As they walked toward the car, Bam focused on Ray Ray with a curious expression.

"Dawg, is you a'ight?"

Ray Ray looked at him and managed to muster up a fake smile.

"Yeah, I'm a'ight dawg. I just don't like when crew members miss our lil homemade family reunions. You know yall is all a nigga got, so yall need to understand the importance of shit like that." His answer put Bam's mind at ease.

"I feel you my nigg, it won't happen again."

They all pulled off in separate vehicles, then ten minutes later, Pooh pulled up down the street from the house they'd just left. He hopped out the black mustang and quickly ran back up in Boon's house. He grabbed the two remaining duffle-bags, then left.

One week later.

"Ay Pee-Wee, answer the door man!"

"Damn Buzz, you know it's your turn to be answerin the damn door, so you need to hurry up and get yo' shitty ass off the toilet."

"Who is it?" Asked Pee-Wee as he approached the door.

"It's Johnny, is yall still straight?"

"Yeah we still straight, whutcha need playa?"

"Let me get two dimes."

"A'ight, hold up a minute."

Pee-Wee quickly ran to the bathroom door.

"Ay Buzz, it's a customer dawg, how long you gon' be?"

"Man just come in and get the sack nigga, don't let dat money get away. The door is open."

Pee-Wee took a deep breath, then rushed in the bathroom to get the sack of rocks. Buzz was sitting on the toilet rambling through his pants pockets in an attempt to locate the sack. Pee-Wee was still trying to hold his breath, but it gave out after about fifteen seconds, and the stench rushed up his nostrils causing him to gag. He quickly pulled his shirt over his nose while Buzz still rambled.

"Damn nigga hurry up, you stank like a muthafucka." Pee-Wee mumbled through the shirt.

Buzz finally came up with the sack in his hand laughing.

Pee-Wee snatched it and ran out of there as fast as he could with watery eyes, gasping for air. He picked up his nine-millimeter pistol off the couch on his way to make the sale. Pee-Wee opened the door as far as the chain would let it open, then passed the smoker two rocks after he was handed a twenty-dollar bill. Buzz came out the bathroom a few minutes after the sale.

A few hours later, Buzz ran to the phone-booth and beeped Pooh. Pooh called back as soon as he saw the code 911.

"Whuddup Buzz?"

"Ain't nothing dawg, I'm just callin to let you know that

things getting low on that tip, so get at me whenever you find time."

"A'ight Buzz, I'll be gettin atchu shortly, holla."

They hung up and Pooh showed up 30 minutes later to pick up his money and drop off a fresh sack of rocks. He then drove five blocks over to meet with a guy name Dre that he was also givin work to. He dropped off ten kilos with Dre because Dre had a heavy clientele and could move the product fast. On the otherhand, his little cousin Pee-Wee and Buzz could only handle a thousand-dollar sack at a time, that's why they didn't receive nothing more than that from him.

"Who is it?" Asked Buzz when he heard more knocks on the door.

"Tenae!" answered the female voice.

Buzz looked at Pee-Wee with a jokingly wide-eyed expression.

"Dawg, it's on now, this bitch is a professional head-hunter and I bet she ain't got no money." He opened the door.

"Whuddup Tenae? Where you been girl?"

The cocoa-brown 35 year old Tenae stood there wearing a tight pair of black Girbaud jeans, and a short white halter-top exposing her flat stomach and petite figure. When she smiled, her missing front tooth kinda jumped out atcha. Other than that, she was a nice-looking woman.

She scratched her face before she answered Buzz.

"Baby I've been in the county-jail for the last couple weeks for boostin, you know how that go Buzz."

"Oh yeah? That's a trip girl, but what's on ya' mind? Talk to me."

Tenae smiled and adjusted her baseball hat that she

wore before responding.

"Baby like I just said, I just got out the county and my money ain't right. But I'm tryna' get high, so let me ease yo' mind while you skeet in mine."

"Is that right Tenae?" asked Buzz excitedly.

"Well let's go girl." Buzz locked the door and tossed Pee-Wee the sack. Then escorted Tenae to the bedroom.

She didn't waste any time getting on her knees and helping Buzz step out of the loose-fitting Gucci sweatpants. She removed her gum and slowly started licking the head of his dick with a steady rhythm in a circular motion. Buzz always enjoyed getting this particular pleasure from Tenae because she knew exactly what to do and when to do it. Tenae took her time as she patiently started inching her mouth over his hardness, taking more inside with every bob of her head.

She held the base of his dick as she continued to swallow more inches. Within moments, her lips were kissing the rim of her own hand, so she slowly slid it back and let it rest on his lower abdominal. Buzz started gripping her head tighter because he felt himself about to come. Tenae took pride in her work, and she loved when she got to the part where she would make men squirm the most, like now, where she suddenly had the entire length of him engulfed in her mouth. Buzz felt his legs starting to get weak, so he sat down on the bed and leaned backwards, resting on his elbows. He watched in amazement as his pipe disappeared in her head so skillfully.

Tenae smirked a little when she realized he was almost at the point of no return. Buzz squirmed and called out Tenae's name as if he was a girl receiving good sex.

"Damn Tenae, aw shit. Hold up a min- goddamn."

As she continued to bob her head and work her mouth, she suddenly heard a loud crashing sound. Buzz and Tenea both jumped to attention.

"Whut 'da fuck was that?" bawled Buzz as he walked toward the door with a swingin dick.

The bedroom door came crashing open just as he approached it. He was in the air, then slammed on the floor with five different caliber handguns in his face before he even realized what happened.

"You are under arrest you piece of shit!" yelled one of the white federal agents with bad breath.

"Damn," squawked Buzz as the second loop of the handcuff was tightened around his wrist.

The agents found the cocaine and took all three of them to jail. Tenae was highly pissed-off because she never gave head for free, along with the fact that she'd really just got out the county jail. And now she was headed right back in.

The feds tested the cocaine just as they'd been doing after all of their recent raids, and when it turned red instead of blue, they all got excited because their plan had worked. This was their biggest break in the case thus far. They interrogated Buzz and Pee-Wee for hours until one or both of them were ready to talk.

Fifteen years for the distribution of 14 grams of crack within five hundred feet of a school zone didn't sound to appealing to Pee-Wee, so he immediately told the feds where he got the cocaine from.

He told them all about what his cousin Pooh was into, and even mentioned Ray Ray as being the ring leader of the crew. The prosecutor agreed to give Pee-Wee four years for his co-operation, but only upon the capture of Pooh. In the meantime, he would have to sit on the original ten year plea until they brought Pooh to justice. Buzz didn't say a word, he just prepared himself to go to trial.....

As Pooh walked out of the MGM Grand Casino, federal agents swarmed him from every direction. He tried to run but didn't get very far before the agents subdued him and took him in.

CHAPTER 14

Raindrops fell lightly against the window as Ray Ray sat at the candle-lit table in his home. Other than the rain, the night was calm and therapeutic in its own way. Ray Ray watched intently as Sheila prepared their food. She carefully placed the thin cut pasta on each of their plates, along with a thick tender grilled chicken breast. She then carefully poured a white sauce over the pasta and the chicken evenly, then placed a basket of fresh garlic bread in the center of the table. She smiled at Ray Ray briefly, then poured two glasses of Remy red wine.

"Chicken Fettuccini miseor." she worded in an Italian accent playfully.

Ray Ray loved the way Sheila prepared this meal. She would always have it looking like it came straight out of a five star restaurant, with the little parsley decorations and all.

And she never went to school for it. She'd always been a natural at it.

"Father I want to thank you for this wonderful life you've given me with a wonderful man. I wanna' thank you for this meal, and every meal that you provide us with Lord. And I ask that you continue to pour your blessing's upon us, Amen. Okay, dig in baby." She spoke playfully.

"I made grace short and sweet because you look

huuuuuunnngry baby!"

"I am huuuuunnngry baby!" responded Ray Ray.

"I ran across some good 'dro on my way to the crib. I'll smoke one with you after we eat."

Sheila laughed before responding.

"Ray Ray you know I don't smoke that stuff."

"Oh, I forgot baby, and guess what? I was actually thinkin about quittin too."

"Fo'real." asked Sheila excitedly.

"Yeah baby, when I'm eighty years old."

She lightly threw a small piece of parsley at him as he bent over crackin his side in laughter.

"I'm just trippin baby. I just might stop sooner than you think, but the quitting process starts with you." Sheila was puzzled.

"What do you mean the process starts with me?"
"Like I said, the process starts with you. Especially if you come over here and feed me the rest of this dinner."

Sheila smiled, displaying her perfect set of teeth before responding.

"Well if I do that, I have an extra request."

"Oh yeah, what is it baby?"

Sheila stood up and turned around in a slow spin, showing off her petite, curvaceous body in the black Prada body dress that would've caused a lot of traffic accidents in public, then she answered.

"Stop smoking weed, and have me for dessert after I feed you."

Ray Ray smiled before responding.

"That's not a compromise baby."

"Why not?" asked Sheila.

Ray Ray pulled her close to him and whispered.

"Because I always have you for dessert."

A long passionate kiss followed Sheila's soft giggle, which landed them between the Louis Vuitton satin sheets on their king sized Versace bed.....

Two hours later, they sat in the oval shaped tub and enjoyed each others company. Sheila leaned forward and got the glass of champagne off the portable stand, then gently rested her back against Ray Ray's chest.

"Ray Ray, have you given any thought to what we discussed a few weeks ago?"

Ray Ray scratched his head in a curious manner before responding.

"Baby you know that I be havin a lot of shit on my mind, so you gotta remind me of what it is we discussed."

"Ray Ray you know what we discussed. Marriage, family business, and financial freedom. I told you we can build our revenue up to a comfortable status, then handle most of our living expenses off the interest rate. And long as the interest rates stay flexible, we would never have to touch the principle. We just can't spend our money carelessly.'

Ray Ray interrupted.

"Wait a minute baby, I thought financial freedom meant that we could spend our money carelessly."

Sheila turned toward him with a mocking expression.

"Baby if we start spending carelessly, we will never be able to sustain financial freedom, ya feel me?"

Ray Ray's mind drifted off. He thought to himself, "*This is a helluva woman, and I'll be damned if I let her get away. I'm a multi-millionare and she don't even know it. I'm gonna tie up all of my loose ends and let the streets have them dumb ass drug dealers. And besides, I can't get to the top-dawg drug dealers if I wanted too. They're a little too powerful, they run the muhfuckin' government.*"

CHAPTER 15

As Sheila walked out the house to get in her Saab, a man with a bouquet of flowers ran up to her and handed them to her along with some car keys. Sheila looked puzzled because she didn't understand. Then the man pointed at the triple white E-420 Benz with the ribbon on it that read "Happy Birthday Sheila." She was ecstatic but still confused at the same time. She opened the door and there was a snow white full-length mink laid across the driver's seat in plastic. Sheila quickly dialed Ray Ray's cell phone number. He answered after three rings.

"Hello."

"Ray Ray, why am I sitting in a triple-white benz, with a snow white mink, some flowers, and a sign that says happy birthday Sheila?"

Ray Ray calmly replied,

"Well maybe they sent it to the wrong Sheila."

Sheila's mouth dropped open.

"Oh my God. Do you think that's what happened baby?"

"Hell naw baby, You know I sent that to you luv."

"Oh my God baby! Wow! You are so unpredictable at times sweetheart. Thank you so much. This is deep." She gasped as she held her hand on her chest in an effort to gain her composure. Then spoke again.

"This is a trip baby, but I need you to explain something to me, because the one thing that I don't understand is why it says happy birthday. You know my birthday is seven months away." Ray Ray laughed before responding.

"Baby-girl you know that everyday is your birthday with me, so enjoy ya'self gorgeous. I gotta go, I'll talk to you later a'ight."

"Okay sweetie, I love you Ray Ray."

"Luv u too baby, holla."

Syann counted the wad of money one more time before placing it back inside the vanilla envelope, then slowly pulled away from the car that sat beside her.......

****

Bam was unexpectedly awakened out of a deep sleep to answer his ringing phone.

"Hello." he groaned sleepishly.

"Whuddup Bam, this Ray Ray."

"Whuddup Ray, what it do?"

"Same ol' same ol' dawg. But check this out, I need you to come holla at me."

Bam sat up and yawned before continuing.

"When dawg?"

"Now." commanded Ray Ray.

"Is it a problem for you?"

"Naw man, but what time is it?"

"It's 3:30 am."

Bam paused for a moment.

"A'ight dawg. I'll be through there in 30 minutes."

"Cool, I'll see you then, holla."

As Ray Ray hung up the phone, he gave Smoke a puzzled look.

"Man, I might be wrong, but I think that nigga know what time it is."

"Why you think that Ray?"

"I think that because he sounded kinda funny."

Smoke laughed and tried to bring some logic to the situation.

"Dawg, maybe the nigga was off in some pussy and you disturbed his groove."

Ray Ray nodded his head in a sarcastic way.

"Well I'll tell you what, that shit might be true, but one things fa'sho and two things fa'certain, we will know in 30 minutes."

They both sat there making small talk for the next hour, then out of the blue, Ray Ray grimaced.

"I told you dawg. That nigga ain't come 'cause he peeped game on where our heads at. And it's a shame because I had decided not to kill the nigga. I was just gon' make him tell me where his brother Spade is at. But now I gotta due'em so we can make Spade come to the funeral, then due his bitch-ass too. Ya feel me."

Smoke gave Ray Ray a strange look before responding.

"Damn dawg, I'm glad we on the same team,'cause you'se a strategic thinkin muthafucka, fo'real."

"Yeah, well you know a guy always gotta stay one step ahead of sucka's and two steps ahead of lames, it is what it is."

Three days later...

Bam was at a BMW dealership getting his 740 Beemer serviced. He admired how Syann looked in the tight fitting Chanel dress that displayed every curve that her beautiful body had to offer. She had her hair in a French wrap, and her big dimples sunk in her face with every smile.

Some of the men who worked at the dealership stared

at her constantly as she moved about. Her burgundy dress and Stelleto pumps matched Bam's burgundy 740. Bam felt himself starting to get an erection as he watched her checkin out all the other model Beemers.

Suddenly, a group of three rowdy looking men walked toward Bam. They were laughing, cursing, and finishing the last of a blunt. One of the men bumped Bam as he passed by without an apology, while the other two men discussed Syann's nice ass out loud. Bam didn't like it one bit, so he nonchalantly called Syann over to him and grimaced,

"Hand me my heater baby."

Syann casually reached in her purse and handed Bam his glock 9mm. Bam stuck it in the front of his pants, then anxiously approached the one who bumped him.

"Yo' my man, you got a problem?"

The man looked at Bam as if he was crazy before he answered.

"Naw man, I ain't got no problem. But if I did, you'd be the first to know."

Bam stepped a little closer to the man, tightly gripping the butt of his gun.

"Well next time say excuse me when you bump into me nigga!"

The man immediately displayed an expression of displeasure, then stepped closer to Bam and shouted.

"Fuck you nigga!"...

Plack!

Blood gushed from his left eye as Bam viciously slapped him across the face with the gun. The other two men quickly ran toward Bam, but just as quickly stopped in their tracks as Bam aimed the gun at both of them, training his aim from one to the other as he shouted.

"Whut you bitches wanna do, huh? I dare one of you bitches to jump." Bam wacked the already disabled man across the face again, dropping him to his knees, then yelled.

"Fuck who nigga! You da' one that look pretty fucked to me! Now get yall bitch-asses up outta here and go to the Cutlass dealership where yall belong."

The other two men helped their friend to his feet, then left. Bam and Syann left 45 minutes later. And as they cruised the Beemer down East Jefferson, Syann suggested they get something to eat so they headed to Fishbones restaurant on Monroe St. in downtown Detroit. Five minutes before they got to their destination, they saw a police car lurking in the area. Bam took precautions and casually slid the glock from his waist and gave it back to Syann to put in her purse.

After the threat of being stopped was over and they made it to the restaurant safely, they ate a cajun fish dinner, sat and chatted for awhile, then decided it was time to leave.

Bam really liked Syann, and he kept asking himself why? He'd never been in love before because he never allowed himself to get attached to females. But lately he had been feeling almost as if he was slowly submitting to the 'L' word, with a stripper of all people. He decided not to let it bother him anymore and just let the cards fall where they fall.

As they walked out of Fishbone, Bam de-activated the alarm on his car. He fiddled with the keys before unlocking the door, then unexpectedly out of the blue, he saw Ray Ray hit the corner in a black SS Impala. He immediately knew what time it was when he saw the look in Ray Ray's eyes.

"Syann! Gimee the heater!" he yelled as Syann stood on the other side of the car transfixed as if she didn't hear him.

When he saw Ray Ray getting closer, he yelled again.

"Syann! Gimme the goddamn gun!" Syann still didn't move.

Bam quickly slid across the hood of the car to where she was at. He snatched the purse from her hand, hurriedly reaching inside, only to come up with the makeup, lipstick, and other miscellaneous items that women carry in purses. Bam savagely looked up at Syann as if to be in pure shock, then yelled.

"You Bitch! You nothing-ass Bitch! Where 'da fuck is my gun?"

And just as he completed the sentence, the flurry of shots that came from the SS riddled Bam's body. Leaving him sprawled out on the pavement in a pool of blood.

Ray Ray winked at Syann, then hit the gas hard. Making the tires screech as him and Smoke fled the scene. Syann had set Bam up for 20 thousand dollars...

Four days later...

Ray Ray and Smoke sat outside Bam's funeral waiting for Spade to show up. Bam's mother had a nervous breakdown during the funeral and had to be rushed to the hospital. Ray Ray and Smoke waited for hours and even went to the burial site, but Spade never showed up.

Later on that night, Ray Ray turned the bottle of Hennessey up while he and Smoke sat in one of their safe houses discussing the latest events.

"Dawg I can't believe that sucka didn't even show up for his own brother's funeral." Smoke remarked as he blew out the smoke from the marijuana joint he was smokin.

Ray Ray sat there with a blank expression on his face, still gripping the bottle of Hennessey. He was trying to sort his thoughts as Smoke continued to elaborate on the situation.

"Dawg, we might not ever get that nigga now, and shit is just fucked up. I called the hospital the other day to check up on Iyonna. They said she is doing better but she still in shock. And they don't know if she will ever speak again. I'm glad I chopped that piece of shit up that messed her up like that. I wish I could kill dat fag-ass lame again, real talk dawg. And these muthafuckas got my face all over the gottdamn news as a muthafuckin child molester, stupid muthafuckas."

The weed had Smoke's thoughts racin' from one to the other.

"Dawg I got a letter from my moms the other day through one of my aunts that I haven't heard from in years. But after I read the letter, I understood why. Man moms told me that her cellmate stole one of my flicks and one of my letters from her and turned it in to the feds. That's how them bitches got a real flick of me and got my address. I wish I knew where that lil bitch was at so I could stick a hot knife up her pussy."

Ray Ray laughed at Smoke's comment because he knew that Smoke would do it in a heartbeat.

"Man you crazy as hell, but I feel you dawg. And I hope yo' mom's get some play on her case, 'cause she been up in that muthafucka long enough. And check this out Smoke, you gotta start layin real low dawg, 'cause everyday them bitches is searchin a little harder, know what I mean."

"Yeah Ray, I know what you mean, and I plan to do that after we tighten up some more of our loose ends, you dig."

Ray Ray suddenly looked at Smoke with a shocked expression as if something had struck him hard.

"Man, I just thought about something. Do you remember when we was over Bam's house lookin at them picture's of Bam and Spade when they was youngsta's."

"Yeah I remember."

"Well check this out. I bet you didn't notice which parent Spade was seen with the most in those flicks?"

Smoke looked dumbfounded before giving a sarcastic reply.

"As a matter of fact, I don't."

Ray Ray moved closer to Smoke as if he had something very serious to say before continuing.

"Man, he was in most of the pictures with his old dude. His father."

Smoke thought carefully for a few moments before responding.

"So whatch'u saying Ray Ray?"

"Dawg, I'm saying that maybe that's where that nigga's heart is at, and that I'm willing to see if he comes to that funeral."

"Whut!" Yelled Smoke.

"Man is you serious? You can't be serious."

"You damn right I'm serious."

"Ray Ray that would be real fucked up to do the old man."

"Yeah. Well it was real fucked up to do my parents nigga. Ain't nobody give a fuck about mines, so you can miss me with that sympathy shit, cause I'm puttin' this down. And if I'm wrong about it, tough luck. And besides, we already spared his moms, and that was plenty, 'cause ain't nobody spare my mom's. Didn't nobody give a Fuck!! So it is what it is, case closed." Smoke decided to end the conversation because he knew Ray Ray's mind was made up and there was no turning back. And even though he didn't fully agree with Ray Ray's next move, he knew that nomatter what, he'd be by his side regardless.

****

Two days later...

"Who is it?" asked Bam's mother in a shaky voice when she heard the knocks on her door. She'd been released from the hospital the same day that she had the nervous breakdown, and was still a little shook up. Suddenly the knocks on the door stopped, so Mrs. Williams stepped a little closer.

"Who is it?" she asked again, but this time she was greeted by the sound of her front door being kicked in.

The door flew open violently, barely missing her as she witnessed two masked gunmen enter her home. One of the men immediately made her lay face down on the floor, while the other one went to the dining room where her husband was sitting in front of his T.V.

The old man was just as he normally is, staring at the television with a blank expression. Ray Ray suddenly removed his mask out of respect, along with the fact that he knew the man's wife was in the other room secured.

The old man looked a little different than he normally did. He looked as if he'd aged ten years within the past few weeks. Ray Ray stepped in front of the old man and spoke in a regretful voice.

"Sorry about this old man. And if you can hear me, I always did like you."

As he aimed the gun, he suddenly noticed what the piece of paper was in the old man's hand. It was an obituary of Bam. Ray Ray slightly dropped his head for a moment, then just as quickly pulled himself together.

"Tell my family I said I'm sorry for takin' on the characteristics of the men who took their lives. And maybe someday I'll be able to change into the man they wanted me to be. So long Pops."

Boh!

A single blast from the snub-nosed 38 left a small hole in the man's forehead, killing him instantly. Ray Ray placed the mask back on then walked past Mrs.Williams as she laid on the floor crying hysterically. She assumed the worst had happened when she heard the gunshot, and thought that she'd surely be next...

Four days later...

Smoke and Ray Ray sat in the back of the crowded funeral home wearing dark Armani shades to match their tailor-made Armani suits. It truly felt odd for them to be sitting in there among Bam's family again within a matter of a few weeks for the same type of tragedy that they were solely responsible for.

Ray Ray really didn't like to see Mrs. Williams in such bad shape, but he couldn't allow himself to entertain that emotion. She sat in the front row in total silence with the same blank facial expression that her late husband wore before he succumbed to his death. A middle aged woman who Ray Ray had never seen before, sat next to Mrs. Williams and held her gently as she laid her head on the woman's shoulder.

They were 45 minutes into the service when Smoke and Ray Ray started getting restless. But they held on because they could tell that the reverend was about to conclude his sermon. Smoke leaned over to Ray Ray and whispered.

"Man, dat nigga ain't comin, let's bounce."

"A'ight, in a minute dawg. We might as well finish payin our respects." Smoke complied and leaned back in his seat.

Ten minutes later, the service was concluded and everyone slowly got up and prepared themselves to go to the burial site. They all walked out into the common area of the funeral home, weeping and embracing those who were visibly distraught.

Smoke and Ray Ray stood up to leave just as the Pall Barrers were closing the casket. Suddenly, a man ran through the door out of breath waving for the Pall Barrers to hold up on closing the casket.

"Gimme a few minutes alone with him man." retorted the man as his eyes shifted from one Pall-Barrer to the other.

They could see the desperation in his eyes, so they gladly obliged. The man stood there in front of the old man's casket with a black hoody over his head. He gazed at the corpse for a steady five minutes before gently touching his face.

He wiped what appeared to be a few tears, mumbled a few words, then headed for the exit.

"Ay my man!" shouted Ray Ray as he slowly approached the man from behind.

"You drop this?"

The man stopped and quickly turned around. And at that moment, they locked eyes for what seemed like an eternity, but in actuality was only a few seconds.

"Finally." said Ray Ray as he stood there with the Sig p226 legion in hand.

He reflected back on all that had been taken from him... all that had been sacrificed...and all that was now tainted forever.

He'd waited on this moment for so long, and now it would finally come. Ray Ray stepped closer to Spade and snarled.

"I asked you a question nigga, I said did you drop this?"

Spade immediately knew what time it was. His past ghost had finally come back to haunt him. And badly as he wished it was all a dream, he knew it wasn't. He was wide awake. He focused on the gun as Ray Ray stood there waiting for an answer to his question. Then moments later, he decided to answer.

"Yeah nigga, I dropped it. Just like I dropped yo-" a rapid succession of holes began to appear in various spots on Spade's face before he could finish the disrespectful sentence that was about to come out of his mouth.

It looked as if he suddenly caught a bad case of chicken-pox in the form of bullets as the 9mm hollow-points penetrated his flesh at point-blank range.

Spade's head jerked backwards, allowing a few of the slugs to rip threw his neck and throat. Then he abruptly dropped to the floor with a loud thud face down beside his father's casket.

And just as quickly as he dropped, Ray Ray rolled him over with his foot, then continued to fire bullets into his face until the clip was empty. Suddenly, Smoke began firing rounds above the heads of all the screaming spectators and family members that started looking in their direction to see who was shooting and what for.

Smoke quickly pulled two ski-masks out of his pockets, putting one on, and handing Ray Ray the other.

"Put this on dawg, hurry up."

Ray Ray seemed to be moving a little too slow for Smoke as he stood over Spade's body transfixed in the moment as if he could watch Spade slide down the tunnel of death forever.

Smoke quickly let off a few more shots as he noticed the heads of two men trying to peep in through the double doors. Now frustrated by Ray Ray's laxed movement, he stepped right up to his ear and shouted.

"Put the Gottdamn mask on dawg and let's get the fuck up outta here." Ray Ray put the mask on and moved a little faster, but Smoke could tell he wasn't completely out of his trance.

As they both ran up to the door about to exit, Ray Ray suddenly turned around and ran back over to Spade's body. He bent down and began to search his pockets.

"I don't believe this shit." mumbled Smoke as he became fed up.

"Fuck is you doin dawg? I know you ain't searchin dat nigga for no money."

Ray Ray didn't respond, he just continued to search until he found what he was lookin for.

He found the state I.D with a Los Angeles address. He had no intention of letting Bo-Bo get away, and he would bet his last dollar that Bo-Bo was at that address. Ray Ray and Smoke managed to make it out of the funeral home by a wing and a prayer before authorities showed up.

When Spade's mother walked in the room and saw her oldest son lying dead on the floor beside her husband's casket, she immediately suffered a massive heart attack and died right where she stood.

CHAPTER 16

"Hold up guy! I told you I don't want that much off the top.""Pee-Wee I heard you the first time, now if you don't be still and let me finish this shit, you gon' be walkin 'round here lookin like you a prime candidate for suicide watch."

A few of the other inmates laughed as they watched Pee-Wee get a taper-fade and complain the whole time.

"Ay Pee-Wee." spoke one of the men in company.

"Did you hear about that dude that got slumped a few months ago, and the niggas who did it let his Rottweiler have it too?"

"Yeah I heard about it, and I'm almost fasho I know who put it down."

"Who nigga?"

"My cousin's boy Ray Ray."

"Man is you talkin about smooth ass Ray Ray ?"

Pee-Wee looked up with his eyes only, in order to not move his head and answered sarcastically.

"Yeah nigga, smooth ass Ray Ray."

One of the other inmates who stood close by and was able to eaves-drop on their conversation had heard all he needed to hear. He never knew who was supposedly responsible for his cousin's death, but now he had a face and a name to put with it. As he walked away from the crowd of inmates, he had a sense of relief that he was only in on a misdemeanor warrant, and only had two days left on a four month sentence. He felt that he truly needed closure because his cousin was his best friend. And somebody had to pay.

"Hey sweetheart, you awake." asked the nurse as she scribbled on a chart beside Iyonna's bed. Iyonna slowly opened her eyes and pointed at the small container of juice that sat on the stand next to her bed.

"You want some juice sweetheart?" said the nurse as she handed Iyonna the Hawaiian punch container.

"Here, let me place this straw in there for you honey, so it will make things a lii-tt-le bit easier."

As Iyonna sat on her bed sippin the juice, the nurse reflected back to the first day she met her. Smoke had came running with Iyonna in his arms, and she was in terrible shape. And when Smoke handed Iyonna to her, she saw something in his eyes that she couldn't put her finger on. All she knew is that it didn't coincide with what the authorities were saying about him.

Riiiiinnnnng!

The sound of the ringing phone shattered her thoughts and startled her at the same time. She took a quick breath then picked up.

"Hello."

"Hey Ebony whassup sis?"

"Ain't nothin up girl, I'm at work being a nurse."

"Well ex-cuuuse me Ms. thang. Anyway, Ebony I really need you to do me a favor. I need you to drop me off at the club 007 when you get off work."

"Tasha when I get off work I be tired girl. And you don't need yo' lil fast ass at no club noway."

"Ebony come on sis." Tasha whined in a baby voice.

"My ride that I planned got cancelled. And Rhonda'nem already had a car full 'cause I had told them I had a ride."

Ebony huffed a few times as if she was tired of the debate, then exclaimed.

"Well alright girl. But I hope you don't expect me to pick you up too?"

"Sis, just get me there, getting back will definitely not be a problem. Especially wit this short, short, Prada skirt. And this cleavage that make a nigga wanna run a credit card through it to see if they can see a little more." Ebony laughed at her sister's remarks.

"Girl yous'a hot lil heifer, I'll see you shortly."

"I know." Groaned Tasha seductively before she hung up the phone....

****

"I miss you too mommi... Yeah baby. Okay, let me hear you say popi one mo' time."

"Popi." she spoke seductively.

"Yeah, that's what I'm talkin' 'bout. I'll see you there, holla." The moment Smoke hung up the receiver of the pay phone, all he heard was

"Stick up nigga! Don't make it no murder."

The youngsta nomore than fifteen, pointed a rusty lookin 38 long at his chest

"Whoa whoa youngsta, take it easy. Don't you know you a little too young to be out here playin wit them kinda toys."

"Man if I wanted a sermon I woulda' went to church. Now gimme yo' muthafuckin ends before I due yo' punk ass!" demanded the youngsta with authority.

Smoke stared the youngsta square in his eyes then calmly spoke.

"Well I'll tell you what youngsta, since you put it like that, I'll give it to you on one condition."

A disgusted frown quickly formed on the youngsta's face that signified, *"If this nigga don't stop playin wit me,"* then he yelled,

"Condition! Nigga ain't no fuckin' condition."

Smoke quickly held up a finger to cut the youngsta's flow of threatening obscenities off before he continued.

"Oh, but it is youngsta. And if you just chill-out for a minute and let me tell you, you can get this money and we both live to see another day."

Tired of the bullshit, the youngsta quickly asked,

"Okay, what muhfuckin condition nigga?"

Smoke smirked a little before giving a reply.

"On the condition that you let me see how fast you can pull it out yo' ass."

There was a slight pause because the youngsta couldn't believe this muthafucka had the nerve. Suddenly, the youngsta screamed as the single shot from Ray Ray's nine penetrated the right side of his buttocks. Smoke snatched the rusty gun from the boy with quickness, then taunted.

"I told you I wanted to see how fast you can pull it out yo' ass."

He opened the gun and started laughin.

"Ray, look at this shit dawg! The lil nigga only got two bullets in this shit."

Smoke squatted down next to the boy as he squirmed on the ground holding his bloody buttocks moaning in pain.

"Let me tell you sumthin young dawg. Don't ever come at nobody like that again. From now on, if you gon' come. Come right."

Smoke stood up and pilled a couple hundreds off his

knot and tossed it to the youngsta. He still couldn't completely stop laughin because he found it so amusing how the youngsta thought he was at the pay-phone alone. Ray Ray had went across the street to the gas station. And being in that line of work, he immediately knew what time it was when he came back. So he crept up behind the boy and damn near listened to the whole conversation.

While still laughin, Smoke gave the youngsta a suggestion.

"You take them couple hundred and buy you a better gun…And no! don't know job come wit' it, this ain't Frank White, this Smoke lil nigga."

Smoke and Ray Ray got in the car still laughin and still clownin the youngsta about his failed attempt at armed robbery. As the car pulled off, Smoke leaned out the window.

"Ay youngsta, if you ever wanna have a shootout wit me, gimme a call, 'cause at least I know I only gotta duck twice."

They burst out laughin again and sped off into traffic.

"Check this out Ray Ray, I hollad at my lil Spanish mommi a little while ago, and she wanna see a nigga tonight."

Ray Ray blew out the Smoke from the Newport before responding.

"So that's why you was using a pay phone huh? So if them people was listenin, you could be ghost by the time they get there."

Smoke's eyebrows wrinkled before he answered sarcastically.

"Okay Einstein, I think you're on to sumthin. Anyway let's swing by the crib so I can put on a little sumthin more appealing to the party scene."

"Whutchu mean the party scene man?" asked Ray Ray rebelliously.

"Man she want me to meet her at the club double-o-seven so we can socialize a little before I bang dem guts out. Dawg you know that club shit is foreplay for them hoes."

"Well you know that club shit ain't me Smoke, so count me outta that one."

"Come on Ray Ray, Man I know you don't like clubs-n-shit, but just roll wit me this one time dawg. We ain't gotta stay long. I'm goin in, mingle for a minute, then we leavin wit that bitch so I can toss her and get my nuts out the sand."

Smoke turned toward Ray Ray to put emphasis on his next statement.

"Dawg, do you realize that I ain't had no pussy in over a week. And you know as well as I do, that ain't like me dawg. So like that song say homie, 'Just gimme the night."

Ray Ray smirked a little at Smoke's desperation plea.

"A'ight nigga, just this once."

CHAPTER 17

"Is that your phone ringing or mine?" asked Smoke as he splashed on a dab of Hugo Boss cologne. He looked in the full length mirror and admired the way his dark Polo shirt, Polo slacks, and Polo boots complimented each other.

"That's mine dawg," said Ray Ray as he picked up the cell phone off the table.

"Hello."

"Whassup baby." Asked Sheila.

"Ain't nothing poppin baby, I'm just missin you."

"Well when are you comin home baby? You know we need to spend as much time together as we can before I go back to school."

"I know baby, and I wouldn't have it no other way. You just sit tight and I'll be home in a coupla' hours, okay?"

"Okay Ray, I'll wait up for you baby, if ya know what I mean." Sheila spoke seductively.

Ray Ray smiled before hanging up and replied,

"You do that baby, you do that."

Sheila blew a kiss through the phone, then hung up. He couldn't wait to get home now. He thought to himself,"*This nigga talkin 'bout he want some pussy, shid, I want some pussy too. Got me goin to this dumb-ass club. I shouldn't even be goin, but fuck it cause I ain't stayin at this shit long.*" Smoke suddenly broke Ray Ray's thoughts with his thinkin out loud.

"Man, I wonder where that nigga Pooh at. We ain't heard from him in over a week."

Ray Ray thought about it for a moment before responding.

"Well you know that me and dawg aint been on good terms lately, cause he get a lil hard-headed from time to time. So ain't no tellin where he at, but that's still my nigg. We'a see if we can catch up with him tomorrow."

"Yeah, tomorrow." Smoke agreed.

"But for now let's bounce"

Thirty minutes later...

Smoke and Ray Ray pulled up at the crowded club, and all they saw were trucks, cars, and motorcycles out front. Systems were pumpin various rap songs. And everybody was dressed to impress.

As they cruised through the bumper to bumper traffic searching for a parking space, two well built females started flirting with them. The light-skinned female with the hot pink Chanel skirt, along with the knee-high Chanel boots to match spoke first.

"Hey cuties, I hope yall comin in so we can get to know each other."

Then just as she got the words out her mouth, her dark-skinned friend with the exact same outfit, only green instead of pink spoke up.

"I like those frames you got on baby. I love a nigga wit good taste."

Smoke laughed before responding.

"Them hoes diggin yo' Fendi frames boy. I told you they was cold. Now I gotta go cop me some tomorrow. As a matter of fact, I'm coppin that whole hookup you got on, cause you dickin' that shit dawg. Look at you,' Smoke playfully swiped towards Ray Ray's head, then continued to comment.

"Wit the cream Fendi bee-bop hat to match."

"Smoke you'a silly muhfucka!" said Ray Ray jokingly.

"You got at lease twenty of these hookups already nigga."

Ray Ray shook his head as he continued to cruise the triple black SL 500 Benz until he finally found a parking spot. They got out and made their way toward the front door with a crowd that was already heading in that direction.

"Ooo girl, look at that fine brother right there." squawked Tasha as she pointed at the Michael Jordan look-alike walkin in the club.

"Bye Tasha! I'll see yo' lil fast butt later." exclaimed Ebony as she sat behind the wheel of a red Neon waiting for Tasha to get out.

"Hold up Eb, girl is my makeup runnin?"

"Naw girl, now go'head on so I can get home, I told you I'm tired."

"Okay Okay, just let me check my lipstick and I'm out girl."

As Ebony sat there restless, waiting for her annoying sister to get out, she glanced around at her surroundings and remembered how she use to be a party girl. She smirked a little at the thought of how crazy she would get on the dance floor, and how her dirty-dancin would attract the wildest dudes. The slammed door abruptly brought her back to the present.

"Bye Eb!" yelled Tasha as she ran past the front of the car headed for the club's entrance.

"Finally." mumbled Ebony as she put the car in drive. And just as she was about to pull off, she suddenly became gripped with fear when she recognized Smoke from the hospital. She quickly put the car back in park and hurriedly pushed 911 on her cell phone. The operator put her on hold.

"Damn." she whispered to herself. She watched Smoke until he faded through the front door of the club. She wished the operator would hurry up and come back, but in the same sense, there was another part that didn't care if the operator ever came back.

She suddenly became angry at herself because she didn't understand it. She rationalized her thoughts while she waited on hold. *"He's a low down dirty child molester, the worst of the worst. That is what the police said, isn't it? He deserves to be under the jail, right? I don't think the police would put out the wrong profile about people, would they? Of course they would, because the time they came to my house for a domestic dispute between my parents when I was young, they said that it was my father who beat my mother. When it was really my mother who beat my father."*

"911 operator may I help you."

"I-, I-"

"May I help you caller?"

The phone went dead. And for the life of Ebony, she couldn't understand why she hung up. She silently prayed about it, then pulled off.

"Ain't nothing but a gangsta par-ty." by Pac and Snoop blared through the speakers as Ray Ray and Smoke stepped through the final door of the club. The whole scene was intense. There were beautiful women in every crevice of the 40 by 20 foot structure.

Ray Ray could tell that most of the people were floatin off ecstacy. Especially the woman who walked up to him as if she wanted to say something but couldn't manage to get the words out. She just grinded her teeth together as she rubbed her hand across his chest. Ray Ray silently thought to himself, *"These hoes on a helluva trip."* And as he walked deeper into the crowd, he noticed the two Chanel girls that flirted with him and Smoke outside. They were dancing with a few dudes in the freakiest manner. And when the light-skinned one saw Ray Ray again, she turned around facing the opposite direction from her dance partner, and started backin dat ass up against his dick with authority.

She wanted Ray Ray to keep his eyes glued on her so she could show him her bedroom skills on the dance floor. When she bent over touching her toes, Ray Ray could see her pink thong peek from under her short skirt. She winked at him while her head was still between her legs. Suddenly, the DJ slowed it down and R Kelly crept through the speakers enhancing the mood.

"It seems like you're ready, I could've sworn you were ready, to go all the way."

Her next move made Ray Ray order a shot of Grey Goose. She stuck her leg out as if she was doing a ballet move, then slowly raised it straight up in the air with ease. A few seconds later she let it gracefully rest on her partners shoulder. They grinded their bodies together while still in that position, then she closed her eyes and made several fuck-faces.

Ray Ray knew he was impressed because he felt his dick get hard. Smoke ran over to him excitedly.

"Dawg, you see that lil flexible bitch? Damn I wanna hit dat." Ray Ray laughed before letting Smoke know the feelings were mutual.

"Me too, but I'm not."

"Smoke! Ay Smoke! Over here poppi!" Smoke looked in

her direction.

"I see you baby, here I come! Ay Ray Ray, that's my pussy for tonight dawg. So I'ma slide over there and see what's what. Holla at me before you bounce so I can let you know which safe spot I'ma toss this bitch at." They gave pounds, then Smoke walked over to where Valencia was. He hugged her and squoze her fat ass.

"I miss you Smoke, where have you been?"

Smoke gave her a silly expression before responding.

"I've been on the run lately baby."

"Well you shoulda been runnin this way Smoke, cause you know how lonely my kitty get without you."

Smoke could tell that she hadn't been watching the news, and he was happy about that because he really didn't feel like explaining that bullshit to her. He just wanted some pussy. Some good pussy at that, and that was Valencia.

The flexible Chanel girl eyeballed Ray Ray from across the room, then moments later approached him in a sleek manner.

"Can I buy you a drink handsome?"

"Why not." replied Ray Ray .

She bought him and her a double shot of XO, then spent the next hour tellin him how deep her throat is. She offered to give him a demonstration if he wanted her too.

Ray Ray was buzzin from the drinks, and had no intention of fuckin her. But he was enjoying her conversation. He bluntly asked,

"If I wanted that head demonstration, where would I get it at?"

She anxiously moved closer to him now before giving an answer. All she thought about was how she wanted to freak with a baller tonight, and he looked like a good catch.

"Do you remember that girl that gave Pac some head in a corner of a crowded club?"

"Yeah, I remember. What about it." asked Ray Ray curiously.

"Well if you want that demo, you can be Pac, and I can be that girl, pick a corner."

Ray Ray started laughin before giving any feedback.

"Damn that sounds temptin' baby, but let's not forget about how o'l girl played Pac in the end. So let me take a rain check on this one."

He stood up and scanned the club for Smoke so he could let him know he was leavin. He spotted him and headed in his direction. He slowly inched his way through the crowd, then right before he reached him, a team of federal agents appeared seemingly out of thin air and swarmed Smoke.

Ray Ray quickly turned to the closest female in proximity and hugged her as if they were a couple. He watched intently as the agents marched Smoke out the club taking him to jail.

"Damn!" sighed Ray Ray as he left the club 5 minutes later.

The feds had found a picture of Valencia when they raided Smoke's house the first time. They matched her nationality with the only Spanish name in his phone book. Then from that point, they put a tap on her phone and a tail on her until it paid off.

CHAPTER 18

"Now listen Mr. McGee, you are facing a very long time in prison. Possibly the rest of your life. You've heard all of the evidence we have against you and your co-conspirators and it's really not lookin good. You guys are responsible for a number of bodies. And I promise you as God is my witness, if you don't cooperate, I will try my damnest to push for lethal injection. Now all we want you to do is wear a wire on your friend Ray Ray. Get him to discuss some of the murders, and we will cut you a sweet deal. So what's it gonna be guy?"

Pooh sat there in the interrogation room calmly smoking on a Newport as the federal agents waited on a answer. The agents were getting restless with Pooh, so one of them walked up to him, snatched the cigarette out his hand, smashed it on the floor, then got in his face.

"Let me tell you something mutherfucker! Did you know that you guys are also facing attempt murder charges on a federal agent?"

Pooh looked up at the red-faced federal agent bewildered.

"What do you mean attempt murder on a federal agent. What agent did we attempt to murder?"

His question was answered five minutes later when Boon came walkin through the door.

"Hey Pooh!" said Boon mockingly.

"I'm special agent Lawson, and it's so nice to meet you."

Pooh wanted to jump up and spit in his face. He couldn't believe this fat piece of shit was a fed.

"Okay Pooh, let me help you see this picture a little more clearer, just in case your vision is blurred. The attempt murder on a federal agent came into play when you and your boys ran up in my house. We know what would've happened if I woulda' been in the house. That's why we set it up to where I wouldn't be there. Then we set the final mouse trap when we planted the chemically laced cocaine to see which mousey wanted a little more cheese than the others. And what'll ya know, it was you. Now you only have two options left. Cooperate, or die in prison"...........

After the seventh attempt to reach Pooh that day, Ray Ray angrily slammed the phone down.

"Where da' fuck is this nigga at?" He mumbled to himself as he poured another shot of Hennessey.

"Ray Ray what's wrong baby?" asked Sheila as she sat on his lap.

Ray Ray's world was collapsing all around him, and this was only the second time in his life that he felt he wasn't in control. He always vowed to keep Sheila away from any of his street activities, but somehow the elements of his circle seemed to be gravitating toward her more and more. Sheila was a school girl, but she was nobody's fool. She was raised in the hood just like Ray Ray and she knew what came with it. And even though Ray Ray always presented himself like he had nothing major going on, she knew that her man was a force to be reckoned with in whatever he chose to pursue. She just prayed that whatever he was into, was something that he could always get out of.

"Baby are you gonna tell me what's wrong?"

"Ain't nothin wrong baby. A nigga just been a little stressed-out lately but I'm straight. Especially since I got you here with me."

He gave her a peck on her full lips and a soft pat on her butt.

"With your brains and my money, we gon' make some helluva shit happen baby."

Sheila laughed a little, then just as quickly, looked at him and spoke sincerely.

"I hope so Ray Ray, 'cause I don't know what I would do if something happened to you."

Ray Ray playfully made his voice sound like Tony Montana from the movie Scarface.

"Me, ain't nuthin gonna happen to me. If the Diez brothers come to get me,... Bang! I kill all those cockaroaches."

They both cracked their sides laughin at his terrible impression, then decided to go get some fast food.

Twenty minutes later, Sheila pulled her Benz in the parking lot of a cornbeef shop on Gratiot and seven mile. They went inside and ordered two cornbeef sandwiches to go. Ray Ray loved their cornbeef sandwiches. He would make it his business to pay them a visit at least twice a week.

After they paid for the food, Ray Ray quickly decided to buy another one for later on that night. Sheila smiled at him and jokingly blurted, "pig!."

"That's me, as long as this place is in bidness."

They left. And right before they pulled out the parking lot, Ray Ray shouted.

"Hold up baby! Them suckas ain't put no damn mustard in the bag."

Sheila came to an abrupt stop, and Ray Ray ran back in

the shop.

After he got the mustard, he pulled out his cell-phone and tried Pooh's number again. He tried the number while still in the shop because he didn't want Sheila to see the desperation in his face. But nevertheless, there was still no luck in reaching Pooh.

"Damn!" he said to himself as he put the phone back in his pocket and walked out the door.

After three short steps toward the car, a man unexpectedly stepped in front of him. And without warning, he casually pressed the nine to Ray Ray's chest and squoze off a series of rounds. The ground was sprinkled with shell casings, and Ray Ray was flat on his back as the gunman skidded off in a gold Malibu.

Sheila couldn't believe what she'd just witnessed. She stepped out the car seemingly in slow motion. She wanted to scream, but the sounds wouldn't come out. She could barely breathe as she ran toward Ray Ray. A stream of tears flowed down her face as she lifted his head and whispered in a strained voice.

"Please don't die baby."

Ray Ray laid there squirming and holding his chest. Sheila called the ambulance on her cell-phone, and Ray Ray steadily kept moving. Suddenly, Ray Ray stood to his feet.

"Baby what are you doing? Lay still, you shouldn't be moving while you're like this."

Ray Ray fell back down, and small trickles of blood could be seen on the pavement underneath his body. Moments later, the ambulance pulled up and the paramedics rushed over to him. Ray Ray grabbed Sheila by the arm pulling her close to him. And through clutched teeth he grimaced.

"Help me up baby! I'm straight."

Sheila didn't understand. She thought he became delusional from the sudden drama and loss of blood, so she quickly shook her head no.

"No baby, just lay still and let these people help you, okay."

Ray Ray displayed the facial expression of a madman, then aggressively grabbed Sheila by her jacket, pulling himself within inches of her face.

"Sheila!" he forcibly yelled.

"Help me the fuck up, I said I'm straight!"

Sheila suddenly realized he wasn't delusional, and that he meant exactly what he said. She immediately helped him to his feet, while the paramedics stood there giving orders not to move him. They moved in closer to try to stop them, but Ray Ray fended them off with his wild swings and constant obscenities.

"Get the fuck away from me!"

"But sir, you're in no condition to-" Ray Ray cut his words off again.

"I said get away from me muhfucka!"

They dialed 911 and backed off.

Sheila finally made it to the car with Ray Ray and helped him in. He layed back from the short exhausting walk to the car, then whispered to Sheila,

"Drive."

They made it to their house in twenty minutes. Once they were inside, things became clearer to Sheila as she helped Ray Ray take off the Kevlar bullet-proof vest that he wore under his shirt.

The only bullet that penetrated was the one that nicked his right leg, and Sheila was able to take care of it with a first-aid kit. Ray Ray had no idea who it was that tried to kill him. And the way his life was led, it could've been anybody. He was thankful that Sheila didn't get hurt in the attack. He knew that she could've easily been in the line of fire, and nothing was guaranteed how things would've turned out. But he always took precautions to change the situation for the better nomatter what. That's why he took all of Sheila's leather jackets and got special made Kevlar installations in the lining of them. Sheila had no idea he did this, and didn't even know that she actually had on bullet proof too.

"Ray Ray, why would somebody try to kill you?" asked Sheila as they sat in a warm tub of water together.

"Sheila I don't know, and I really don't feel like talkin about it."

"Well what if they don't miss next time Ray, huh? What about me?" asked Sheila angrily as tears rolled down her cheeks.

Ray Ray climbed out the tub and walked out because he felt that he had enough drama for one day.

CHAPTER 19

Ray Ray knew that some serious moves had to be made, and time was running out. He decided to make a few business calls while Sheila was over her mother's house. The phone rung twice before a heavy accented voice picked up.

"Whussup main, who dis?"

"Nigga this yo' cousin Ray Ray."

"Ah whussup main, my muhfucka! What's really good witcha' main?"

"Same fight different round baby, you know how the story go. But check this out couz, I need to know is you still shootin moves to Cali?"

"You know me Ray Ray, always in it, always wit it main. Why, whussup couz?"

"Man I need you to check out a situation for me the next time you shoot that way. In the meantime, write down this address."

"Hold on main, let me get sumthin to write wit."

When Gabe came back to the phone, Ray Ray eagerly gave him the address that he got out of Spade's pocket.

Gabe lived in Houston, Texas and he was well established. He controlled one of the largest dog fighting rings throughout the west coast, and he was one of Ray Ray's best kept secrets. Ray Ray had moved to Houston with Gabe and his mother after his parents were killed.

Big Ray only had one sister, and she was Gabe's mother.

She took Ray Ray in and wanted him to live with her in Houston as long as they were there. But Ray Ray moved back to Detroit when he turned fifteen because he wanted to be with Sheila and handle some unfinished business. He also didn't like the fact that Gabe started selling dope. Ray Ray reflected back to the time Gabe took him along to cop a half of bird. He had no idea that they were meeting the dude called Slim to get drugs from him. They all met up at a local park. And after they walked away, Gabe pulled out a half of kilo of cocaine.

Ray Ray was furious and he let Gabe know that he wanted him to stop indulging in that game. Gabe agreed because he loved Ray Ray, but he continued to cop from Slim anyway. Ray Ray finally had a discussion with Gabe's mother about his desire to move back to Detroit, and she respected it and let him go.

Gabe's connect 'Slim' was found in an abandoned building with two slugs in his head a week before Ray Ray left. Whoever was responsible left two kilos in his duffle bag right next to his body. Gabe never sold drugs again, and he also realized the fact that it was too many other hustle's out there. He always did suspect Ray Ray as the one that handled Slim, but he never knew for sure.

"A'ight cousin Gabe, I'll holla back atcha' soon, holla." Ray Ray hung up the phone and limped to the bathroom. He cursed to himself as the pain and soreness ran through his leg from the scraping bullet. Halfway through his piss, he heard someone knock on the door.

"Damn." he whispered as he tried to force his piss to come out a little quicker.

"Who da' fuck could this be."

He finally finished, then washed his hands and went to

the front door.

"Who is it?" he asked in a stern voice.

"Pooh!"

"Who?" Asked Ray Ray again as if he didn't here correctly the first time.

"Pooh!" exclaimed Pooh a little louder the second time.

Ray Ray anxiously opened the door and let him in.

"Whut the hell up dawg, where you been?"

"Man it's a long story," answered Pooh. He glanced around the room in a sort of frantic behavior. Then just as Ray Ray was about to say something, Pooh quickly threw his finger to his lips as a gesture for him to be quiet. Then slid over to the entertainment system and put in a Tupac CD. The song *'So Many Tears'* crept through the speakers as Pooh walked back over to Ray Ray and got directly in his ear. And as close as he was, if somebody else would've seen it, they would've thought it was queer-related.

Pooh whispered.

"Ray Ray, man I fucked up. I fucked around and got greedy and did something that you specifically told me not to do. Now the shit done came back and bit me in the ass Dawg. I don't have a whole lot of time, so Imma make a long story short. I've been back-trackin on our missions gettin' the work out the cribs. The feds peeped it and set me up, now they want me to set you up."

Pooh held up his finger again, then suddenly yelled out

"Ray Ray! Hurry up and get out that shower man!" then he took one step backwards, opened his shirt and showed Ray Ray the transmitting device, then got back in his ear.

"Man you know we've had our differences, but you know I would never sell you out for them bitches. Oh, and guess what dawg? That fat piece of shit Boon is a federal agent. He was they plant. But fuck'em, he got that off, just like I'm 'bout to get this off. I'm 'bout to get ghost on they ass, so ain't no tellin when I'ma see you again. But you know me, I'ma be a'ight. You just lay low and watch yo' steps 'cause they want you bad. Much luv my nigg, 'til we meet again."

Ray Ray handed Pooh the keys to his white Dodge Viper, gave him a hug, then whispered.

"Before pops died, he told me that every person in life will meet a true friend once in a blue moon. My nigg, today I saw that moon. And if you need me to help you put something together, you know how to find me. Much luv my nigg, I'll holla."

Pooh pulled back the curtain and peeped out the window, then ran to the back door. He waited for a few minutes to make sure it was clear, then slipped out.

As the agents sat in the control van, one of them let out an annoying sigh.

"What the fuck is this guy doing? All I hear is that guy Tupic, Pok, or whatever his name is. He needs to cut that shit off and start working on getting a confession from that scumbag."

Suddenly, the white Viper came speeding down the street and came to a sudden stop when it got to the van.

Pooh held up the 'Fuck You' finger, then pushed the pedal to the floor. This infuriated the agents, and the commander of the operation quickly radio'd their backup-units giving a description of the Viper with the order to pursue.

Several cars responded, but a call came through approximately ten minutes later informing the commander that they lost the suspect somewhere in traffic. The zero to sixty in 3.4 second Viper was a little too much for them. Originally they were going to wait to apprehend Ray Ray, but being that they were so pissed, they decided to raid his house anyway.

Five minutes later.

"Freeze Gottdamit! Put your fuckin hands where I can see'em. Don't you fuckin move mutherfucker!" yelled the red-faced agent.

Ray Ray submitted without a fight, and as he laid stretched out on the floor, he was thankful that Sheila wasn't there to witness the arrest. They ransacked the house and found nothing, then took him into custody.

After he was processed in the Wayne County jail, he tossed his linen on the bed, then picked up a three day old newspaper off the floor.

"Ay my man, that's my paper dawg!" replied the man standing directly behind him.

Ray Ray quickly turned around in defense-mode ready to confront the man, but suddenly, a smile appeared on the man's face.

"Whassup youngblood."

Ray Ray looked a little closer at the man's face, then excitedly shouted.

"Sporty! Is that you?"

"In the flesh baby boy."

"Damn dawg! Long time no see, what's been up witcha' Sporty?"

"Aw man I've been tryin my damnest to stay outta these white folks penal system. But it's always an uphill battle, you dig? But I'm only here on some unpaid traffic violations, so I should be bouncing up outta here in a few weeks. Now what's the deal with you youngblood, what you doin in here?"

Ray Ray scratched his head as if his answer would be complicated.

"It's a long story playa, long story."

Sporty looked at Ray Ray sarcastically for a moment.

"Check this out youngin. For the past two years, I've been what the underworld considers a square. After my last three-year stretch in the joint for petty larceny, I decided it was time to call it quits. Nomore druggin, nomore boosin, and nomore games. I got myself a decent old lady, we saved up some money and bought a small building, renovated it, and turned it into a little hole in the wall convenient store. We've been struggling with it from day one because those slimy-ass Arabs make sure the suppliers keep us understocked with the most demanded products. They don't want no competition on the block, especially black competition. So business has been real shady. And it's to the point where we think we might lose the place. But it's okay, because I'm the type of man that's built to fail and bounce back from it. And guess what? My woman is just like me, that's why I chose her. She compliments my character, you dig? And that's the only time a man is suppose to make a lifetime commitment to a woman. But that's another story youngblood, my point is this, just because I'm not in the streets, don't mean I ain't got my ear to the street. And to be truthful, I'm surprised to see you standin here."

"Why is that Sporty?" Ray Ray asked curiously.

Sporty offered him a cigarette before answering.

"No thanks man."

He lit his cigarette and took a hard drag, then continued.

"Youngblood, I say that because I overheard a lil youngin runnin his mouth about how his boy Clyde was gonna touch you for killin his cousin in a armed robbery. He supposedly overheard a lil youngin name Pee-Wee discussin you and ya' boy Pooh's business. And the word on the street is that Clyde took it to you at a cornbeef joint on 7mile and Gratiot, and you are supposedly six feet deep."

"Oh yeah Sporty?"

"Yeah youngblood, but you ain't here it from me."

"Ay yall, it's time to eat!!" yelled another inmate.

"Ay youngblood, I'll holla atchu about that situation later, okay. I'm 'bout to go get this grub."

Sporty took a few steps in the opposite direction, then stopped and looked back at Ray Ray with a sincere expression.

"Ay youngblood. You more like ya' old man than you'a probably ever know. He was a helluva guy." Then Sporty casually walked away.

Ray Ray laid in his bunk throughout the night and thought about the things that Sporty had ran down to him. Sporty was a street-smart individual, and it was good to see him after all the years that passed. Ray Ray knew that Sporty highly respected his father, which is the only reason he put him up on who it was that tried to kill him. Sporty didn't like dealin with the younger generation too much, because he said they were too watered down. And his favorite sayin was, *Lettin yall youngins in the game is what made me rush to get out."* Ray Ray thought to himself, Sporty definitely had a point. 'Cause even though he was in it from a different angle, the game had definitely changed.....

The next day, the county officer escorted Ray Ray off the rock and delivered him to the awaiting Federal Marshall's. They drove him to the federal building, and never said a word during the short trip.

When they finally made it inside the building, they

got on an elevator and rode to the ninth floor where six federal agents were waiting for him the very moment they stepped off. They escorted Ray Ray down a long corridor until they finally made it to the designated room. When they went inside, they directed Ray Ray to sit in a steel chair in the middle of the room, then all of the agents left back out.

Ray Ray glanced around the room and was marveled by the oddness of it. It had no furniture, tables, or anything in it like most federal rooms. All it had was a octagon-shaped screen that almost encircled the only chair in the room, which was the one that he was sitting in. He also noticed that there were no windows in the room. There were no door knobs or visible means of exit or entry. And the entire room resembled a cloudy day because it was painted a dull gray.

After sitting there for 30 minutes without any human contact and total silence. Ray Ray began to think to himself. *"What the hell is these clowns up to."* Suddenly, all the lights went out and the room became pitch black for about ten seconds. Then the entire octagon shaped television screen popped on.

A white man appeared on the screen holding his credentials in front of the camera.

"My name is special agent E. Burns. And this footage is a part of the mayhem caused by a group of individuals who we believe are responsible, and sad to say still at large. We believe that this individual is the ring leader of their crew. His name is Raynard Thompson, aka Ray Ray."

A picture of Ray Ray appeared on the screen. Then moments later, they showed a man sprawled out on the floor with multiple gunshot wounds to his head.

They let it stay on the screen for 60 seconds before it

was replaced by another dead man who's eyes and entire body was swollen from a cocaine induced overdose. That scene also stayed on for 60 seconds before being replaced by another man with multiple gunshot wounds to his face. Ray Ray finally understood the point that they were trying to make. They were playing a psychological game with him. In hopes that he would break down mentally and not be able to properly defend himself. It was a good strategy because it caught Ray Ray off guard, but it wasn't enough to totally discombobulate him. He sat through all 38 bodies that they showed with a blank face. He assumed they had some sort of hidden device that they were watching him through to monitor his reaction, so he displayed none. Ray Ray also knew that he wasn't responsible for all of the bodies that they were showing. Because being in the streets, he was aware of the fact that if the authorities got you accounted for fifteen bodies, they would add at least five unsolve's to your tab. That's a game they've been playin for years.

After the horror show, the six agents re-entered the room. The agent that was standing the closest to Ray Ray snobbishly spoke first.

"So how does it feel to see your handy work killer?"

Ray Ray didn't respond to the remark, so one of the other agents shared his thoughts as well.

"Mr. Thompson, you might as well co-operate with us because you will never see daylight again if you don't, so here's our proposition. We are willing to let you plead guilty to half of the bodies, in exchange for your testimony against your codefendants. You won't get the death penalty, and you will be an old man when you get out, but at least you'll get out."

Ray Ray looked up at the agent and calmly stated,

"I'd like to keep exercising my right to remain silent." and he never spoke another word during the entire interrogation. They took him back to the county-jail frustrated because of his stubbornness, and promised him he would surely get the death penalty...

When Ray Ray returned to the cell-block, Sporty introduced him to the slim, dark, red-eyed man known as Trell. He explained to Ray Ray how Trell could get to Pee-Wee because he was a county trustee and had access to any floor. Ray Ray talked with Trell for awhile and agreed to pay him ten thousand dollars for the hit. Ray Ray knew the feds were bluffing, and could only hold him for the standard 72 hours. Because without Pooh, they had nothing but hearsay from Pee-Wee.

Two days later.

"Raynard Thompson, pack yo' shit!" yelled the county dep.

"Alright youngblood, I'll catch you on the rebound baby boy." said Sporty as he gave Ray Ray some dap.

CHAPTER 20

"Time served!" yelled the black female judge as she slammed the wooden mallet against the gavel. Yvonne immediately hugged her two high-powered attorneys that Smoke had hired for her, then said to them,

"Now let's go see about my son." Yvonne had won her case on an appeal and she was overjoyed.....

****

As Pee-Wee sung 'Get Money,' by Junior Mafia and Biggie while taking a shower, Trell continued to mop the floor and work his way toward the two-man shower. When he finally reached it, he mopped around the area until the other inmate came out.

He swiftly placed two 'wet floor' custodian signs in front of the shower, then took a brief glimpse around the area before quietly slipping in. The moment he heard the shower stop, he quickly pulled out the thin piece of guitar string, gripped it tight with both hands, then flipped it over Pee-Wee's head around his neck.

Pee-Wee kicked and jerked as he desperately tried to break free from his attacker. Trell had done time most of his 42 years on earth, and this wasn't his first time putting down a demonstration like this. He had no family, and never had any outside support during none of his bids. So he would always do whatever it took to make ends meet while in prison. He once broke a man's jaw for twenty dollars. And most of his hits were simple like that. But this was his biggest payday yet, and he wasn't about to let it get pass him.

He pulled the wire so tightly, that he damn near severed Pee-Wee's head. Pee-Wee finally stopped moving, and his lifeless body fell limp. A few beads of sweat appeared on Trell's forehead and nose as he stood there breathing heavy. He carefully peeped out the shower, and when he saw that the coast was clear, he rejoined his mop-bucket and slipped out of the area just as smoothly as he came in.

When Ray Ray got the word that Pee-Wee was dead, he sent Trell ten, one thousand dollar money orders just like he promised. Then sent Sporty the same thing with a note saying,

"Get yo' store off the ground man, it ain't enough black owned stores in the hood noway."

Sporty was grateful, and he vowed to take his place of business to another level. Ray Ray knew the feds were gonna keep comin at him until they could make something stick, so he started making preparations for the worst.

As Sheila was sitting at the table checking over her credit score, Ray Ray was on the phone talking to the high-powered lawyer that he hired for Smoke. Ray Ray tried to hire Johnny Cochran, but he was busy at the time with another case. Smoke and Ray Ray kept their contact limited because the authorities had no idea Smoke was one of the Get Flat members. Ray Ray chatted a little longer with the attorney, and soon as he hung up, his cell phone rung.

"Hello!"

"Hey, is this Ray Ray?" asked the woman on the other end.

"That depends on who wanna know."

"Ray Ray baby this is Smoke's mother Yvonne."

"Is that right?" asked Ray Ray excitedly.

"Whussup Yvonne, how you doin?"

"I'm doin fine now cause my black ass is outta prison."

"Whuud! You out!"

"Yeah, I won my appeal. And now I need to get with you so you can fill me in on what's what with my son."

"Check this out Yvonne, where you at right now?"

"I'm on 2636 Navahoe."

"I'll be through there in about 30 minutes cause I'm at one of my other cribs on Whitcomb and Grand River okay?"

"Alright Ray Ray, I'll see you then."

When Ray Ray hung up the phone, Sheila blurted out,

"Somethin ain't right with these calculations, them people overcharged me for certain items or somethin. I gotta call my girl cause they is not about to play me like that." She picked up the phone and called her friend who's a credit-card consultant. Ray Ray just smirked a little and shook his head as he walked out the door.....

Ray Ray pulled up in front of one of Smoke's houses on Navahoe 30 minutes later. He got out the white Cadillac Escalade truck and trotted up to the door. When Yvonne answered, she immediately gave him a tight hug. Ray Ray was amazed at how prison had preserved her. She looked ten years younger than what she really was. She'd always been a nice looking woman with a pretty dark complexion, but now she was enhanced in every way. And Ray Ray could tell that she had been working out because her waist was a size 28', and she had a figure like a coca-cola bottle. Her hair was cut short like Anita Bakers, and her skin looked soft and replenished. Ray Ray traded information with her about Smoke's situation, then he took her shopping at the Fairlane Mall. He took her to one of Smoke's safe houses in Clinton Township and gave her the keys to all of his vehicles. He told her they'd be in touch, then left.

CHAPTER 21

As Rashia climbed off Pooh and walked toward the bathroom, Pooh cringed and replied,

"Goddamn girl you got some good pussy." He closely watched her naked body strut with grace to the bathroom. She looked back smiling, then stopped, slapped her own ass and said, "I know." then proceeded on.

When she came out, she sat on the side of the bed and accepted the blunt that Pooh passed her. And soon as she hit it, her phone rung. She pronounced "hello" in a strained voice.

"This is the AT&T operator with a collect call from an inmate in a county jail by the name of Buzz, will you accept?" Rashia looked backed at Pooh before answering the operator's question and whispered, "shshsh, be quiet, this Buzz."

Then said, "yes, I accept."

Buzz was patched through.

"Whuddup doe sis?"

"Ain't nothing up boy, whussup?"

"I got that change you sent, and that was good lookin out fo'real. You must've ran up on a big trick lately, cause you ain't never sent me that much since I've been in the county."

"Boy shut the hell up, yo' ass betta make it last 'cause I

ain't sending you nothin else for awhile."

"Well that's a'ight 'cause this five hundred should keep me straight for a minute, real talk. Anyway, have you seen that bitch Toya lately?"

"Nope."

"Well if you do, tell that bitch I said get at me. I only got one letter from her since I been here."

"Boy stop sucka-strokin and press yo' bunk." squawked Rashia as she tried to hold back her laughter.

"Fuck you girl, wit yo' peanut head ass." Buzz retaliated.

Suddenly, Pooh began coughing from the blunt. Rashia quickly tried to cover the phone as she looked back at him with an astonished frown.

"Who is that?" asked Buzz.

"None of yo' gottdamn business Buzz, ol' nosy ass nigga."

"Girl that sounded like Pooh, and if that's him, you need to let me holla at him."

Rashia shouted.

"Well you won't be hollerin 'cause it ain't him. As a matter of fact bye, 'cause you don't want shit noway." she hung up the phone then looked at Pooh with a devout expression before addressing him.

"Baby you can't be slippin like that. You know them people is lookin for you heavy."

Pooh took another pull off the blunt before responding.

"I hear you baby, but that's only lil Buzz, he straight. So stop trippin."

Rashia scooted closer to him and lifted his chin so their eyes could be evenly leveled in the debate.

"Pooh, I love you baby. And when I love something or someone, I protect it at all cost. That's why you are sittin here now. We can't trust nobody! Okay, and I mean absolutely nobody!"

She stressed her point precisely and seriously, and Pooh had to respect it. Pooh knew she loved him, and although he wasn't the lover-boy type, he actually felt strongly for her and appreciated the way she felt about him. He considered her a loyal friend, and loyalty meant the world to him. He gave her the money to send Buzz because Buzz was working for him at the time of his arrest, so he vowed to make sure his books would be straight for however long he would end up being in prison.

Pooh playfully dove on Rashia, and as he sat over top of her, he looked at her intently and decided to reverse the vibe of the situation.

"I feel whutcha' sayin hot mama, but talk to me about it when we seventy years old and you rubbin my back with bengay from bangin dat ass out like a savage!" They both burst out laughin, then immediately fell into another steamy sex session....

Buzz walked away from the phone and thought to himself, *"I know that was Pooh over there. Rashia think I'm stupid... That dumb bitch Toya been playin games, and she know I will fuck her up...I gotta get outta here... Fuck this shit... The feds is lookin for that nigga heavy, and I think they even got a reward out."* Buzz walked to his cell as his thoughts continued to dance in his head. *"Man, dat nigga ain't did shit for me since I been here, and for all I know, he probably set me up"* Buzz looked down at the federal agent's number on the torn piece of paper in his hand, then suddenly exclaimed,

"Fuck dat nigga, I'm goin to the crib."

The District Attorney pushed for a speedy trial for

Smoke after he turned down the plea bargain of life that was offered to him. The feds stepped all the way out of the case and let the state deal with it. Smoke sat in solitary confinement as he thought about the different chain of events that had taken place, as well as the ones that would take place in the following weeks to come. He was more than happy to know that his mother was free, he just wished he was able to be there to share it with her. Ray Ray had sent word to him that he was gonna watch the outcome of his trial from a distance, because he didn't want the authorities to connect Smoke to him and bring more heat on Smoke. He already had enough problems, and if they found out he was one of the invaders, they would probably come at Smoke with two lethal injection needles instead of one. So Smoke understood and rolled with the program....

Ray Ray slowly rode across Gunston down Wilshire street until he approached the red brick house near Conners. He parked on the opposite side of the street, then got out and walked up to the front door. He paused momentarily when the car with the bright headlights approached.

After it passed by, he knocked on the door and waited for someone to answer. A few seconds later, the porch light popped on and a female voice yelled,

"Who is it?"

Ray Ray responded.

"Is Jameisha here?"

"Who?" asked the female voice.

"Jameisha." said Ray Ray again.

"Don't nobody live here by that name."

There was a momentary pause, then two shots rung out and the door flew open from the force of Ray Ray's kick. Two girls around the ages of seventeen and nineteen screamed and held their hands up when they saw the masked gunman. Their mother and father came running down the steps with their robes on. Ray Ray quickly grabbed the closest girl to him, which happened to be the seventeen year old when he noticed the shotgun in her father's hand. The man pushed his woman aside and kept coming down the stairs. Ray Ray instantly fired two shots, hitting the man in his left leg stopping him in his tracks.

The heavyset man screamed out in pain but he didn't drop the gun. Ray Ray gripped the girl tight from behind and kept the gun trained on the man.

"Drop that shotgun old man."

The man laid there slouched on the steps with blood pouring from his leg and a firm grip on the shotgun as if he didn't have any intentions on dropping it. His wife and the two girls cried and yelled,

"Please don't hurt us" as the scene unfolded.

Ray Ray focused on the man and pointed the gun with emphasis. He motioned the gun forward with every word and demanded, "Put!...The Gottdamn Gun!...Down!" The man didn't budge from Ray Ray's demand. Suddenly, Ray Ray pointed the gun at the girl's head. He pressed it hard against her temple and snarled,

"Muthafucka you got about a half a second to drop that gun or you can kiss this lil bitch goodbye." The man quickly read Ray Ray's eyes as best as he could, and what he saw made him put the gun down just as quickly.

"Smart man." yelled Ray Ray.

"Now, where the fuck is Clyde?"

Everyone just stared at Ray Ray, still weeping and wiping tears without answering. He looked at them with an irritated expression, but managed to let his words come out calmly.

"If yall just tell me where he is, we can all walk away from this in one piece. Now let's not all speak at once."

The 19 year old wiped a few more tears, then raised her hand as if she was in school. Then after permission from Ray Ray was granted for her to speak, she spoke in a trembling voice filled with fear.

"He dead."

Ray Ray looked at her with a puzzled expression before responding.

"I know you didn't say what I think you just said."

The girl was fearful of repeating herself, but she did. "Yeah, he's dead, really."

Ray Ray paused for a moment then squawked,

"Do you really expect me to believe that shit?"

No-one said anything in reference to his comment. Then moments later he pulled the already subdued girl a little closer to him and pressed the gun to her head hard enough to leave an imprint from the barrel.

"Yall must don't love her. Cause I'm bout to show yall what her brains look like up close. Now watch closely."

"No!! wait a minute!" yelled the nineteen year old.

"Please!" Then she raised her hands up as she walked toward the fire place as an indicator to Ray Ray that she meant no funny business. Once she reached it, she grabbed a piece of paper and slowly walked toward him with it. Her sister cried profusely and prayed that Ray Ray wouldn't accidentally pull the trigger due to his anger.

The nineteen year old constantly held one hand up in the air as she handed Ray Ray the paper. He took it and silently read the words. "In Loving Memory of Clyde Thompson." Ray Ray paused for a moment and instantly went into deep thought. Something bewildered him about what he'd just read. And it wasn't the fact that it was an obituary and dude was really dead, it was something else. Something that made him reflect back to a time when his mother mentioned her sister Dorris that she'd never met. She would always say, *"It's a shame that I don't know my only sister and she lives right here in Detroit."*

All she knew is that Dorris was with a man named Robert, and that she had a boy and two girls by him but they never got married. Ray Ray looked at Clyde's last name again, which was the same as his, and asked the trembling mother,

"What is yo' name?"

She nervously answered.

"D-Dorris."

Then he looked at the man and asked,

"What about you?"

Through clutched teeth from the pain of his wound and anger from the situation, the man answered.

"Robert."

Ray Ray immediately knew that he was in the midst of his aunt, uncle and first cousins. He took one hard glance at them, then casually pushed the seventeen year old in the arms of her sister.

They held each other and cried in relief when the situation appeared to be coming to an end. Ray Ray suddenly asked,

"How did he die?"

The nineteen year old sniffled a little before briefly explaining what happened to her brother.

"Last week, him and his friends ran up in a dude house trying to rob him, and one of the dudes that was there with old-boy crept from one of the back rooms and shot'em five times in the chest. His boy Ed got hit and died too."

After hearing the story, Ray Ray slowly backed up toward the front door with the gun still trained on them.

"Close yall eyes and count to a hundred slowly." he demanded then left.

As he rode pass the incoming police cars that one of the neighbors had called, he thought about how ironic life could be at times. His first cousin attempted to kill him at a cornbeef shop, and now he was dead due to leading the same lifestyle as his. Ray Ray felt a little disheartened about the situation in it's entirety because even though Clyde tried to kill him, he was still from his bloodline. And had he known Ray Ray was family, their may have been a different outcome. And besides all that, Ray Ray felt that Clyde may have been a good asset to his relentless crew. He shook it off and continued to put distance between himself and the scene. He snuck back to their house a few days later and paid a thirteen year old boy to put a small paper bag that contained ten thousand dollars in the mailbox, ring the doorbell, and run.

CHAPTER 22

As Rashia wiped herself with the tissue, she flushed the urine-filled toilet then washed her hands. As she turned to walk toward the door, she suddenly jumped back, letting out a short scream when she caught a glimpse of the white face that quickly ducked away from the bathroom window. She ran to the bedroom where Pooh was at and quietly shook him out of his sleep. When he sleepishly sat up, she whispered in his ear.

"Pooh, I just saw a white man outside by the bathroom window, he ducked when he saw me."

Pooh yawned and groggily mumbled.

"Are you sure?"

"Yeah I'm sure boy. I know what I saw."

Pooh reached under the pillow and grabbed the glock nine millimeter, then walked to the front door wearing only his boxers. He peeked out the window to see if he could see anybody, then opened the front door and stepped out on the porch. He stood there for a minute as the night breeze made small chill-bumps appear on his arms. Then he made a complete round around the perimeter of the house. He didn't notice anything strange, so he headed back toward the front door. Instinctively he stopped, and then walked a little closer to Rashia's car. He made a complete circle around it, and his thoughts immediately began racing when he noticed all four of her tires were flat. Then after only a few seconds of processing the scene, he struck out and ran up on the porch as fast as he could. Just as he opened the door, a series of gunshots rung out in his direction, missing him by inches. Bright lights suddenly shined through their front windows, and a federal agent's voice blared through a bullhorn.

"Marcell McGee, this is the FBI. You are completely surrounded, so make this light on yourself and come out with your hands up."

Pooh quickly slipped on some pants, a shirt, and some shoes. He pulled the fully automatic AK-47 and the M-14 out from under the bed. Rashia immediately started to cry.

"Pooh, don't do it baby, you know them muthafuckas will kill you." Pooh ignored her statement and continued to pull out weapons and ammunition. Once he had everything in place, he pulled Rashia close to him and wiped her tears.

"Rashia, check this out baby, I need you to be strong for me right now. Don't let them break you down, you need to keep that pretty smile wide and bright just the way I like it."

Rashia tried to muster up a smile through her constant flow of tears, but it was dampened by the already sorrowful look on her face.

Pooh walked to the window and without hesitation he open-fired on the entourage of law enforcement. The agents quickly took cover, then immediately returned fire. Pooh turned the heavy oak table over and pushed it in front of the couch. Then pulled Rashia behind it in an attempt to shield her from the incoming bullets.

The barrage of projectiles shattered windows and

ricochet off walls barely missing them. And when it momentarily stopped, the voice over the bullhorn demanded that anyone who was presently in the house, to come out with their hands up or they would open fire again at will. With the sole intentions of taking out any living targets. Pooh looked at Rashia with confidence in his face and spoke with justification in his language.

"Baby, them muthafuckas really want me to snitch on my dawg. They just don't give a fuck about nothin but what they stand to gain. Fuck them bitches, they can get my testimony from the grave. Now listen and listen closely. I want you to run to the basement with me as fast as we can on the count of three, a'ight. One, two, three!"

They both dashed to the basement in a hurry. Once they were there, Pooh grabbed one of the sheets from the dirty laundry basket and tore a long strip from it. He looked at Rashia intently before giving her a casual command.

"Cumeer baby."

Rashia was puzzled and didn't fully understand his actions, but she still came to him. He quickly tied her hands behind her back, then gently rubbed her braided hair and cocoa brown face. He put his head down momentarily, as if letting a certain pain subside before expressing himself.

"Baby, the federal government got a fucked up law called conspiracy. And all it means is if they think you are a part of whatever crime their suspect commits, they charge you too, with or without physical evidence. So what I'm doin right now is necessary, because I don't want you gettin fucked around in they racist-ass system because of somethin that I did. So roll with the program, and let them bitches know I held you at gun-point against your will the whole time, okay."

Rashia attempted to shake her head no, but was quickly stopped by the firm shake Pooh gave her while looking her directly in her eyes.

"Listen!" he pronounced with a little more authority.

"This ain't no game 'Shia. Now I need you to promise me that you gon' do what I told you to do."

Rashia stared back at him deeply without a spoken word, letting two full minutes lapse in time before answering.

"Okay Pooh, I promise."

Pooh unexpectedly tongue-kissed her aggressively, then stared in her eyes for a few moments with the same affection that she'd just displayed for him. He placed a piece of duct tape over her lips, then slightly ripped the front of her gown in an effort to make it look like there was a struggle. He never told Rashia verbally that he loved her, but she saw it clear as day in his hazel brown eyes. Pooh gently sat her in a chair, then walked away. Rashia's eyes quickly filled and overflowed with tears. And as she watched him fade out of sight up the stairs, she caught a glimpse of a red spot about the size of an orange on the left side of his shirt. Then she looked down at the floor and noticed the long trail of blood that led from where she sat, over to the last four steps that was in her view.

"Oh my God." she said to herself when she realized Pooh was hit.

Suddenly, she heard another flurry of gunshots, and she could tell that it was coming from inside the house. She sat there for the next twenty minutes and painfully listened to Pooh exchange gunfire with the agents. Suddenly, she heard the gunfire stop. And for the next fifteen minutes there was total silence.

Rashia's mind was crowded with confusion as she

wondered what was going on now, and what was gonna happen next. She prayed that Pooh would be alright, and she vowed to herself that nomatter how much time they'd give him, she would always be by his side. She totally eliminated the fact that it could possibly end more tragically, because denial had took over her ability to rationalize.

A loud crashing sound suddenly broke up her thoughts.

"Freeze!" yelled the first agent who entered the house with the combination of a bullet proof shield, vest, hard hat, and AR-15. Followed by ten more agents in exactly the same attire. Pooh sat there against the wall losing blood from three different holes in his body. The entering agents could only see a small portion of his body because the table and couch were blocking the view.

The agents slowly crept around the couch in tight formation with their guns eagerly trained on every particle in their path, living or non living. Threatening or non threating. They steadily inched their way closer to Pooh. And when they felt that they were in the preferred range, two of the agents silently agreed to simultaneously snatch the table and couch partially aside to create a line of fire. They looked at each other and silently counted to three, using fingers only. The moment the third finger was flashed, they both snatched at the two pieces of furniture with a strong tug, while the other agents immediately drew down.

"Drop it!" yelled one of the trained gunmen as Pooh sat there with the barrel of the 40 caliber pistol resting against the side of his own head.

"Drop it gottdamit!" yelled one of the agents again.

Pooh suddenly began laughing, and his laughter grew in volume as the agents steadily commanded him to disarm himself. Pooh's laughter held a sinister element, and he continued to laugh until he suddenly held up the "Fuck You" finger and nonchalantly snarled,

"Did you muthafuckas really think I would give you the pleasure of killing me, ha! ha! ha!" Boh! He pulled the trigger, painting the wall, furniture, and carpet with spattered blood, fragments of his skull, and exposed brain-matter. The agents immediately rushed over to him and removed the weapon from his hand. One of them silently said to himself,

"Damn, I wanted to see you rott in prison mutherfucker."

The other agents quickly searched the rest of the house, and when they found Rashia with her hands bound behind her back sitting in a chair, they quickly untied her and escorted her to one of their vehicles. Rashia sat in the back of the Crown Victoria in a state of shock as she thought about how the only man she'd ever loved went out. It all happened so suddenly, and her mind didn't want to accept the fate that had already played out its earthly role. She hated the fact that Pooh was gone, but the principle in which he stood on made her proud to be in love with a man like him. She marveled on the fact that he'd rather die than to snitch on his friend. That was unheard of in this day in time, being that there were more snitches in the federal system than soldiers. The federal system was the perfect weapon against black people. They set black unity back a couple hundred years, just when we thought we were seeing a little progress.

The feds went for Rashia's story about her being held against her will. And every derogatory sentence that she had to spit out her mouth against Pooh made her skin crawl. And the only reason she went through with it is because it was Pooh's wishes.

But she really wanted to tell them that she would've gladly accepted an invitation from Pooh to be right by his side doing battle, firing slugs at them and happily dying by his side. She contacted Ray Ray shortly after the incident and informed him on what had taken place. Ray Ray met her in the parking lot of a public eatery and gave her an undisclosed amount of money. She moved to a new house in the suburbs and focused on starting over. Rashia later found out that it was Buzz who gave up Pooh to the feds. And even though he was her only brother, she vowed to never associate with him again and disregarded him as family.

Buzz was on a different floor from Pee-Wee, and when he heard the news of Pee-Wee getting slumped, he became terrified because he figured it was Pooh and Ray Ray's work. And now that Pooh was dead, he knew anything could jump off, so he checked himself into the protective custody unit of the jail for his own safety.

CHAPTER 23

As Ray Ray sat in one of his safe-spots in downtown Detroit, he almost came to tears when he thought about what Pooh had done for him. He was deeply distressed about the entire situation, and he knew that he'd probably never experience loyalty to that magnitude ever again in this lifetime. He gazed out of the large picture window as he blew smoke from the Newport against it, taking in the tranquility of the rain that sprinkled its outer-surface leisurely.

He could see the federal and state court buildings from where he stood, and he wished he could be over there to support Smoke, but he knew it wasn't safe. As his thoughts progressed, he took another sip from the cognac in his cup, giving a slight frown from the burning sensation it gave his throat. He smashed the rest of the Newport in the ashtray after taking one more pull, then picked up his cell phone and dialed a number....

Smoke's mother Yvonne carefully placed the earphone plug into her ear, then softly answered.

"Hello."

"Yvonne whuddup, this Ray Ray, how is everything goin?"

"Everything is okay so far Ray Ray." whispered Yvonne.

"But I can't talk right now baby because we are in the middle of court and they are just lookin for a reason to throw any of his supporters out. So don't worry yourself baby, I'll call you as soon as we get a recess or something, okay?"

Ray Ray agreed and they hung up.

The prosecutor continued to make Smoke look as bad as Jeffrey Dolmer and the Son of Sam. Smoke sat there and listened to the horrible lies that were told, and he could tell by the looks on the juror's faces that they were buyin it.

"I call my next witness, Ms. Ebony Sutton,' yelled the prosecutor.

Smoke watched as the attractive honey-brown nurse from the hospital took the stand. He mentally noted that she looked much better out of her work clothes. The Sean John jeans she wore hugged every curve that her 130pound body had to offer. Her eyes seemed to be green from one angle, and lemon-tea brown from another. Her sandy brown hair was in a French wrap style, and her teeth were bright white and straight as if she wore braces as a youngster.

After she was sworn in and interrogated all over again by the prosecutor, she stared at Smoke and took in his appearance in the present compared to how she last saw him. His smooth dark complexion was a little lighter, due to lack of sunlight. And his brush waves appeared to be a little less wavy. His gotee was a little thicker than he normally kept it, not to mention the orange county jumpsuit that he was wearing wouldn't win him any fashion competitions.

Which is exactly one of the points that his lawyer tried to argue for him, stressing that it was bias toward the jury's judgement of him because it made any innocent man look guilty. But despite his rugged looks, Ebony still noted to herself, *"He is kind'a cute. And he still didn't strike her as the man the prosecutor and authorities said he was."* She felt that it was safe to assume he probably had some ugly skeletons in his closet, but child molestation just didn't fit his demeanor. Smoke nodded his head at her as a gesture of appreciation as she left the stand, because her testimony actually helped him rather than hurt him. The prosecutor was coming at Smoke with everything he could. But his next pitch would surely put Smoke deeper in the pit of persecution....

When everyone returned to the courtroom after the fifteen minute recess. Smoke's heart skipped a beat when he saw special agent Nathaniel Lawson, a-k-a Boon, sitting in the courtroom. He wondered what in the fuck he was doing there. He quickly leaned toward his lawyer and whispered.

"Why is that federal agent sittin' in here? I thought they gave the state jurisdiction over the case."

The Jewish lawyer displayed a puzzled look on his face before responding.

"Just relax for a moment and I'll go check it out."

He walked over to the prosecutor, mumbled a few words, then they both approached the bench that held the white female judge.

"Your honor, I've just been informed that the prosecution plans to use a federal agent to provide some sort of testimony against my client, knowing that it is a clear violation of the initial agreement in this case."

"Is that true?" asked the judge to the prosecutor.

"Sort of your honor."

The judge quickly displayed a sarcastic expression and squawked,

"Sort of, Mr. Wyatt we don't deal with sort of's' in my

courtroom."

"I totally understand." said the prosecutor as his pale face turned red.

"But your honor, the federal government has recently come up with newly discovered evidence pertaining to the defendant that would clearly establish the criminal element in his character. And once this is established, they also plan to re-indict him on the additional charges that we are going to present to the court today within his testimony."

The Jewish lawyer interrupted.

"Your honor, being that we've already come to an agreement with the government, and he's a federal agent, this testimony should not be admissible."

The prosecutor quickly cut back in.

"Your honor, he's not acting as a federal agent in the presentation of his testimony. He will be in equal accordance with your average citizen." Smoke's lawyer stepped a little closer aggressively, then quickly calmed himself down in order to not make a fool of himself on his next statement.

"Your honor, citizens don't just waltz into courtrooms and give testimonies against people with the professionalism of a federal agent."

The judge gave a nod as if to say, it makes sense. Then the prosecutor cited a case that would show cause as to why the agent's testimony is permissible. The judge exhaled a heavy breath, demonstrating annoyance over the whole argument, then flatly stated.

"Since it is documented case-law that this particular situation is in fact permissible, I'll allow it."

"But your honor!"

"No but's counselor, that's my decision and that's the

way it's gonna be. But what I will do for you is put this testimony on hold to allow you and your client sufficient time to prepare for the new addition to this trial."

Smoke's lawyer looked disappointed, but felt that at least they got that. So he grumpily asked,

"And what do you consider sufficient time your honor?"

"48 hours." she stated boldly as they concluded the discussion.

CHAPTER 24

Ray Ray picked up the phone after the third ring.

"Hello."

"Ray Ray whuddup dawg?"

"Who dis, Smoke?"

"Yeah man it's me."

"Whuddup doe baby boy, how is everything lookin?"

"Man shit just got worse. Today that connivin ass prosecutor went up on me by a few points because that punk-ass federal agent Boon came walkin in the courtroom."

"Whut!" shouted Ray Ray.

"What happened man?"

"Man I don't know, but my lawyer tried to fight the entry of his testimony, but the best he could do was get a 48 hour preparation period for our defense."

"Oh yeah?"

"Yeah dawg, and you know as well as I do that whateva' he say, it can't be good. So like I said before, 48 hours dawg." said Smoke. Putting emphasis on the 48 hour part.

"Yeah I feel you dawg, and time is a terrible thang to waste, but I got you. And by the way, how did you call, I didn't hear no operator."

"I'm on my moms three-way."

"Oh, okay. Well check this out my guy, I got some a.s.a.p bidness I gotta handle. So until better days, hold ya' head and stay on yo' research. Holla.

After Ray Ray got off the phone with Smoke, he thought to himself.

"That piece of shit Boon is 'bout to really fuck up the program. I can't let Smoke go out like that. Now how do I fix this problem?"

Ray Ray jumped in his Escalade and drove over to his part- time accountant's office. He hired the accountant a few years ago to help him manage a few money issues. Ray Ray's father always told him to make sure you keep an ace in the hole at all times, meaning that you indulge in certain business that none of your associates knew about. And separate it from your illegal ties to the streets, if there ever was any. So Ray Ray invested a hundred thousand dollars in the stock market and hired a broker to oversee the progress because he didn't really have a lot of knowledge about the market. But once it grew to a half of million, it was time to hire the accountant. The guy was very intelligent in the field, but Sheila's knowledge of the money management game far exceeded his. She was brilliant, so going to see his accountant was a part of him tying up all of his loose ends. He let him know that his services were no longer needed, and paid him a hundred thousand dollars to transfer all business interests in Sheila's name.

The accountant handled everything that needed to be handled, and they shook hands and went their separate ways.

Ray Ray drove to all of his different spots and gathered up all of his mattress money. He took it all to one house, then called Sheila and gave her directions to meet him there. As he sat there placing stacks of money on the king size bed, he received a call from his cousin from Texas telling him that he was in L.A and he found Bo-Bo. Ray Ray was overjoyed and told him that he'd be on an express flight to L.A within the next few hours. Sheila arrived shortly after the phone conversation, and Ray Ray was happy to see her because she would always provide him with the solitude that he desperately needed at times. He embraced her, then went to the kitchen and brought her back a cup of her favorite Mocca Cappuchino with marshmellows floating in it. He stared her up and down and admired how her gray Prada slacks complimented her small waist and nice hips. The Prada turtleneck matched the band that held her hair in a pony tail, and the platinum key-shaped earrings blended perfectly with the color.

Sheila slid off the gray Prada boots and sat on the couch sipping her drink, smiling at Ray Ray with her bright smile and slightly large eyes.

"What is it baby, why are you looking at me like that?" she asked as she sat with her legs folded comfortably underneath her. Ray Ray didn't answer her right away, he just continued to gaze at her and think about everything they'd been through together and how far they'd come. Sheila was a phenomenal woman, and Ray Ray knew they were meant to be together. He reflected back to a time when they were eleven years old, and he had gotten into a fight on the way home from school. Sheila ran up and damn near knocked his opponent out with her book bag.

And she didn't even know him at the time, she just knew what she wanted. And when Ray Ray had looked at her face, he remembered that she was the one who lil Ron tried to hook him up with. That's when he knew she was his kind of girl because she had his back. He felt that Sheila was his soul mate. She offered every positive characteristic there is to offer in a relationship. She offered companionship, confidence, psychology, guidance, friendship, love and affection. And Ray Ray was ready to come all the way clean with her. So after a few minutes of gazing at her, he suddenly responded.

"Cumeer Sheila. Come walk with me for a minute."

Sheila got up and followed him to the bedroom. When they walked in, she suddenly came to an abrupt stop with both hands covering her open, but silent mouth.

Moments later, she started taking slow, calculated steps toward the bed as if it was necessary for her to approach it with extreme caution. Ray Ray stood there and watched as Sheila was in awe over the large sum of money that laid scattered, covering the entire king-size bed.

"Oh my God!" was all she could manage to get out. She pointed at it and looked at Ray Ray with an overly concerned facial expression.

He knew she had a thousand questions computing through her head, so he decided to break the silence and start explaining.

"Check this out Sheila, I know you trippin right now, and I would be trippin too if somebody brought somethin like this to my attention. So I'ma be straight up with you and let you know what's up. I love you baby, and I just felt that it was time for me to be all the way real with the woman I'm gonna spend the rest of my life with. The woman who's gonna give birth to my children, and the woman I'm gonna grow old and die with." He paused momentarily, letting the words from his last statement sink in, then continued.

"Sheila, this money basically got blood all over it. I'm sure you already assumed it, but so does every other American dolla' on this planet. It's all fucked up. So all

I want you to do for me right now is look at the bigger picture. Self preservation is not just a way of life for me, it's the only way of life for me. And every time I spilled a man's blood, I hated myself for it. But every time I looked in your eyes and saw the love you had for me, it would always balance me out and help my focus get a lot clearer. Baby I can't change what's already been done, but I do have the power to change most of the discomfort that's gonna come into both of our lives real soon, if you are willing to take the next step with me. I've never read the bible Sheila, but I remember my father telling me about the story of Sodomn and Gamorrah. He told me that a man named Lot had a wife that looked back while God was destroying the cities, which was forbidden because God specifically told them all to not look back. So her punishment for her disobedience was gettin turned into a pillar of salt in the instant she looked back. I never really understood the significance of that story until recently, so let's apply it to our lives Sheila and never look back. That's 7.8 million dollars on the bed, and I just had a half-a-million from a legitimate investment transferred in your name a few hours ago. But we'a go over the details later, if there is a later for us. So what's it gonna be Sheila? 'Cause my back is against the wall right now. Pooh is dead, Bam is dead, Smoke is facing lethal injection, and the feds wanna do something to me ten times worse than everything I just named."

Sheila stood there with a stream of tears flowing down her face as she pondered on everything that Ray Ray had just laid on her. She always knew he wasn't a saint, but she had no idea that things were as deep as they were. And she could only imagine how much blood was probably spilled to accumulate all that money. Sheila cried more as she thought about what her man had become. She also cried for Pooh, Smoke, Bam, and all of the victims of one man's pain.

She knew that Ray Ray was never the same after his parent's horrible death, and she had no idea if he ever would be. All she knew is that he was the love of her life, and that she couldn't imagine turning left if he was turning right. He was her everything. And if this is what it's come to, she would accept it along with whatever consequences that came with it. Sheila walked up to Ray Ray and gently slipped her hands into the palms of his, looking him straight in his eyes before venting.

"Baby, you were my first, and you are my last. It started with you, and it's gonna end with you. That's it."

She slowly slipped into his arms in a warm, passionate embrace after finishing her final statement. Ray Ray was happy that she decided to strive toward the finish-line with him, even though it was still questionable as to whether they would make it or not. The odds were stacked against them in the damnest way, and they were running outta time.

CHAPTER 25

As the jet landed at the LAX airport in Los Angeles, Ray Ray made his way to one of the many cabs that was sitting in front of the terminal. He quickly placed an upfront twenty dollar bill in the slot, assuming that the driver preferred it that way. He smiled to himself when he realized his assumption was right. The Korean driver took the twenty from the slot with no hesitation, then pulled off headed for the address Ray Ray had given him.

Ray Ray took in the sights of L.A. as the cab cruised through the inner city down Vermont Ave. He'd never been there before, and it was a trip to see all the palm trees that he'd heard about. L.A. was beautiful, but the darkside of it stuck out like a sore thumb. The junkies, winos, and gangbangers that roamed the streets just confirmed the fact that every city got a ghetto.

As they made a left turn on 59th and Budlong, home of the rollin 60's, Ray Ray glanced at the eerie looking John Mere Highschool and suddenly didn't feel so far from home.

"Keep the change!" yelled Ray Ray as the cab driver attempted to place the four dollars and odd cents in the slot. He glanced around the area of the designated spot as he stepped out the cab, but he didn't notice anyone or anything familiar... Suddenly, a darkskinned guy with cornrows to the back came walking toward him. Ray

Ray's heart-rate immediately increased and he had to refocus his eyes until the man opened his mouth and asked, "You Ray Ray?"

"That depends on who wanna know." Answered Ray Ray on the defensive.

"Check this out cuz, I'm down wit' yo' cousin Gabe, and I was told to meet you here and bring you to him."

Ray Ray breathed a sigh of relief at the mention of his cousin's name, because there were two things that had him tensed up. The first thing was the fact that dude looked identical to Spade, minus the missing tooth. And the second thing was the fact that he was approached by a stranger at a time he wasn't strapped. Even though he knew that his cousin Gabe would put him in good hands, it still didn't out-rank having yo'self in good hands.

Ray Ray climbed on the passenger side of the SUV and rode for another ten minutes until they pulled up in the parking lot of a grocery store. The man got out and instructed Ray Ray to follow him. Moments later, they were both walking through the busy grocery store. Ray Ray noticed his escort nod a hello to the Korean man behind the bullet-proof glass of the skybox that sat two feet off the floor in a corner of the establishment. They walked through two double doors in the back of the store past the meat section and full-size freezers. As they continued on, their walk soon turned into a journey as Ray Ray found himself walking through door after door, stair-case after stair-case and down several corridors. Finally they entered a door that appeared to lead them to a small underground arena. It had a seating capacity that would hold about five-hundred people. There was a small gated cage that sat directly in the middle of the room, and dried up blood decorated portions of the gate. Ray Ray followed the man to an office that sat in a distant corner from the seats. When he walked in, the first thing he saw was a wide-grinned smile displaying two platinum covered teeth with a few diamonds encrusted in them.

"Whuddup main!" Gabe spoke excitedly as he walked up and locked hands with Ray Ray, giving him a shoulder to shoulder embrace. Ray Ray smiled at Gabe and playfully tapped his bulging stomach.

"Looks like you been eatin' good couz." Gabe smiled at Ray Ray's comment.

"Yeah, you know I gotta get mines couz."

Ray Ray's smile disappeared momentarily.

"Just how have you been getting yours couz?" Gabe knew what he was thinking, so he quickly responded on the defensive.

"Whoa! Whoa! Big fella, don't get ya'self all worked up thinkin I'm still fuckin wit' that white girl. I haven't fucked wit' that shit since the last time I saw you main. I makes my paper electronically baby, that's the new game. I clone phones and give good prices on computer software. I also run one of the biggest dog-fightin rings on the west coast in case you forgot. Now do I get to keep my hard earned dough couz, or should I prepare myself to make way?" Ray Ray smiled at him and laughed a little at the same time, then replied,

"That's whussup, get yours dawg."

Gabe stroked a brush over his short brush waves, then rubbed a hand across his dark face with a facial expression that said,

"I'm one cool cat." They all burst out laughin, and soon as the laughter subsided, Gabe looked at Ray Ray seriously and said,

"Now let me take you to the lil bitch you've spent

a lifetime chasin." Ray Ray didn't say a word, he just returned an overly anticipated look on his face and made a hand gesture to Gabe that meant,

"You lead, I'll follow."

Gabe led him to another room that was two doors away from his office. When they walked in, a strong odor smacked them in the face and it almost made everybody throw up except Gabe, because he was use to the horrible smell that lingered in that room at all times from all the gruesome events that took place in there. Bo-Bo sat in a chair blind-folded and duct-taped. And a couple of Gabe's boys snickered a little when they noticed that Bo-Bo had pissed and shitted on himself.

Ray Ray walked over to Bo-Bo and snatched the blind fold off. Then a half of a second later, he snatched the tape off his mouth. Bo-Bo let out a sissified moan from the sudden pain it caused, then squinted his eyes from the light and took a few moments to refocus his vision. Ray Ray walked behind him and looked down at his tied hands, and seeing the 'G-life' tattoo was confirmation enough that this was the right man. Bo-Bo looked a little different than he use too. His face was a little fatter, and he looked ten years older than he really was.

Ray Ray stepped back around in front of him and stood there until Bo-Bo's eyes absorbed the new light and allowed him to see clearly again. He looked up at Ray Ray with a constant irritated blink, scanning his face to try to jog his memory as to where he knew him from. Once he realized Ray Ray's face didn't, and probably wouldn't ring any bells, he casually blurted out...

"Man can you please tell me what this shit is about."

Ray Ray immediately slapped blood from his mouth then grabbed him by his shirt and grimaced,

"Look at me and look at me good you lil bitch, 'cause you came into my crib and took everything I stood for. My mama, my ace, and my-," Ray Ray paused for a moment as he felt a build up of tears about to erupt. He gave himself a few seconds to regain control, then finished his sentence.

"And my pops. That's what this is about you bitch-ass nigga." Bo-Bo's facial expression quickly formed into a portrait of pure fear as he reflected back to the night he participated in the triple homicides. He took a deep swallow, then tried to run a weak game of psychology to possibly get out of the situation.

"Lil Ray Ray!" he began.

"Damn man I can't believe it's you. I really thought it was you who Spade killed that night. Now I'm glad to see that it wasn't. And check this out man, I swear to God that Spade made me do it with him. He had his boy holdin my mama and lil sister hostage in they own crib, and he said that if I didn't go along with the program, they would kill them both. So I had too dawg. What would you do in a situation like that? Huh?'

Ray Ray just stared at him coldly, then answered.

"The same thang that I'm 'bout to do to yo' ass now."

"Hold up dawg!" Bo-Bo shouted frantically.

"Man I'm tellin you the truth. And on top of that, it's been over ten years since that jumped off. I can't believe you is still trippin on that."

Ray Ray had heard enough, so he casually leaned toward Bo-Bo and grimaced,

"Nigga! It ain't never no statue of limitation on shit like that, and never will be. Maybe you'a get that through yo' big ass head in yo' next lifetime, cause you played ya'self on this one dude."

Bo-Bo suddenly let out a scream mixed with a moan

as Ray Ray leaned the weight of his body into the force of one of the hardest punches he ever threw in his life. He instantly knew Bo-Bo's jaw was broke from the loud cracking sound it made. Ray Ray slipped off his black Pelle and looked at Gabe with bucked eyes. And in the voice of a frantic junkie in need of a fix, he asked,

"You got a hammer around here couz? Gimee a hammer or a screwdriver couz."

Gabe held up his hand and replied,

"Hold up a minute couz, don't even sweat that cause I got somethin real special in mind for this lame. This room was designed for muthafucka's like him, that's why it smells the way it smells, now come with me."

Gabe led Ray Ray and the other two associates into another room that was adjacent to that room. They stood behind what looked like prison bars, and still had a clear view of Bo-Bo. They was so close that they could reach through the steel bars and touch him. Gabe announced that he'd be back shortly, then left the room. One of Gabe's associates pulled out a blunt and asked,

"You ever Smoke any of this good Cali greenery cuz?"

"Yeah, but it's been a minute." Answered Ray Ray.

"Well let's get yall reacquainted cuz, cause you sho'l gon' need it with the demo that you 'bout to witness."

They fired up the blunt and smoked half of it by the time Gabe came back. He walked in the room where Bo-Bo was at and left the door open behind him. He then stood directly in front of Bo-Bo so he would have his undivided attention.

"I'd like you to meet somebody. Lucifer!" he called out, and a muscular jet-black pitbull with charcoal eyes encompassed by a dark red cornea, casually strolled in the room and obediently sat down beside Gabe.

"Now I'd like you to meet somebody else. Satan!" he called out. And another jet-black male pit of the same description strolled into the room and sat down next to the other one.

"And last but not least, Ebliss!" said Gabe in a voice filled with confidence, then a third identical dog made his way in the room beside his brothers. Gabe cleared his throat, then took one step forward.

"Now before we begin this most anticipated session main, let me give you a little history on these three gentlemen." He casually swayed his hand in the direction of the dogs to let Bo-Bo know he was referring to them when he said gentlemen.

"Their mother came from England, and their father came from Paris. They were the only three survivors from a litter of six. They was sick at birth main, and they was the only three pups who was jet black and identical to each other. Now, one of my bidness associates called me from Germany and told me that he'd just nursed three rare pits back to health, and wanted to know if I was interested in purchasing them. I immediately jumped on it main, especially when he told me the mother was from the Snoody bloodline, and the father was from a Kobey. And when he paused over the phone and told me there was one small problem, I was like aw shit main, whut is it? Now peep this. He said that the mother had a slight brawl during her pregnancy, and nobody realized she ruptured somethin inside her intestine. And she bled internally for the last 30 days of her pregnancy until she gave birth and died. Now here's the tripped out part main, the puppies was feedin' off the blood from the small wound inside her. That's why they was so sick at birth. And after all kinds of studies from my veterinarian friend, it was discovered that they would only eat raw flesh, preferably human flesh."

Bo-Bo immediately began to sweat profusely at the mention of the flesh-eating beasts. Gabe laughed a little before continuing the story.

"Then my friend asked me in a serious tone main, do you think you can keep them a fresh supply of human flesh? Main I laughed hard as hell at the top of my lungs and said, main, with all the sucka's, scandalous niggas, scandalous bitches, and snitches in the world, consider my puppies rich on human flesh playa. And after that, the rest was history." Gabe clapped his hands together a couple times as if to say, moving right along.

"Now, I haven't fed them in a week, because I was originally waiting for the law to give two of my workers a bond. But it looks like the law's is gettin' a little more strict on gettin' caught with truck loads of software, so we'a have to settle for you." Bo-Bo instantly started squirming in his seat.

"Ey mun, chill ut' wit dat shit mun, don do dis to me."

His words could barely be understood because of his broken jaw, but he still squawked and pleaded.

A few seconds later, Gabe formed what almost appeared to be a crip sign, and Lucifer leaped forward immediately. He locked on Bo-Bo's already bloody mouth, and savagely tugged and shook his face from side to side. He screamed and kicked until he fell out the chair with the dog landing on top of him. Moments later, another signal was given, which instantly made Satan join the attack. He locked on one of Bo-Bo's bare feet, and it was only a matter of seconds before you could hear the sound of cracking bones in his foot. He screamed what cries he could get out as the two demons chewed away at his flesh. His hands were still tied behind his back, and he had dislocated his right shoulder from the fall. When Ebliss was finally given the command, he ran up and bit down hard on Bo-Bo's abdominal section. And on about the second tug, he came up with a mouth full of Bo-Bo's intestines.

Ray Ray and the two bystanders quickly turned their heads away momentarily from the gruesome sight of the bloody guts in the dog's mouth.

"Ha Ha, what yall pussies lookin away foe main? Yall betta' watch my babies devour this bitch."

They all stood there and watched in amazement at how the dogs constantly tore and ate flesh from Bo-Bo's body at the same time. But Ray Ray was the most amazed because he'd never seen nothing like that in his life. It resembled a national geographic program with lions devouring a gazelle. Bo-Bo died within the first twenty minutes of the attack, and the dogs steadily ate until they were full. They left a half of a leg, an arm with a missing hand, three toes and two fingers. The rest was just skull, bones, and shredded clothes. Gabe gave the command for them to go to a neutral corner and sit, while Ray Ray and the others walked past them out the door. Ray Ray looked at Gabe as the door shut behind them and asked,

"What about the rest of those remains?" Gabe smiled then answered.

"Don't worry 'bout dat couz, they will be finished with that before the night is out."

Ray Ray was fully satisfied with Bo-Bo's punishment for killing his parents. He thought about Sheila and hoped that everything was going as planned with her. She was cool with a black professor at Michigan State University, and he would always talk about how she reminded him of his daughter. He took a liking to her in a fatherly type of way, and the more he started seeing Ray Ray come up to visit with her, the more he would hit her with talks about wrong and right choices.

He didn't know Ray Ray on a personal level, but he assumed he was just another typical drug dealer who would go to prison for a long time, or get killed and leave her lonely. And judging by the different cars Ray Ray drove, and the stylish clothes he wore, the professor figured he had some heavy money. He would always drop hints to Sheila about hiding major money and making dirty money clean. Saying things like, *"If you were my daughter, I'd make sure I showed you where one of the safest bank's in the world is located at. I know because I have an account there. It's just off the coast of the Camen Islands, so if you ever plan on taking a vacation around that area, give me a call and I'll introduce you to some people over there that can be very beneficial to you under the right circumstance."*

Sheila knew exactly what circumstances the professor was talking about. And she knew that she needed help on securing all the money that Ray Ray had, so she called him and told him a story that was not all true, but was enough to get him to help her make major moves.

Sheila combined her financial knowledge along with the professor's, and within a twelve hour period, she had secured 4.5 million of Ray Ray's dollars through various internet back-channels that the professor hipped her too. It was like being in the Camen Islands without actually being there. He used a lot of his resources to make it all work.

Sheila kept the rest in cash and spreaded it out evenly in three different safety deposit boxes throughout the city. Everything went smooth for her, now she would just lay low until she heard from Ray Ray.

CHAPTER 26

The spectators yelled and cheered through the thick clouds of tobacco and weed smoke as the two pitbulls fought a brutal battle. The one with the tiger-stripes held a steady lock on the white pits throat, cutting off the flow of oxygen, which caused the white pit to make a wheezing sound with every strained breath.

Mostly everybody in the room were baller's, and they held up fists full of money as they jumped around in excitement or disappointment for their chosen dog. One of the dudes wearing a blue Nautica track suit with blue chucks ran up to the cage and yelled, "Finish'em killa! Poppa need a new ride." The brown tiger-striped pit continued to shake his opponent until he fell limp in his grip. He felt proud of his win, so he violently shook the lifeless dog to finalize his defeat. Then boldly waited 'til the lock-breakers came in the cage and forced his mouth open with a object that looked like a crowbar.

Ray Ray was more than ready to leave at this point, mainly because he still had unfinished business to attend to. He only stayed as long as he did because Gabe asked him to stick around for a couple dog fights. Gabe took him to the airport himself, and just as Ray Ray was about to board the express flight, Gabe called out to him.

"Ay couz, hold up a sec." Ray Ray turned around and walked up to him.

"Whuddup couz, what's on ya' mind?"

Gabe scratched the side of his head with a curious expression before responding.

"Main, let me ask you something." He made direct eye-contact with Ray Ray before posing his question.

"Would you happen to know who was responsible for my past coke connect gettin' found slumped with two slugs in his dome, and two untouched kilos left beside his body?"

Ray Ray paused for about five seconds, then simply smirked, winked, and walked away.

Gabe smiled and shook his head and yelled,

"If you was tryna' scare me out the game main, it worked."

Ray Ray acknowledged Gabe's statement by raising two fingers as he walked in the opposite direction, then faded in the distance.

****

Ray Ray made it back to Detroit at a satisfying time, and he only had one thing on his mind, *"getting agent Nathaniel Lawson to not testify against Smoke."*

He knew that the agent had the kind of evidence that could get Smoke put under the prison, so he contacted one of his resources in the fifth precinct and quickly devised a plan. He met with Sheila to find out how everything went with her, then gave her a few last minute instructions to set the stage for possible failure on his final mission. Sheila cried her eyes out because she didn't like the mere thought of them not coming out on top of this situation together. But she understood his disposition, and would do everything that he asked her too.

Later on that night, agent Boon paid the lady at the drive-thru window for the two Coney Island chilli dogs, then pulled off. As he rode down east Jefferson in his white GS 300 Lexus that he bought from a police auction, he ate the chilli dogs and thought about how fortunate he was to get a snapshot of Smoke from the automatic surveillance camera that he had set up outside of his decoy house. The photos had clear shots of everybody except Ray Ray. And it really pissed him off because he and his co-workers really wanted to put Ray Ray away, but lack of evidence wouldn't let them.

Boon felt that he still had a chance at getting him, because he figured that whenever he put the pressure on Smoke, Smoke would snitch and make things a lot easier for them. As the agent made a left on Garland, the flashing lights in his rearview mirror made him angrily mumble,

"What the fuck do these peons want. They'a get some act-right as soon as I flash this federal badge and make'em feel like K-Mart security guards."

He abruptly pulled over and waited for them to approach the car. The black officer climbed out of his squad-car and walked up to the driver-side window.

"Hello sir." said the officer. "May I see your license, registration, and proof of insurance?"

Boon positioned himself in his seat so that he'd have direct eye-contact with the officer.

"First of all officer, why did you stop me?"

The officer displayed a little agitation before responding.

"Sir, you failed to use a turn signal."

"You're a damn lie!" shouted agent Boon.

"Sir you need to calm down and produce the

information that I asked you for."

Agent Boon aggressively pushed his FBI I.D within inches of the officer's face.

"There! You happy man, that's my information."

"Sir, that's not what I asked you for." The officer spoke in a calm tone, and agent Boon became furious. He angrily snatched open his glove compartment and pulled out his paperwork, then produced his license and gave it all to the officer with a slight shove.

"When this little bullshitten game is over, I want your badge number guy, cause this is some bullshit and you know it."

The officer nodded in agreement then casually walked back to his squad-car to run a check on him. Agent Boon was angry because he usually gets out of traffic tickets whenever he flashes his federal credentials. But he realized it wasn't working this time, and he wasn't too happy with that. At first he was gonna play the race card, but that woulda' looked real silly being that both of them are black. So he would just result to using his rank to inconvenience the young officer in the near future instead.

After running a check on the agent, the passenger officer walked up to the agent and handed him his license and paperwork back. He kept the flashlight pointed at an angle where it would slightly irritate a person's eyes. Boon snatched his paperwork and added,

"You know, you should really talk to your partner about these kind of inconveniences toward a man of my position, 'cause it could easily come back to haunt him in the damnest way."

The officer handed him a ticket then replied,

"Yeah, I know whatch'u mean about things comin back

to haunt a man. Especially pieces of shit like you."

A frown suddenly appeared on Boon's face, and he squinched his eyes in an attempt to see the smart-mouth officer clearly.

"What in the fuck did you just say to me?" he asked, wanting to clarify whether he heard him correctly or not.

Ray Ray casually moved the light from his face and grimaced,

"Yeah you heard me right you piece'a shit. And one things fa'sho and two things fa'certain." He pressed the gun against Boon's head, then ordered,

"Now ask me what the answer is?"

Boon hesitated before slowly mouthing,

"What's fa'sho and what's fa' certain?" Ray Ray smirked and replied,

"You won't be testifyin against my boy in this lifetime!" then squoze off five quick rounds in his head, then casually reached inside and retrieved the bloody traffic ticket. The two men pulled off in the squad-car, leaving the Lexus sitting idle under the dimly-lit street-light.

They drove to Boon's house, broke in, and got all of the surveillance photos and any other evidence that could link Smoke to the home invasions.

Ray Ray sat in the car and destroyed the evidence, while his police friend Smitty listened to the dispatcher call for all units in the area to respond to an attempt car-jacking and possible homicide in a white GS 300 Lexus. Ray Ray had paid Syann to go to the scene, call it in, and act as a witness to the crime. She made up a bogus story about how she had pulled up over a friend's house on the same block, and saw two black dudes jump out of a black cutlass and demand the man to get out the Lexus. And when he refused, they shot him and left the scene. The authorities bought the story, and Ray Ray paid his crooked police-friend Smitty Branch twenty-five G's in cash to conclude the deal.

CHAPTER 27

When the news of agent Lawson's murder came in, the prosecutor was furious. Not because he was a friend or anything of that nature, but because his testimony was vital to the prosecution's case. The prosecutor was suppose to receive copies of everything the agent had the very next morning, but the tragic event left him empty handed.

He sent other agents to search Boon's house meticulously for any of the documents, but there was still no luck. In turn, he was forced to withdraw from introducing any federal issues throughout the course of the trial, because all he had was allegations with no proof.

The trial went forward, and the prosecutor had done a good job so far of painting Smoke as a real monster to the jury. Smoke clearly looked like a child molester and murderer, and the only plea-bargain that they were offering was sixty years to life.

For eight long days it was a real dog fight between the prosecutor and defense. And so far, the prosecutor had won every round... Smoke's lawyer repeatedly gave the jury significant insight on the tragic loss of his little sister, in order to establish the fact that Smoke would never commit such a twisted crime. But despite how convincing he'd sound, it was all to no avail as the jury sat there expressionless...

On the final day of the trial, the prosecutor was more than convinced that he'd won the case, and that he would surely see Smoke sentenced to the rest of his natural life behind bars. He wanted to put icing on this cake to make it sweet as possible, in hopes that the jury would see his guilt beyond a shadow of a doubt. So he allowed young Iyonna Brown to get on the stand to finalize the grand finale.

The crowd of spectators sat attentively as Iyonna's mother escorted her to the stand. She kissed Iyonna softly on the cheek and whispered,

"Just nod yes or no for the man baby, and whenever you don't feel like being up there anymore, mama will come get you, okay?"

Iyonna nodded yes to her mother.

"I love you sweetheart. And we want to make sure we put this man away for doing those horrible things to you. So don't be afraid to help the prosecutor reveal the truth."

She kissed her once more, then went back to her seat.

The pale prosecutor approached the stand in a subtle fashion, making sure the jury took in his sincerity, warmness, and kindness to a little girl as he softly spoke.

"Iyonna, do you like candy?" He asked. And when she nodded yes, he handed her a cherry lollipop, then immediately turned to the jury for discussion.

"Ladies and gentlemen of the jury, what you've just witnessed is just how easy it is for the many predators in our society to approach our vulnerable young people with masks of generosity. Pretending to be kindhearted citizens for the sole purpose of taking their precious, innocent, fragile little bodies for their personal enjoyment and disturbed fetishes. They harbor perverted thoughts and sick pleasures in their sick minds, then move on them the way this animal moved in on this nine-year old little girl."

The prosecutor pointed at Smoke with aggression.

"Objection your honor! He's speculating." Yelled Smoke's attorney.

"Sustained." Replied the judge.

The prosecutor continued.

"This little girl will never be able to speak again, because the horrible ordeal that she experienced left her in shock. People, I want you to recognize the fact that her life has been reduced. And if you all would just close your eyes for a moment and try to imagine a fraction of what she went through, there would be no doubt in your minds as to where the person responsible belongs. Iyonna, would you please point to the man who brought you to the hospital."

With her head slightly tilted towards the floor, Iyonna slowly raised her hand and pointed her finger at Smoke.

The prosecutor stepped a little closer to Iyonna, responding to her expression of fear.

"Its okay sweetheart, you don't have to be afraid anymore. No one's gonna ever hurt you again. Now sweetheart, I'm gonna ask you one more question, and I'm gonna try to make the question as painless as possible, okay?"

She nodded her head yes, seemingly in slow motion.

Her unsteady nerves made her constantly swing one of her tiny legs, which caused her barretted pig-tails to slightly bounce from the continuous movement.

The prosecutor walked over to his table and took a few swallows from a glass of water as if he was revin up for his next question, then returned to Iyonna. He looked at her with the most sincere facial expression that he could muster up, then asked,

"Iyonna, did this man ever touch you sexually?"

Iyonna's mind immediately went to the man who did touch her sexually, and she suddenly burst into tears. She began to cry outloud in a steady "Aaaahhh!" Her cries were similar to a young child that had just been spanked. The volume of the courtroom quickly turned into a bunch of "oow's ah's oh's and damn's."

"Order in the court!" yelled the judge. "Let this be a warning that I want my courtroom quiet during these proceedings."

Iyonna continued to cry, and Smoke immediately began to mentally prepare himself for the long stretch in prison that he knew was coming. Because the present scene definitely shitted on any sympathy that the court may have had for him... The prosecutor casually turned to the judge with a display of confidence and said,

"I have no further questions your honor." Then he approached Iyonna and told her that she didn't have to answer anymore questions. He took her tiny hand and slowly helped her off the stand. As she walked toward the aisle with him, she suddenly stopped. She looked directly at Smoke for about two full minutes, then pointed at him aggressively trying to utter undescribable words at the same time.

The prosecutor quickly bent down and whispered,

"It's alright sweetheart, he's not gonna hurt you again."

Then he tried to continue the walk toward her mother, but Iyonna refused to move. She continued to stand there and point at Smoke, uttering the same babble that couldn't be interpretated by nobody in the room.

"Ee, a-mee, ee-a-mee." The prosecutor suddenly figured that he knew what she was trying to say, so he gave his interpretation loud enough for everyone to hear.

"We know he raped you honey. And justice is definitely gonna be served here today. Now let's go to your mommy so we can fix this problem."

Iyonna still didn't budge, and tears constantly flowed down her face as she continued to strain her voice in an effort to be clearly understood. At this point, her mother got up and walked toward her with an equal share of tears.

Many of the spectators were now visually assassinating Smoke with the mean stares they shot in his direction. And Smoke, as well as his lawyer could feel defeat smothering the room. Suddenly, just as Iyonna's mother reached out for her hand, Iyonna snatched away from the prosecutor and ran toward Smoke as fast as she could, unexpectedly jumping in his arms, wrapping her tiny arms around his neck as tight as she could. The courtroom erupted in awe, and the bailiff immediately ran over to Smoke and Iyonna to insure her safety. All he was able to do was standby along with the prosecutor and Iyonna's mother, because Iyonna refused to let him go.

The prosecutor quickly turned to the judge moments after she restored order in the courtroom and pleaded.

"Your honor, she's been through a lot' and I can assure you that she's just confused right now."

Smoke whispered in Iyonna's ear.

"Hey lil mama, you remember me after all huh?" Still holding him tight, she shook her head yes.

"Sweetheart, I'm in a lot of trouble here. And I don't wanna make things any worse, so I want you to do me a favor and go to your mommie okay." Iyonna rose up and positioned herself on him where she was now looking him directly in his eyes. She touched his face while ignoring her mother's demands to come to her.

Then a few moments later, she turned toward her mother and spoke as clearly as if God himself had just touched her vocal chords.

"Mommie, he saved me." The courtroom erupted once again, and Iyonna's mother rushed over to her with a confused expression, barely able to control her flowing tears.

She stared in amazement before her words were able to come out.

"Oh my God, you're talkin' again baby."

Iyonna just paused momentarily, then repeated herself.

"Mommie, he saved me." The prosecutor was furious, and he kept on fighting until Iyonna got back on the stand and cleared Smoke completely of the child molestation charges. However, he was still found guilty of murdering the real child molester, and was sentenced to 7 years in state prison for manslaughter.

Ray Ray was a little sad about his friend going to prison for 7 years, but he knew it was a blessing considering everything they'd done. And he was relieved that it was finally over.

Ebony, the nurse from the hospital told Smoke that she knew he was innocent all along, and that she'd be willing to be a friend to make his bid more comfortable. All the pieces to the puzzle seemed to be falling in place, even for the feds because they weren't through with Ray Ray just yet. They had lifted a partial fingerprint from one of the crime scenes that they were almost certain was his. But the discrepancy was, the set of his prints that they had on file didn't provide the necessary angle, so they gambled and immediately issued warrants to re-arrest him.

Sheila sat on the plane in tears when she finally realized Ray Ray wasn't gonna show up. She was told to use the one-way ticket whether he showed up or not, and that's exactly what she did.

She cried herself to sleep and woke back up about two hours into the flight. After returning from the bathroom freshening up, she opened up her laptop and checked the internet to see if Ray Ray had boarded any of the late flights under his assumed name. After exhausting all of her remedies, she closed the laptop and sunk back into the seat feeling helpless and betrayed. Betrayed by her man and all the forces that wouldn't allow him to be there. And even though she had millions of dollars to insure a comfortable life for herself, it didn't mean nothing without Ray Ray......

Ray Ray placed a few more items in his suitcase, then made one last phone call to one of his business associates to finalize all of his business interests. After hanging up the phone, he took a sip from the bottled water, then went to the bathroom to urinate.....

Meanwhile, the feds slowly formed a position outside of the house on Ashland and Jefferson. They slowly crept up on the porch, and the body warrant for Ray Ray was handed to the leading agent. He looked it over one last time to make sure everything was legit, then on a finger-count of three, they bombarded the front door and stormed into the house......

Four days later...

Sheila stood in front of a small pond at a park, watching fish swim gracefully through it while in deep thought. She thought about how she would pick up on her schooling where she left off, and how awfully lonely her life would be without her soulmate.

She contemplated on jumping on a plane heading back to Detroit, but she thought about how firm Ray Ray was in his instructions for her to never return nomatter what.

And it literally ate her alive to think that he was somewhere in the world in a desolate predicament and she couldn't even be there for him through whatever discomfort that he might've been experiencing.

The more she thought about it, the harder it became for her to hold back the frequent tears that she'd been shedding lately. She'd never before experienced pain like the pain she was feeling during these times, and things didn't seem as if they would ever get any better.

Sheila produced a slight smirk when one of the fishes quickly dove out, then landed right back into the water creating a soft splash. She had always been fascinated with anything dealing with wildlife every since she was a little girl. She would often visit Sea World and the Detroit Zoo with her mother and watch the dolphins and other animals for hours. She smiled at the thought of how she would always throw tantrums when it was time to go. That's where most of her spankings would derive from. Sheila wiped her tears and came to grips with the reality that she'd have to pull herself together and get ready to face the world with strength, just as Ray Ray would want her too. She picked up her Prada purse and closed her light overcoat. And just as she prepared to walk away, a pair of hands covered her eyes from behind.

'Guess who?' mumbled the disguised voice. Sheila suddenly felt her legs get weak. She felt faint and thought she was losing her mind. Because even though the voice was in disguise, she still knew it all to well. She'd heard it all of her life and prayed religiously that she'd someday hear it again. She quickly turned around. And to her surprise, it wasn't a dream. He was real and he was in her presence.

"Oh my God, Ray Ray it's you!"

"You damn right it's me bae."

She hugged him so tightly, almost to the point of knocking him down, then she pushed herself back to look at him again.

"Baby I thought you wasn't comin! I thou-," he put his finger to her lips as a gesture for her to settle her anxious flow of words.

"Baby I know what you thought, but I wouldn't leave my baby out here by her lonesome for nothin' in this world. So get use to lookin' at this ugly mug, cause daddy here to stay. Now I think this calls for a celebration, don't you?'

"Yes, yes." Sheila answered excitedly

He grabbed her hand and smiled.

"Well let's go to my favorite establishment." Ray Ray called the service people to pick up the rental Sheila had, and they pulled off in the one he was in.

As they rode through the streets of their new home, Ray Ray thought about how shitty the feds must've felt when they ran up in the wrong house. And when they finally did run up in the right house on Nottingham and Mack, they were furious when they found a note from Ray Ray sitting under a empty water bottle that read:

Dear Mr. FBI,

I personally wanted to thank you for your persistence in pursuing a nigga like me. I commend you hoes on your effort to bring me to justice, because I am in fact, not a very nice person. I've done some things that I will never be proud of, and if the other hell really does exist, I'll more than likely be sent first class on an express flight. So if it makes you lames feel any better, I'll be properly judged one day for my sins by forces greater than yourself. I know you probably say to yo'selves, 'what could drive a man to reek so much havoc on the society that he grew up in? Well let me enlighten you. Da' hood was the artist of my life, and It painted me into all that you see in me today, so, many of us don't choose the way of life that we find ourselves trapped in, the life chooses us. And people like you are too stupid and naïve to recognize the real problems, and much too weak too participate in the solutions. And according to the way the system is set up, I was actually goin' with the grain rather than goin' against it. This country was built on blood. Otherwise, it wouldn't be as mighty as it is. Now I have a question for you. Where would the economy truly be without the criminal element? 'Cause without criminals, there's no need for all the different law enforcement agencies yall got. It would be no need for lawyers, judges, Co's, counselors, case-managers, jurors, or wardens. It would be a disaster, wouldn't it? So to conclude my letter, I want yall to thank me for bein' a good sport and puttin' food on yall families table. Oh, and by the way, I left a full finger-print on this water bottle for you clowns to match up with that partial print you found at that crime scene, it wasn't mine. But I felt it was time to leave anyway because everybody knows that yall are sore losers. So, so long muthafuckas, it's been real."

Ray Ray snapped out of his thoughts as they got out the car to enter the store. Sheila flashed a cordial smile at the white lady coming out walking a brown Pomeranian dog, then leaned over to Ray Ray's ear and whispered,

"I want one just like it, okay?"

When they walked in, the lady behind the counter smiled and took Ray Ray's order. The store was built like a restaurant, and whatever you purchased, you could either sit down at a table with, or take it out with you.

After sitting in the place for twenty minutes, Ray Ray found himself tickled at Sheila's behavior. And he could tell by the silly look on her face that she enjoyed her first order.

"Damn baby, where you goin?" asked Ray Ray.

Sheila didn't say a word. She just strolled up to the counter with a silly grin and said,

"Excuse me miss, can I have another order of that purple haze. But this time I'd like a half-ounce."

The lady behind the counter smiled and replied,

"Will that be for here or to go?" Sheila spoke softly through her silly grin and red eyes.

"To go please."

Ray Ray cracked his side in laughter, then walked up to her and whispered,

"Do you still want me to quit smoking baby? Cause this Amsterdam thang ain't 'gon let me."

Sheila looked up at him with the same silly grin and stated,

"This Amsterdam thang ain't gon' let me quit either baby, its home now."

When the flesh-eating dogs refused the half of raw pig that Gabe threw them, he looked at them with a puzzled expression and mumbled,

"What da' fuck is wrong wit' them fools today?"

He stood their looking at them for a moment, then spoke out-loud.

"You crazy muthafuckas ain't ate in days, and you mean to tell me yall ain't hungry." He looked at them as if he expected an explanation, but after a few moments, he shrugged it off. He turned to walk to the door, and in one smooth motion, Lucifer leaned forward and snapped his powerful jaws, then proceeded to chew on Gabe's pinky-finger as he walked away.

It took Gabe a few seconds before he realized his finger had just been bit off.

"You muthafucka!" he shouted as the realization allowed the pain to kick in. And before he could get another word out of his mouth, Satan and Ebliss charged at him, knocking him to the floor. Gabe swung at them wildly while constantly commanding them to back off, but it was no use, they kept comin. Gabe suddenly felt a chunk of flesh rip away from his left arm, then another finger disappeared from his left hand.

It was the first time since he had the dogs that he regretted getting their teeth specially sharpened to a razor point. As the attack progressed, Gabe knew that he was dead if he didn't fight a lot harder and get the hell up outta there. So with that thought in mind, he gave a vicious, hard kick to one of their heads, which allowed him to reach the pocket-knife in his back pocket. He swung it wildly as the dogs tried to clamp down on any of his vital organs. And just as Lucifer was in motion to clutch down on his stomach, Gabe stuck the knife deep in his right eye. Lucifer let out a loud squeal mixed with a sinister growl as he backed off momentarily. Gabe took advantage of the favorable opportunity as he retracted the bloody knife, then slashed it across the two other dogs, then ran to the door as fast as he could. As he fell through the door, he felt another chunk of flesh being ripped from his left buttocks. The pain was excruciating, but he was thankful that he made it out the room alive. He cursed out loud as he used the wall for balance while dragging his left leg and bleeding from different areas of his body. Once he retrieved the AK-47 assault rifle, he eagerly limped his way back to the room. Before opening the door, he mocked the words of Tony Montana from the movie Scarface in his own voice.

"Okay, you bitches wanna play rough, okay, let's play rough. Say hello to my little friend." He snatched the door open and fired on all three of them. Emptying a thirty round clip, violently killing them in less than thirty seconds.

He leaned against the wall and wiped the single tear that fell from his eyes. He loved his dogs, and hated the fact that it had to come to this. But he was realistic, and always knew in his heart that puttin' them down could someday be a possibility. Because the fact of the matter was, they were ironically born diabolical.

CHAPTER 28

Five years later:

A man stepped off a plane in Amsterdam with a photo of Ray Ray and Sheila. And after checking into a hotel, he went to the store that allowed people to purchase marijuana over the counter. He strolled up to the counter and got the female clerks attention.

"Excuse me miss... Do you know these two people?"

The woman smiled before replying,

"Yes I do. They're my best customers."

With that being said, the white federal agent smiled and told the clerk he'd be intouch.

He went back to his hotel room and looked over the warrant he had for Ray Ray again. And this time he felt a sense of relief because they finally had something concrete after all these years.

The agent sipped his coffee and reflected back to the night they got their break. *"Officer Branch, you are from the fifth precinct, is that correct?"*

"Yes, that's correct."

"Well we've been investigating your department for quite some time now, which brings us to the reason you are here being interrogated today. We have you on numerous counts of robbery, extortion, assault, narcotic distribution, and a host of other things that will make sure you go where a lot of the same men that you put away are, prison. But if there's

anything that you can tell us that's worth listening to, the prison option just may be compromised."

Officer Branch cleared his throat before responding.

"As a matter of fact, there is. Do you remember the federal agent Nathaniel Lawson who was killed by an apparent car-jacker in his Lexus about five years ago?"

"Yes" answered the agent.

"Well I know who did it because I was there. In fact, I was twenty-five-thousand dollars there.".......

Agent Burns displayed a devilish grin as he concluded his thoughts. He continued to sip his coffee and analyze the warrant.....

****

As Smoke walked out of the maximum security state prison in Ionia Michigan, his mother Yvonne and Ebony embraced him at the same time. They were overjoyed to see him as a free man. Tears quickly formed and streamed down Ebony's face. She'd waited for him the whole time, and ironically did it faithfully. Smoke was about twenty pounds heavier than he was when he went in. His muscular body showed well through the plain white t-shirt he wore.

"Let's get the hell up outta here yall, we'a finish our welcome home's when we get to the crib."

They all snickered a little then got in the black Navigator and pulled off.

Sixty minutes later.

Smoke smiled to himself when he saw the big welcome home sign with a large crowd of people standing in front of the yard waiting to greet him. The first person he noticed was Iyonna. And even though she was fourteen now, she still wore a distinguished scar just above her right eye that came from her attacker. She was a lot taller and a little heavier, but she still had her same little girl face. Smoke walked up to her and gave her a big hug.

"Whussup lil mama?"

"Hey uncle Smoke."

"Babygirl you gettin big on me, and it looks like I came home just in time to keep them sucka's away from you."

Iyonna smiled before responding.

"I keep them sucka's away from me anyway unc."

"Good girl." complimented Smoke.

"Iyonna, I kept all of your letters, and we gon' go through them together later on okay."

"Okay unc."

Smoke didn't know half the people that were there, but the men kept walkin up givin dap's and handshakes. And the women walked up giving hugs and friendly kisses. Smoke took in the scene and mentally noted how some of the little girls that he left behind were all grown up, especially little Tamera. She looked like she came straight off the pages of smooth magazine. And she constantly winked and blew kisses to let Smoke know she's game for whateva.' He just shook it off and made his way toward the bar-b-que pit.

As he was approaching the grill, he noticed a dark-complected man with a few missing fingers flash a diamond and platinum smile at him.

"Whussup main, remember me?"

"Vaguely dawg," answered Smoke. "Refreshin my memory."

"It's me main, Ray Ray's cousin Gabe from Texas."

"Aw whuddup dawg, long time no see." said Smoke as he remembered Gabe.

"Man, the last time I saw you was at one of yo' dog-fights in Cali. And if you don't mind me askin, what happened to yo' fingers?"

"Main, them damn dogs turned on my ass and I had to put'em to rest."

"Damn dawg, they must'a been some vicious muhfuckas."

"Yeah main, nuthin less than the devil."

"Anyway, what brings you to Detroit these days, is Ray Ray back or somethin?"

"Nah main, he still out the country and I ain't seen him in years, but dig, I'm here because I wanna holla at you about somethin heavy."

Smoke smirked a little before responding.

"Damn dawg, I ain't been out the joint a good 60 minutes and you wanna holla at me about somethin heavy already. I'm damn near scared to hear what it is."

"Aw cut it out main, you can tell that shit to them busta's, cause the Smoke I know ain't never scared."

Smoke smiled then replied,

"Dat Smoke might still be in the joint, and if he is, I ain't never tryna' see his brave ass again."

They both burst out laughin.

"Main let me find out them folks dun' got my nigga shook."

Smoke rubbed his head and replied.

"That just might be the case dawg, so let's not rule it out. Anyway, what's on ya mind Gabe?"

"It's like this main, I don't do my software and dog-fightin' thang nomoe. I'm on some other shit these days, but I need a strong right-hand man on my team fa' me to get the kinda' paper I'm tryna get. I got a sweet plug on some yae. The ticket is gravy and I know we could clean up."

Smoke gazed at Gabe sincerely before responding.

"Man, you know that ain't my thang. That ain't never been my thang."

"Aw main come on baby-boy, it's time for a change anyway. And if you thinkin' 'bout playin ya' old gig again, you need to think twice because these niggas ain't lettin' niggas run-up in they shit like that nomoe main, fo'real."

"Gabe is you trippin man, it ain't a sucka on this planet that I can't get."

"A'ight main, whateva' you say, but I'll be around wheneva' you ready to get this fa'sho money." Smoke nodded in agreement then blended in the party.....

Later on that night when Smoke and Ebony finished their intense love-making session, he pulled out all the photos that Ebony had sent him while he was in prison. He picked out his favorite ones and watched Ebony blush as they reminisced. Ebony still held her job at the hospital as a registered nurse, and Smoke admired her for being so career oriented.

He'd left a lot of money behind, and although most of it was gone, she hardly spent any of it. His mother made a few bad investments that left Smoke with a little under a hundred G's, which is considered broke in his circle.

After Ebony fell asleep, Smoke laid awake pondering on the things he would have to do to get back on top again. He felt as desperate as any other hustler would feel after getting out of prison, and his mind was made up to re-visit his past occupation. A few days later, Smoke jumped in Ebony's red grand prix and cruised through the city, giving himself a tour to see all the changed faces and changed land development that happened during his absence. It felt good to be free, and he was amused at himself when he compared the super fine females in the hood, to the female CO's that he use to lust over in the joint. And even though it was a few fine co's in there, he was now convinced that prison really can make a man delusional.

He rode throughout the city a little longer, then decided to swing by Valencia's house. He hadn't seen or heard from her in years, and he wondered if she still had the same almost perfect body that she had when he use to hit it. When he pulled up across the street from her house, he saw Valencia standing on her porch talking to a dark-skinned man about nineteen years old wearing a baseball hat, baggy jeans, and Timberland boots. A few moments later, a blue Camry pulled up, and she ran off the porch, climbed in on the passenger side for a few minutes, then ran back up on the porch handing the youngsta something.

Her face was still beautiful, and she still had that long curly Puerto Rican hair. But she had lost about twenty pounds, and it made her look sickly. Smoke started to get out and go over to her, but the constant traffic that came to her house made him quickly change his mind. Smoke eventually came to the conclusion that Valencia's house was a drug spot, but he didn't know if she was selling or using until a black 745i Beemer pulled up. The driver looked like the rapper biggie smalls, and soon as Valencia got in, she immediately started suckin the man's dick.

As she continued to suck him, he tapped his horn then motioned for the youngsta to come to the car. The youngsta stood at the driver's side window and conversated with him for about five minutes before handing him a large roll of money. Valencia kept sucking him until he held the back of her head steady, and his body began jerkin.

The youngsta started laughin as he watched the fat man cum in her mouth. Smoke pulled off thinkin to himself, *"Damn I wonder who turned her out."* Then all thoughts of her faded just as quickly as they'd came. He stopped at a neighborhood store and picked up a six pack of Heineken and a pack of Newports. And when he came out, he noticed a youngsta about eighteen years old walkin toward him fast. He thought to himself, *"Not another one of these silly ass youngsta's tryin some sheisty shit. And I ain't even got my heat wit me."* But the closer the youngsta got, the more teeth he showed from the wide grin he was forming.

"Smoke! Is that you dawg?" asked the youngsta with the nappy braids excitedly.

"That depends on who wants to know." Smoke answered on the defense.

"Man it's me, lil Scoop. I use to stay down the street from you, and you use to let me make a lil money washin yo' cars and keepin yo' grass cut. I was about thirteen when you went to the joint."

The more the youngsta talked, the more Smoke remembered who he was.

"I'll be damn, whuddup lil Scoop. How yo' moms doin?"

"She doin a'ight man, but that diabetes is still kickin her butt."

"Sorry to hear that young dawg. Tell her I said hi. Now what you been up to these days?"

"Nothin major man, I just been makin a lil change here and there, but nothing major."

"Well all that might change real soon, cause I might have a proposition for ya, but I'll get back witcha in a few days on it, okay?"

"A'ight Smoke, I'll holla back"...

Three days later...

Smoke, Yvonne and Scoop rode to the grocery store to pick up some items for an up coming cookout that one of Yvonne's friends was havin. They parked, got out, and went in. Once inside, Scoop flirted with a big-butt dark-skinned girl while Yvonne and Smoke scanned the meat section checkin out some beef ribs. Yvonne picked up a few slabs of ribs, and just as she was about to hand them to Smoke, she caught a glimpse of a familiar face in her peripheral vision. Her heart started racin' as the reality kicked in of who it was. Her breathing became heavy as she fought to spit the name out her mouth. 'Brenda!!' she yelled frantically with her eyes bucked like a psycho. Brenda squinched her eyes while looking at Yvonne, trying to recognize the person who called her name. Suddenly, a look of fear covered Brenda's face when she remembered who Yvonne was. She immediately took off running toward the front door, and Yvonne took off behind her. Yvonne looked ahead and saw that she was headed in Scoop's direction, so she quickly yelled out,

"Scoop! Get Dat Bitch!" Scoop looked up just in time to football tackle the high speed Brenda. She went to the floor hard with Scoop landing on top of her. She struggled with Scoop until Yvonne and Smoke got there.

Yvonne didn't waste any time stomping and kicking her in the face.

"Bitch! I shared everything with you, I even gave you my last, and you still betrayed me and snitched on my son you triflin bitch!"

A puzzled expression formed on Smoke's face when he realized the woman was his mother's ex-cellmate. He immediately joined in and commenced to kickin' her too.

As Brenda curled up from the constant blows, individual packs of meat began to fall from under her jacket. She'd been boosting whatever she could to support her crack habit.

The arab owner of the store ran over to the scene with a pistol in his hand yelling for them to stop the assault and get the hell outta his store. But the moment he noticed the packs of steak that constantly fell from her jacket, he slapped her across her forehead with the pistol.

Blood leaped from the instant cut, and Brenda's loud screams echoed throughout the establishment.

"You filthy beetch, how dare you steal from my store!" another vicious slap with the pistol drew more blood from Brenda's already bloody face. Yvonne was furious at Brenda, but for some moralistic reason she felt bad for her. She felt that Brenda had enough punishment, so she motioned for Smoke and Scoop to not hit her anymore. Then she stepped in front of the still swinging arab man when she noticed Brenda lose consciousness.

"Okay, that's enough man, that bitch got the message."

"Move beetch! Before I give you some of this! She's a fuckin thief. So I beat her like thief, now move!"

Yvonne formed a menacing expression before responding. And just as the words were about to come out her mouth, a can of corn came crashing into the side of the man's face, instantly dazing him.

"Who da' fuck you talkin to like that? That's my moms muthafucka!" Smoke yelled as the man bled from the blow and struggled to stay on his feet. He wobbled and attempted to point his gun at Smoke, but just as his barrel locked in on its target, another barrel pressed aggressively against the arab's temple.

"Please buck so I can paint this muhfucka wit'yo

brains." grimaced Scoop.

"Go 'head, shoot muhfucka! I luv this shit!" The arab man knew he couldn't win, so he gently lowered the 45.

"Gimee this shit!" squawked Scoop as he snatched it out the man's hand.

"And just for playin us like that, empty the ends outta all seven of these cash registers, now!" Smoke immediately instructed Yvonne to go to the car. She helped Brenda outside while Scoop and the arab went to every cash register retrieving the money.

People in the store began to scurry toward the front doors, but Smoke blocked the entrance with a weapon in-hand and wouldn't allow anyone to leave until they finished. Scoop slapped the owner across the head one more time and made him lay face down after they had all the money. Then they both hurried outside where Yvonne waited for them out front with the car running.

She drove straight to the hospital to drop Brenda off, and Brenda regained consciousness by the time they arrived.

"Get out" snarled Yvonne as she looked at Brenda with a disgruntled expression.

Brenda hesitated as she attempted to find the proper words of consolation to say to Yvonne, but she couldn't. And her condition didn't make her effort any easier.

"Get the fuck up outta' here!" grimaced Smoke as he pressed the arab's 45 to the back of her head.

"Chill out Smoke. We ain't gon' stoop to her level baby."

"Nah Nah mama fuck this bitch. I should kick one of these hot ones in her head right now."

Smoke cocked the gun as if he was fed up, and Yvonne frantically yelled "No Smoke! I said No! We are not gonna stoop to the level of this bitch. I know it was fucked up what she did, but she's payin for it in a major way. Look at her, she's nothin but a low-life junkie. And if I would'na been leading with my heart instead of my intuition, I woulda' easily recognized her basehead character. But that's history baby, it's behind us now, so let's move on and let God deal with her scandalous ass." Tears fell from Brenda's bloody face as she began to mumble pitiful apologies.

"I'm sorry Yvonne, I'm so sorry. I know I was wrong and I can't take back what I did, but God knows I'm sorry." Yvonne cut her off.

"Look Brenda, I don't wanna hear it. Now this is my last time tellin you to get out. Sittin here bleedin all over my seats-n-shit, just go girl."

Brenda stepped out, still clearly shaken up from the double beat-down and loss of blood. She slowly started to stagger away, then suddenly stopped and turned around.

"Yvonne, can you help me with cab fare, 'cause I don't have a way home when I'm done here?" Yvonne paused for a moment, thinkin, *"This bitch got the audacity to ask me for some money. I ain't givin her nothing."*

A few moments later, Yvonne found herself pulling a ten dollar bill from her purse to give to Brenda, but Smoke quickly stopped her while grumbling 'Hell naw ma!' Then he balled up a one-dollar bill and slung it at her aggressively. The bill hit her in the face and fell to the ground, then Yvonne hesitantly pulled off........

Later on that day, Smoke and Scoop sat on Smoke's front porch smokin a blunt and reflecting back on the drama-filled day.

"Ay Scoop, check this out young dawg. I respect yo' gangsta and all, but the way you handled shit today ain't how I get down dawg. I know it was probably a spare of the moment thang for you on the robbery tip to basically add insult to injury, but that petty larceny shit ain't gon get you nowhere. And check this out, I appreciate you steppin up to the plate when that sucka had the drop on me, but what I don't appreciate is you lyin to me about havin heat on you when you got in the car with me and my moms. You know I just got out, and I can't afford to be ridin dirty like that unless I'm in one of my crookmobiles or something stolen that I can crash in a high-speed chase, know what I'm sayin? And dawg, I want you to realize how serious and thick this shit would be right now if it wasn't for Detroit Edison shuttin off half of the store's power to fix some other shit. I didn't know shit was gon jump-off the way it did, but I did peep the Edison truck soon as we pulled up. But we definitely woulda had to grab the surveillance tapes, real-talk. Otherwise, we woulda been on the news by now. Man I ain't tryin to go back to the joint over no chump-ass shit, ya' feel me. I can't see it."

Scoop nodded his head in agreement as he listened attentively and puffed the blunt.

"And like I said before, my ol'girl was in the ride nigga, and I'll be damned if I let her get caught-up on some weak shit like that. She done too much time to go out like that. So what I'm sayin is this, as long as we associate with each other, don't never lie to me again... Hold up, let me rephrase that. Don't never let me catch you in nomore lies again, comprende?"

Scoop didn't appreciate being checked like that, but he had enough respect for Smoke to not challenge him. So he nodded in agreement as Smoke continued.

"Let me put you up on game young dawg. When I was in the joint, the veterans that's been on lock every since you was in diapers use to always say, if a snake bite you once, shame on that snake. But if a snake bites you twice, shame on you. And we talkin rattle snakes youngsta. And being that I already been bit a few times in my life, I'm to the point that I'm leery of anything that rattles... And I thought I heard a little rattlin in yo' game, which is the very reason we havin this discussion, know what I mean fella? But I'm through wit' it. I just want you to be aware of your surroundings so you won't make the same mistakes twice, you dig. Now check this out, on another note, I see its a few lil sucka's around here that's gettin money. And you know it ain't no secret that I'm tryna get mine. So I need you to point out who's who so I can re-employ myself dawg, fa'real."

Scoop displayed a silly facial expression before responding.

"Man, I know two suckas right now that we can get. They keep over three-hundred G's in they spot at all times, and it's a easy lick cause the only heat they keep is a full-length 12 gauge, straight up."

"Is you fa'sho dawg?"

"I'm tellin you Smoke, I put dat on everything."

"A'ight then, we gon go at that change tomorrow, so be ready."

"I'm always ready Smoke."

The following day, Smoke pulled up in front of Scoop's house and sat there for ten minutes while the mixed attractive female finished twisting up the last three cornrows in Scoop's hair. Scoop gave her a soft pat on her butt and replied,

"Thanks boo, I'll holla back later."

She placed her hands on her hips irritably and displayed a sassy pouty-lipped expression which caused Scoop to answer her body language before she could get the words out.

"Yeah yeah I'ma bring back some Ghanja a'ight, damn! Let's bounce dawg."

Smoke smirked and pulled off.

As they rode toward their destination, a million thoughts ran through Smoke's head. He felt odd because this was the first time he ever attempted to pull off a robbery without any of his childhood homies. He also felt odd because Ray Ray and himself would normally do homework on a mark and watch him for months before they would approach the situation. That's how they had such a high success rate at what they did. Now he found himself laxing a lot because in the back of his mind, he always felt that a mark could get got, with or without Ray Ray's approach.

"Oh my God! Please don't hurt me!"

"Shut up bitch!" yelled Smoke as he slapped the big-butt girl to the floor while Scoop searched the rest of the house for occupants.

"I know you got the combination to this safe, so open it up and stop bullshitten."

The high-yellow girl fumbled with the digital buttons on the safe trying to open it in a hurry. She was unsuccessful on her first couple attempts, so she dropped her head and began to cry like a little girl because she knew she would die at any moment if she didn't get her thoughts together and open the safe.

Just as she took a deep breath and tried again, Scoop came in the room.

"Ain't nobody else here dawg."

"Good." answered Smoke. 'Watch this bitch right quick while I run to the bathroom to take a quick shit, my stomach still ain't use to this free-world food yet.'

Scoop laughed before responding.

"A'ight nigga, I got it."

Smoke left the room and Scoop ordered the girl to stand up. When she did, he put the gun under her chin and exclaimed,

"Bitch, do you know the combination or not?"

The frightened girl answered.

"Yeah, I I-."

"Well why in the fuck is it takin' you so long to pop that shit open?"

"Cause I'm sca- scared. I'm soo scared."

Scoop rubbed the gun down the side of her face slowly.

"You scared bitch? Well you got a right to be scared. And that's what you get for fuckin wit' bitch-ass niggas. What's yo name?"

"Christina." mumbled the trembling girl.

"How old are you?"

"Twenty two."

"Oh yeah? My bitch is twenty two too. But her ass ain't as fat as yours."

Scoop lifted the back of her t-shirt up over her butt with the gun, admiring the plumpness and roundness of it, not to mention the way her panties hugged it.

"I love it when a bitch walk around the crib in a t-shirt and panties like this. It keeps this dick hard, know what I mean?" Scoop asked in a sinister tone of voice. Then suddenly displayed anger when he realized she didn't answer him. He grabbed her by the back of her neck and yelled,

"Bitch! I said do you know what I mean?"

"Yeah, Yeah! I know what you mean." answered the girl frantically.

"Let me see if you really know what I mean." Scoop got a firm grip on her panties, then yanked them off with one snatch. He stood behind her, pushed her forward, demanding her to place both of her hands on the wooden table that sat beside the safe. She did as she was told, then Scoop unzipped his pants and pulled out his already erect flesh.

He rubbed it between the lips of her slit and forcefully pushed himself inside her. The girl let out a sorrowful grunt, and Scoop began to hump her like a madd man.

"Damn you got a fat ass. And dis' pussy good too. You like this dick? Huh?"

The girl's hesitation to his question made him instantly cock the 45 and place it to the back of her head as he continued to hump.

"Bitch! Don't let me have to ask you again."

"Yeah, it-it's good," moaned the crying girl. She felt violated and humiliated at the same time while the stranger pleasured himself inside her.

As Smoke entered the room, his mouth dropped open when he saw Scoop's butt cheeks suddenly tighten up and his body go into what seemed to be mild convulsions as he emptied his semen inside her.

He slapped her on her butt and groaned,

"Goddamn baby, I gotta fuck that pussy again someday soon."

Smoke walked over to Scoop with a grimacing expression but didn't say a word.

He made the girl finally open the safe. They took the twenty G's and left........

On the ride home, Smoke contemplated on pulling the car over, pumping two rounds in Scoop's head and leaving him on the side of the road. Scoop violated every rule of the game that Smoke was accustomed too. The amount of money that was supposed to be there was way off. Nothing was in the house like Scoop described it. And on top of that, he takes some pussy and don't even use a rubber.

Smoke thought to himself, *"If he was anything like he use to be before he went to prison, he would've killed Scoop thirty hours ago. But if the prison experience had taught him anything, it was how to be patient with youngsta's."*

He casually looked over at Scoop and calmly asked,

"Man why you violate that girl like that?" Scoop blew out the smoke from the Newport before answering.

"Cause she had a fat ass and I wanted some pussy."

"Well why didn't you wear a rubber, what if she get pregnant or give yo' young dumb-ass a disease?" Scoop smirked a little then answered.

"I don't give a fuck if she get pregnant, I ain't gotta' see dat bitch nomoe. So I ain't gotta pay for no abortion or raise no kids. And if she gave me a disease, she can cancel Christmas 'cause I know where she live. She'a be one less bitch on the set."

Smoke didn't even allow himself to get angry from the senseless, carefree answers. He just made a mental note that the curse on the younger generation is definitely real.

CHAPTER 29

"Boom!" was the sound as the double doors flung open, and the federal agents hurriedly poured into the cozy mansion in the suburban part of Amsterdam. They deployed throughout the house searching for any residents, but found none. The leading agent stopped in front of the fire place and calmly inspected the photos that were on display. He picked up a picture of Ray Ray and Sheila's wedding day, and another picture of Ray Ray, Sheila, and their two little girls. He smirked to himself as he analyzed the photos. The family seemed so harmless. And they probably were, all except Ray Ray.

Special agent E. Burns searched the house thoroughly and found nothing illegal, but he did find evidence of someone leaving in a hurry. Clothes were scattered across the bed in the master bedroom, with more clothes hangin out of a suitcase that had to be left behind. There was a phone number written down on a piece of paper on a night-stand that had urgent written over it. Agents instantly took interests in it. Agent Burns dialed the number, and after four rings, a heavy accented Jamaican man answered.

"Hellow mon, who dis be?" Agent Burns cleared his throat before speaking.

"This is a good friend of Ray Ray's."

"Ah mon, tell him dat everyting's ready for his arrival,

he's all good."

Agents Burns grinned to one of the other agents before responding.

"I'll be sure to tell him."

After hanging up the phone, he smiled at the closest agent and remarked,

"I wish our leads could always be that easy, that clown is headed for Jamaica."

As Ray Ray sat on the 747 airplane, he reflected back to the call he received from the owner of the marijuana shop, telling him about the inquisitive federal agent. He wondered what they actually had on him to make them hunt him five years later when things were going so good in his life. He'd become a successful business man, a husband, and a father. Now he had to just up and leave it all because of something in his past that came back to haunt him. He and Sheila owned five fitness centers, a consulting company, and a seafood restaurant. They were considered some of the most respectable citizens in Amsterdam.

Sheila had went back to school and received her bachelor's degree in business-management, and ended up rubbing shoulders with a few big-shot politicians over there. And although their positions wouldn't carry any serious weight in the U.S, it was still beneficial to her in that particular arena in the world. Sheila made a lot of business investor's rich, and others richer. She was definitely establishing herself gracefully in the corporate world, and was definitely headed for some major things.

Ray Ray squirmed uncomfortably in his airline seat as the thoughts of his sudden departure sunk in deeper. And even though the new situation was a big inconvenience in his life, he always kept in the back of his mind that most of the gangsta's that he knew, never really got away completely. And he would always ask himself, what made him any different. That's why he took certain precautions and was always smart enough to throw a bloodhound off his trail, if only temporarily. He'd called one of his friends in Jamaica and coached him on what to say when the feds called, cause he knew they would call after he set out the bait. He wrote down a Jamiacan pay-phone number on a piece of paper and wrote 'urgent' on it, which automatically made the feds think his eagerness to get away allowed him to make a careless mistake, and it worked like a charm. Now the feds were on their way to Jamaica, and he was on his way back to the U.S, to hopefully find answers, and prayerfully find solutions.

"Ehhhh! Ehhhh! Daddy! Daddy!" Sheila instantly woke up when she heard the cries from her two-year old daughter.

"Ray Ray will you get her." She mumbled sleepishly.

"I got her." answered Ray Ray as he made his way over to her.

"Come on baby, daddy is right here."

Her crying subsided as she was lifted up and cradled by Ray Ray.

"What's wrong wit' daddy's little princess, bad dreams, huh?"

The two year old named Love didn't answer, she just laid in her fathers arms and dozed right back off to sleep. Ray Ray glanced over at his four year old daughter Myonly, and she was still sound asleep as well. His daughters meant the world to him, and he never wanted them exposed to the world he grew up in. But his entire life always seemed to be an uphill battle, and the mountain that he climbed seemed to only get steeper.

****

"Smoke! Baby come get the phone." yelled Ebony.

"A'ight hold up, let me catch this last replay of the game."

Smoke stood there excited as the rookie for San Antonio guarded Kobe and rejected his shot as he executed to the basket.

"Yeah baby!" cheered Smoke.

"That's what I'm talkin 'bout. Don't get me wrong, Kobe's a bad muhfucka, but I'm just an underdawg kinda guy. Hello."

"Whuddup Smoke, dis Scoop."

"Whuddup Scoop. Why you ain't hit me on my celly?"

"Dawg I just dialed the first digits that came to mind cause I needed to holla atchu in a hurry. Anyway check this out, I need you to come swoop me up right now. I got a sweet lick for us, but we gotta do it now cause these niggas is slippin."

"A'ight nigga I'm on my way, and it betta' be some real cheddar involved this time or this is my last time fuckin wit you on that tip. I'll see you in a minute." Click.

The moment Smoke hung up the phone, he headed for the front door. Ebony gave him a detestful look, but he ignored it and headed out the door regardless.

"No! I will not hold, wait! –goddamit!" Yvonne barked as the lady on the receiving end of the phone put her on hold.

"I am so sick of goin' through this dumb shit wit' these people, Lord excuse my French." Yvonne mumbled to herself as she impatiently waited for the EPA representative to click back over to her line.

Eight minutes later...

"Sorry for the wait mam, now would you kindly explain your issue to me again."

Yvonne sighed irritably before responding.

"Listen Ms. I am a significant investor in the Environmental friendly section of your agency, and if my memory serves me correctly, Congress specifically stated in the environmental protection policy, act 5.b220 that under no circumstances will the EPA allow hazardous chemicals of any kind to be instituted into any natural wildlife areas. Particularly in the Northwest region. Now all of a sudden, certain government investors are allowed to run oil pipelines through The Wilderness Tours of America Inco. In Alaska, which happens to be the place where I have a considerable amount of stock and shares in that company. There was no warning of this, and my establishment is in a frenzie."

"Ms. Broxton, I understand your argument, but actually it's implausible because the re-introduction of the policy-act you're speaking of was in fact made public information in timely accordance with our guidelines."

"That's bullshit!" shouted Yvonne. "I was given specific and precise predictions."

"Ms. Broxton, please forgive me if my next statement sounds a bit sarcastic, but not even God can give specific and precise predictions these days. So if you have any more questions pertaining to an unsatisfactory investment, please come down to our office and see us in person-"

"For the hundredth time." blurted Yvonne.

"-As I was saying. You'll be speaking with our department head Mr. Steinbeck. Our office hours are from-"   "I know all that bullshit, and thanks for nothing!"

Click! She slammed the phone down and took a couple valiums to calm her nerves. She flopped her head down on the table and spoke out loud to no one in particular.

"I can't believe this shhhhhhitt! Ray Ray left enough money for me and Smoke to live comfortable for the rest of our lives. Not to mention the money that Smoke already had. We were straight. But I sat my entrepreneurial ass in prison and thought of a million different businesses that I wanted to get into, and jumped straight into'em with no parachute. Now I'm damn near broke. Uhhhh huh huh huuu."

Yvonne started crying as she reflected on her mishap.

"I failed my son, I failed myself, and I failed all the people who believed in me."

Her voice suddenly went lower, and her eyes became heavy as the valiums took effect.

"Oh God, I don't know what to do. I just don't know."

It seemed as if her words were in slow motion as they faded out with her last statement.

"God help me."

Plack!

"I said lay down nigga, and if I gotta tell you again, dat's yo ass."

Scoop demanded and pointed the gun at the man he'd just slapped to the floor. The man squirmed as he laid beside the five other men and held the bloody gash near his temple.

The room was cloudy from the marijuana and cigarette smoke. And it smelled of alcohol and cheap cologne. Smoke took in every detail, and upon further observation, his nose flared and he began to perspire from the instant anger that was forming fast inside him.

He focused on the decks of cards that sat on the wooden table, then on the four to five thousand scattered dollars. Then to the pair of dice that sat on the table, along with the other four pair that they pulled from a few of the dude's pockets. The reality of the situation dawned on him as if it was a two-ton weight. They were in the act of robbing a gambling house, which is equal to robbing a five dolla' crack house according to Smoke. And just as the thought hit him, the rapid shots that came from the direction of the kitchen didn't allow him to entertain them long.

"Aaaah! Uhgg!" yelled Scoop as the bullets spent him and sent him tumbling to the floor. Instinct mixed with a surge of adrenaline made Smoke immediately aim the Calico in the direction of the kitchen and open fire. At that instant, one of the apprehended men on the floor saw the chaos as an opportunity to vacate the premises, so he jumped to his feet and sprinted toward the front door.

Smoke quickly trained the gun in his direction and sprayed him down, then crept toward the kitchen in a cat-like manner. The unseen shooter suddenly peeped around the corner, and Smoke seized the moment.

"Aaaah!" screamed the man as the first bullet caught him in the side of his face, spinning him into full view.

Boh!

"Ugggh."

Cac! Cac! Cac! Cac! "Muthafucka!" groaned Smoke through clutched teeth as the man fell dead. He gripped his bloody shoulder, then ran over to the man and kicked the smokin gun out his hand.

He then ordered the remaining men on the floor to run away as fast as they could, and promised that the first one to look back was a dead man. Scoop was still alive but barely. Smoke knew he couldn't be moved, so he kneeled down and whispered,

"Check it out young dawg, your wounds is too bad for me to move you, and I'm losin blood fast from mine. So I'ma bounce and call some help for you, and when they come, tell'em somebody tried to rob you and shit got ugly. I'll check back with you at a later date, keep breathin youngsta, you gon' be a'ight. I'll holla."

Smoke made it home in ten minutes, and when he got out the car, a sudden pain caused him to swiftly clench his wound. He leaned against the car for a few seconds until the pain subsided, then rushed inside the house.

"Ebonaay!" he yelled the moment he was inside. Ebony came running from the kitchen when she detected the urgency in his voice.

"What is i- Oh my God, baby what happened? Let me call the ambu-."

"Naw Eb, no ambulance, just go get your first-aid kit and get busy. The bullet is right at the exit point, I can feel it at the skin, so it shou- ahh, be easy to get out."

"But baby that's a gunshot wound, and without the proper medical attention, a major infection can set in and-"

"Ebony! You'a goddamn nurse right!-right?"

"Yes."

"Well do what the fuck nurses do and stop bullshitten!"

Ebony immediately went to work on Smoke. And being that she was a nurse, she had a better than average first-aid kit.

It took her about 45 minutes to get the bullet out and stitch him up. Her skills allowed her to thoroughly clean the wound and put a professional dressing on it. The prescription drug Vicodin that she kept for sudden emergencies came in handy for the pain relief, and if the bullet would've been in him four inches deeper, Ebony would not have been able to help him because nurses don't specialize in internal surgery.....

Smoke slept for three days, and when he finally woke up, his head felt like it weighed a ton. His mouth was dry as the Mojave Dessert, and pain traveled from his wounded shoulder throughout his entire arm. Ebony was sitting beside him when he opened his eyes.

"Hey sleepy head." She joked as she immediately pushed another pill in his mouth with a sip of water to wash it down.

"I know how you are feelin Smoke, and what I just gave you is a milder form of what I gave you before. You'll feel better in about fifteen minutes, but now you gotta eat up, so open up."

She forked a portion of the scrambled eggs in his mouth.

"Mmmm! Baby you did yo thang wit' these eggs, keep'em comin, I'm starvin."

She sat there and fed him 'til the eggs, turkey sausage, and cheese grits were gone. After washing it down with Ocean Spray cranberry juice, Smoke lit up a Newport and drifted into thoughts of Scoop. He assumed Scoop died because no police showed up at his door, otherwise, he figured he would've been in custody by now because the youngsta's these days seemed to think snitchin is cool.

Bling Blong, Bling Blong!

The sound of the doorbell shattered his thoughts and put him on defense. He pushed himself up into a more sturdy position, then reached under the covers and came up with a Baretta nine millimeter.

Bling Blong!

"I'm comin! I'm comin!" yelled Ebony as she rushed toward the door.

She peeped through the peephole and saw an attractive bi-racial female. She was slightly puzzled because she didn't know her, so she placed the chain-lock on, then cracked the door.

"May I help you?"

"Yeah, is Smoke here?"

Ebony's temper instantly flared while looking at the attractive young woman asking for her man. She instinctively attempted to say something foul, but quickly decided to stay calm.

"May I ask what you would like to see him about?"

The girl instantly recognized the *"Don't fuck with my man"* expression written on Ebony's face, so she countered.

"Oh no! no! no! it's nothin foul Ms., my name is Precious, and I'm Scoop's fiancé."

Ebony felt a blanket of relief but tried not to make it so obvious. She let Precious in and offered her refreshments, then took her to the bedroom where Smoke was at and they both listened attentively as Precious informed them on Scoop's status.

"Scoop is in the hospital and the doctors said he is gonna live, but he's paralyzed from the waist down and he will never be able to walk again. When I first went to see him, two detectives stopped me at his room door and asked a bunch of questions about his gambling habits. They said Scoop told them somebody tried to rob him and his boys while they were gambling, and that the two dead dude's killed each other. At first they were thinkin' about charging him with both of the bodies, but they didn't because that area was known for things like that. And plus, didn't nobody else ever come forward and say anything different. Scoop's been in and out of consciousness, so I haven't really been able to have a full conversation with him. But the last time he came too, he asked about you, and I told him I would check on you so I came over.'

Smoke entertained mixed emotions as she concluded her story. From one standpoint, he was pissed at Scoop for getting them caught-up in such amateurish work. But from another standpoint, he appreciated Scoop for keepin his mouth closed and stickin to the script. Smoke got out the bed, went to his stash, and gave Precious five-thousand dollars to give Scoop.

"Tell him I said I will catch up with him in a couple months and kick out somethin decent for his pockets, but in the meantime, to just rest and stay focused on gettin well and walkin again, fuck what the doctor said."

CHAPTER 30

One week later.

"Whussup main, how is that shoulder feelin?"

"Much better Gabe, much better."

"Main I'm glad you finally ready to stop playin games and get this real paper, cause I need a real nigga on my team for the level I'm tryna get to, ya dig? So check this out, like I told you before, I got a sweet plug on dem' thangs main. My connect give me a thousand birds at a time, so I'll split the ticket down the middle with you and let you control five-hundred of'em at your convenience, bet?"

"Bet dawg, and if you don't mind me askin, what's the quality layin like?"

"Aw main, you know how them Cubins come wit' it, it's that P-flake baby, dat butter, a'ight?"

"A'ight dawg, let's get paper."

Gabe and Smoke gave daps, then got in their cars and left the riverfront.

As Smoke drove away, he had an eerie feeling because he'd just agreed to go against everything he ever stood for and join forces with the people he once considered his eternal enemies, drug dealers.

His body shivered momentarily at the thought of Ray Ray witnessing this.

"I'm glad dat nigga is still in Spain or whereva' da' fuck

he at, cause I ain't tryna here nuthin. It's a new day, and eatin is eatin."

Smoke turned up the radio and let Scarface 'Man Cry' thump as he concluded his thought.

Two months later.

"Smoke! I'm not gonna tolerate this, I waited too many years for you, and now you wanna put my life in jeopardy playin these silly ass street games. You are just what that prosecutor said you are."

Smoke cut off her words

"I don't rape little girls, I sell drugs!"

Ebony's face tensed up before she responded.

"You are equal to a rapist, because you rape people's mind with that shit you sell them. You rape them of their dignity, their morals, and their self-respect."

Smoke snapped. He ran up to her and viciously slapped her across her face. Then just as quickly, grabbed a handful of her hair, pulling her stinging red face closer to his.

"Let me tell you somethin bitch! You don't know shit about me, and you don't know shit about the streets. And you betta' not ever in yo natural born life compare me to a muthafuckin rapist again, or you'a see a side of me that won't allow yo' bitch-ass to live to tell about it. Now let me hip yo green ass to the difference between a drug dealer and a rapist. A drug dealer gotta be witty, skillful, keen, sharp, clever, and alert. He gotta be able to read muthafuckas as if he was a psychologist, because somebody's always out to do him a disservice in his game. Whether it be his friends, the police, jealous competition, or his bitch. On the other hand, a rapist is nothin but a sick predator who get off on violatin a person's body.

He don't gotta' have no organizing or leadership skills, it's just him and the victim. And he is actually some of those females first sexual experience, now where does that leave a person's morality and dignity? He's the lowest form of human existence, period! Now get the fuck out my face you simple muthafucka! Before I stump a mudhole in yo stupid ass!"

He aggressively shoved her away from him displaying an expression of disgust. She quickly ran to their bedroom and slammed the door, while Smoke jumped in his black SL-500 and skidded out the driveway.

CHAPTER 31

As Ray Ray pulled out the parking lot of the new corn beef shop on Mt.Elliot and Gratiot, his passenger side window was suddenly blitzed with a flurry of knocks. He instantly reached in his pants for his gun, but kept it concealed when he saw the joyful smile on the woman's face.

"Whuddup doe Ray Ray! It's me, Syann."

Ray Ray relaxed a little when her face and name registered. He hit the release-lock button on the door and let her in, then parked.

"Woman you almost got popped just then, runnin' up on me like that."

"I know how you roll Ray, but whut's been up, long time no see, damn."

"Aw ain't nothing special poppin, I'm just out and about gettin a lil grub for me, my wife and kids."

"Whuuud, wife and kids, I hear ya' Mr. family man, go 'head witcha bad self. Anyway, I heard you had moved out the states."

"Yeah I did, but I'm back on business."

Syann quickly formed an 'I'm still down' expression then asked,

"Is it the kind of business that I can help you with?"

Ray Ray paused for a moment before answering.

"Naw, but if so, I'll look you up, a'ight."

"A'ight Ray Ray, I'm here."

"So what you been up to these days Syann, cause from the looks of that expensive jewelry and that expensive-ass cranberry mink, I'd say you doin' pretty good fa' yaself girl."

"Yeah, well I'd say you guessed right. Just call me a high-price hooker, cause I run a underground escort service, in which I get paid to hang out with big-money ballers for however long they request my services. My services include everything from vaginal, oral, anal, and S-n-M pleasures. I developed a prestigious reputation a few years ago when I pussy-whipped one of the big-money ballers in the game. A rumor quickly spread that I was gettin' a ten-thousand dollar weekly allowance from him, so I capitalized off the gossip and made a living off of it. I still do private strip shows too, only now I get top dolla 'cause the stock went up.'

She flashed a bare thigh with her million dollar smile to put the period behind her sentence.

Ray Ray thought to himself, she is still beautiful, and her big deep dimples highlighted her flawless beauty. He also made a mental note that ice-water still ran fluently through her veins. And although she appeared to be harmless to the average Joe, she had the heart of a venomous snake. Ray Ray often asked himself why he never eliminated her after they concluded their grimy business together. Maybe because she always displayed loyalty, and never gave him a reason to react aggressively toward her. And, he always felt that he might need her again, because she was skillful at what she did.

"Ray Ray, you must be Mr. Untouchable."

"What makes you say that?"

"Because everytime I hear about the laws lookin for

you, you seem to just make the situation disappear."

"Be more specific Syann."

"Well, you know, like when the feds came through here a few months ago flashin your picture askin' folks do they know of you or your whereabouts. And they didn't do it 'til they busted that crooked cop you use'ta deal with. But like I said before, all of a sudden I didn't hear nomore about it, it kinda' just went away, and here you are now ridin around like it never happened."

Syann had just answered the million dollar question for Ray Ray. It was now clear to him why they were suddenly lookin for him. And little did she know, he was still being heavily hunted by the feds. And once they'd find out he was back in the states, the hunt would definitely intensify.

The man in the silver 745i tapped his horn lightly, causing them both to look in his direction.

"Ray Ray I gotta go, that's one of my clients, but listen, here's my number. Call me if you ever need me for anything, okay. And I mean Nnn-E-thing." Ray Ray smirked at her advances toward him.

"A'ight girl, I will." Syann suddenly stopped and turned around as she was getting out.

"Ray Ray, have you seen ya boy Smoke since you been back?"

"Naw, did he get out?"

"Yup, he got out alright. Him and a platinum tooth, three fingered muhfucka name Gabe got the city on lock wit' 'dat work."

Ray Ray instantly formed an expression of confusion, not sure if he heard her correctly, then asked through his strained face.

"What did you just say?"

"I said, him and a nigga name Gabe with a three-fingered hand and platinum teeth, got the city on lock wit' 'dat work."

Ray Ray couldn't believe his ears. His thoughts raced in a million different directions. *"Drug dealers!" "What in the hell happened while he was away, and what the hell was Gabe doin' in Detroit".* The honk from the car horn snapped him out of his trance. Syann held up her finger to let her client know she was coming.

"Syann, can you get intouch with Smoke?"

"Baby I can get intouch with who'eva you want me to get intouch with."

"Well check this out, give dawg my number and tell him I said get at me in a hurry. And don't tell nobody else that you saw me, a'ight?"

"Okay Ray baby, your secrets are always safe with me. We'll be intouch."

Ray Ray went straight to the temporary home he bought where Sheila and the kids were, and contemplated on how he would approach the situation. He felt totally betrayed by Smoke and his cousin, and he vowed to straighten the situation out.

"Myonly, you and Love go to bed."

"Aw daddy."

"Aw daddy nothing, its bedtime. I'll be right behind yall to tuck yall in, okay?"

"Okay daddy."

Later on that night after the babies were tucked in and sound asleep, Ray Ray laid wide awake next to Sheila in deep thought.

"Baby, you still up?" asked Sheila unexpectedly.

"Yeah, I guess so." answered Ray Ray dryly. Sheila scooted her body closer to his, so his ear would be leveled with her mouth, then softly spoke.

"Ray Ray, I'm scared."

"Scared? Scared of what baby?"

"Scared of me and the kids losing you forever."

Ray Ray re-adjusted his pillow, then turned toward Sheila to look at her eye to eye in the semi-darkness.

"Baby listen. You don't gotta be scared of nothing. I refuse to let anything happen to us, okay?"

Sheila didn't answer right away, then moments later she mumbled out a reluctant yes.

"Ray Ray I miss our old life. I want the best for our babies, cause this ain't no way for them to grow up. We gotta-"

Ray Ray cut her off.

"Shshhh. Baby I know, trust me, I know. And I'm gonna fix this problem, and we gonna have our old life back with much more."

Sheila re-adjusted herself before responding.

"Ray Ray, just tell me when it's gon' end." She asked softly with tears now streaming down her worried face. Ray Ray leaned toward her and placed a gentle kiss on her lips, then whispered.

"Soon Sheila, I promise. Now go to sleep baby."

CHAPTER 32

Smoke hurriedly made his way over to Gabe through the crowded club known as Club Med.

"Yo playboy, I need to holla atchu on some serious shit like now."

"Goddamn main, don't you see I'm 'bout to be seduced in a minute by these two luvelay thangs right here."

Gabe pointed at the two gorgeous women by his side wearing gator boots for girls, tight body dresses, with swinging gator purses to match.

"Now let me introduce them to you. This chocolate delight right here is Dominique. Her mother is Indian and her father is black, that's why she got straight hair wit a ass like she straight off'a phat azz dot com. And according to her gear 2-night, we know she likes purple."

Both girls instantly burst out giggling, then Gabe pointed at the other one.

"Now this green-eyed mocca princess is Sheena. She's all black as far as nationality and she call herself waitin on some nigga in the joint. She say she ain't did nothing in nineteen months since dude been gone, and dude got a ten-piece to do. So if my calculations serve me correctly, tonight is the night that she breach that agreement, cause tonight is the first night she spent more than five minutes wit a boss playa main, ya dig? Now like I told you a minute ago before I was rudely interrupted, I'm the type of nigga

236

that will respect the game, meaning, I'll except dude's collect calls in the morning, and even shoot'em a little commissary money from time to time. Now how many niggas would do that?"

"Not many!" they blurted simultaneously.

"Well that's what I'm sayin baby, I'm in a class by myself. And I like to be recognized as a service provider, so whenever you allow me to provide my services, I promise, you won't be disappointed."

The girls started gigglin again.

"Dawg, I hate to break up yo lil party, but like I said five minutes ago, I need to holla at you outside."

"Humph." Gabe sighed as he became frustrated with Smoke's annoyance.

"Will you ladies excuse me?"

"Yeah." They both answered.

"Order whateva' yall want, and I'll be right back. And as for you green eyes, hold on to this for me baby. And when I come back, I'ma tell you the whole story of how I had to fly all the way to Miami to get it because it was out of stock everywhere else at the time a'ight?"

She smiled as he placed the black Dobb with the burgundy band on her head. The band around the hat matched his gators, and the two ladies groaned, 'ump humph umph, he is wearin that suit girl.' As him and Smoke walked outside.

"Now whussup main, whut's so important that you gotta' drag me away from some pussy?"

"Man fuck them bitches."

"That's what I plan to do main."

"Listen dawg, I talked to Ray Ray today."

Gabe's eyes lit up.

"Oh yeah main, whussup wit' dat nigga, is he a'ight?"

"Yeah, he a'ight, he back in town and he wanna have a meeting slash reunion with us."

"Aw main that's good, I wanna see my cousin anyway."

"Yeah me too, but check this out Gabe, he found out that we major playa's in the game. And you already know how he feel about that."

"Whut! You mean to tell me he still trippin' 'bout that?

Well fuck 'dat shit main, he gon' have to get over it, 'cause I'ma get my grind on regardless. So set up the meeting and let's see where his head at. I hope and pray couz ain't still trippin doe, fo'real."

Three days later.

Ray Ray pulled up at the riverfront in a low-key dodge intrepid. He parked next to the black SL-500, then got out.

"Whussup couz!" Spoke Gabe as he walked up to Ray Ray lockin hands with him, giving a shoulder to shoulder G embrace... Smoke followed suit, then smiled at Ray Ray.

"Boy you look like you gained a few pounds." said Smoke playfully.

"I'm tellin you main, look at his face." They all laughed momentarily.

"Smoke you look like you gained a few pounds too." added Ray Ray.

"Yeah dawg, but mine mostly muscle. It came from eatin' all them potatoes and pumpin that iron when I was on lock. I was bigger than this, but I fucked fifteen pounds of it off soon as I got out."

Ray Ray glanced at Gabe's odd hand and noticed the missing fingers.

"What happened to yo' hand man?"

"Aw main, them evil ass dogs finally turned on me. And it hurt me to my heart to put'em to rest. But they made sho' they gave me somethin' to remember'em by."

He held up his mangled hand.

"Yup, everytime I finger-fuck some pussy wit' this hand, I think about'em."

They all erupted in laughter. Then a few seconds later when the laughter subsided, Smoke displayed a serious expression, then stated,

"So what's on ya mind playa?"

Ray Ray returned the same serious expression before responding.

"If you askin me what I think about yall niggas bein' in the game, you already know I ain't feelin that shit."

Gabe interrupted

"So whut you want a nigga to do main, just stop eatin cause you back on the scene?"

"Somethin like that." said Ray Ray sarcastically.

'Well I'ma tell you like this couz, I ain't 'bout to stop eatin for nobody, so I suggest you get over yo' lil phobia main. 'cause it's a new day, and if we don't do it, somebody else will."

Smoke followed Gabe's approach.

"Yeah Ray Ray, we ain't kids nomore dawg. And as long as we are responsible for what we do, our business shouldn't concern you. It ain't like we askin you to be down wit us, we just askin you to live yours and let us live ours. The way we choose too." added Gabe matter of factly.

Ray Ray stared at them both for thirty long seconds without sayin a word, then suddenly blurted.

"A'ight dawg, do what yall do, just respect what come wit' it."

He jumped in his ride and skidded off.

"Aw shit main, I can't believe this nigga really trippin. Fuck dat nigga main, cousin or not. If he wanna take it to that level, we gon' take it to that level."

Gabe turned toward Smoke to stress his feelings belligerently so Smoke wouldn't miss his point.

"Main, you know what we gotta' do, right?"

Smoke returned a puzzled expression before responding.

"Naw man, tell me."

"Main we gotta bury his ass." Smoke snapped.

"Nigga is you crazy! Ain't no way in the fuck we gon' do that. I know he is trippin and all, but he still my dawg, so get that silly shit out yo' head."

"Main I'm tellin you, if we don't kill him, he gon' kill us. And I ain't about to sit back and let nobody! Get dat off on me. And since you actin' like you ain't wit' it main, you can get some too nigga!"

Smoke instantly jumped in Gabe's face.

"Whut you sayin dawg? You threatenin me, Huh?"

Gabe pushed Smoke out his face and grimaced,

"Take it how you need to take it main, fuck you and fuck Ray Ray."

"Fuck you nigga!" Smoke quickly snapped back.

"Fuck you main!"

"Fuck you nigga!"

"Fuck you!"

"Fuck you!"

"Fuck this,"

Gabe swiftly pulled out a Sig Suaer 45 and fired two wild shots that barely missed the charging Smoke. Smoke managed to get a grip on Gabe before he could get another shot off and commenced to slangin' him around viciously, trying to make him release the gun. Suddenly throughout the tussle, Smoke lost his footing and slid to the ground in one direction, while Gabe and the free gun slid in another.

Smoke went for the gun, then quickly re-thought it and headed toward his car when he realized Gabe would beat him to it.

Pocka! Pocka! Pocka! Pocka! Pocka! Pocka! Gabe riddled the black Benz as Smoke skidded off wildly into the night.

As Smoke drove down the freeway, he thought about everything that had taken place in his life. He wondered how things had come to this point, and was too afraid to imagine where things would eventually go. It was tonight that he finally realized Ray Ray's mental condition was actually a sickness that was too far gone. He didn't know the proper medical term for it, but he knew it stemmed from being severely traumatized as a child. And although Ray Ray was definitely outta' control, Smoke couldn't see himself killing him. He looked at Ray Ray as if he was his blood brother. Now Gabe had officially declared war on them, and Smoke knew if he moved carelessly, Gabe would kill him with ease.

CHAPTER 33

Two weeks later.

As Ray Ray, Sheila, and the kids pulled up to their house from the grocery store, the first thing they noticed was the swarm of federal agents in front and throughout their house. Ray Ray glanced at the scene, then quickly blurted,

"Yall want some ice-cream?"

"Yeah daddy, we want some ice-cream, let's get some ice-cream daddy."

Sheila glared at him, trying to conceal her worried expression. But at the same time, letting him know she was aware of his tactic in diverting his daughters attention to avoid them from witnessing the manhunters invade their space.

Ray Ray casually drove by the ambush, thankful to not be a part of it, and even more thankful that his babies never noticed it.

After getting the girls some ice cream and checking into a motel, his mind drifted back to the earlier events. He wondered how the feds found out he was not only back in the states, but back in Detroit so soon. No-one knew about that house, and he didn't recall telling anybody about it. He laid on the bed and racked his brain trying to figure it out until something suddenly dawned on him.

"Ay Sheila, cumeer!"

Sheila walked in the room two minutes later.

"Yeah bae, what's up?"

Ray Ray sat up before answering.

"Check this out baby, remember that night I pulled up at the crib about a week ago, and you was talkin to that dude who delivered that pizza?"

"Yeah, why what's up?" Sheila asked curiously.

"Well I noticed that you talked to dude a little longer than you normally would, who was he?"

"Oh, that was just a lil nerdy dude that I knew when I was goin' to Michigan State. And I was surprised he still remembered me after all this time."

"*Bingo*," said Ray Ray silently in his mind. He didn't need to hear anymore, because as far as he was concerned, that's how the feds knew. 'Cause not only were they flashing his mug shot around, they were flashing hers too.

"I'll be damned." He groaned as he flopped down backwards on the bed....

"Sheena, spin around for me one mo' time baby. Damn I like the way that mink look on you girl, it match them pretty green eyes of yours."

Gabe turned towards the sales woman and replied,

"Yeah, we will definitely take it."

"Oh thank you baby." said Sheena joyfully as Gabe paid cash for the lime green three-quarter length mink. They left the Northland mall with almost a dozen shopping bags. Gabe de-activated the alarm on the pearl white 745Li beemer, as the man who spotted him from afar came approaching at a hurried pace. Finally he made it to the car before Gabe could pull off.

"Yo G, is that you?" he asked excitedly.

Gabe gripped his nine as he searched his memory for the man… The man assisted by snatching off his baseball hat to reveal more of his face.

"It's me man, Ty from Inglewood."

"Aw main whussup witcha baby, damn it's a small world. Whutchu doin in these parts main?"

"I got people that live here, so I came through to kick it for awhile. But check this out G, is you still doin yo thang wit' the dogs? Cause I'm tryna get me a thoroughbred fa'real."

"Naw main, I let that game go years ago, but if you still want some of the same quality action that I was comin wit,' here's my man Larry outta Miami hookup. Get at'em main, he a straight-up guy so don't play no games wit'em."

"A'ight G, good lookin playa, I'll holla."

As soon as the man walked away from the car, Gabe pulled out his already erect pole and ordered Sheena to wrap her pretty lips around it. Sheena didn't hesitate, she removed the piece of gum she was chewing, then slipped her mouth over the head.

She slowly inched her way down, working her jaws methodically as Gabe tilted his head back and enjoyed the session. Sheena sucked until she felt him cumin, then pulled back and started jackin him off.

"Naw naw baby." said Gabe as he quickly pushed her head back down on him.

"All the money I spent today tells me you gon' swallow every drop of this good protein."

He held her head steady as he released his load, and she didn't let a drop get away and licked him clean afterwards.

As they pulled off, Gabe reminded her,

"Don't forget to drop that money order in the mailbox for yo man in prison sugar."

"I won't." She answered reluctantly.

Fifteen minutes later when they pulled into the KFC drive-thru, the grey corolla that followed them all the way from the mall pulled up too... Gabe handed the cashier a hundred dollar bill to pay for the 24 piece bucket of chicken that he'd just ordered, then looked over the food as he waited for his change.

Suddenly, as he reached toward the woman for his change, he caught a glimpse of Smoke running toward him through his rearview mirror. Gabe immediately hit the gas. Boca! Boca! Boca! Boca!

Boca! Boca!- Boca! Boca!... The back window shattered as the car spent out in traffic barely missing oncoming cars.

"Damn!" cursed Smoke when he realized he missed....

Smoke dialed Ray Ray's number to warn him of Gabe's intentions, but there was no answer, so he dialed his mother's number afterwards. Yvonne picked up on the third ring.

"Hello."

"Hey ma, whussup."

"Ain't nothin up baby, I'm just still beefin wit' them damn corporate assholes about my money."

"Mama let that shit go, we back on top again so we don't need that chump-change noway."

"Yeah I hear ya' Smoke, I just don't like let'em get over on me."

"And I hear you too ma but we straight. Anyway, is everything a'ight over there, did you get use to the house yet?"

"Yup, I'm right at home."

"That's good to here. Where is Ebony?"

"She's in the living room crocheting a blanket to keep herself calm cause she's still pissed at you for makin her take two weeks off work because of this lil situation you got into."

"Well fuck how she feel, she'a get over it. It's just too dangerous for her to go to work right now, so she can just keep poutin and crocheting til I straighten this shit out. Tell her I send my love and I'll be home in a few days okay, holla."

CHAPTER 34

Tiny snowflakes fell lightly as Ray Ray and his family pulled up to the motel they were staying in. Ray Ray carried Love as she slept, while Myonly and Sheila followed closely behind. A scraggily-lookin homeless man unexpectedly approached them begging for money.

"Excuse me Miss, can yall spare some pocket change, please."

Sheila stopped and gave the man three dollars, then caught back up with Ray Ray.

"Why you give that clown yo' money? He looks like he livin better than us. And on top of that, he'a youngsta. Which means he can get off his lazy ass and make somethin happen."

"You are so grouchy at times Mr." Sheila remarked jokingly as they went to their room.

Just as Ray Ray got to the door, his cell-phone rung.

"Hello."

"Ray Ray whuddup dawg, this Smoke, where you at dawg?"

"Why, what you want guy?" asked Ray Ray in a firm tone.

"Man I just wanted to tell you that yo' cousin Gabe is trippin. Dat nigga tried to kill me 'cause I didn't agree with killin you, so I tried to kill him and fucked around and missed. Now he tryin to kill me and you, so watch yo'self man cause this shit don' got thick. And one last thing before I go, nomatter how hard you call yo'self trippin, I still love you like a brother and always will. Give Sheila and the kids my blessings, holla."

After hanging up with Smoke, Ray Ray somewhat felt defeated because he could tell that Smoke knew he would never hurt him unless he truly had too. Smoke was the only one of his childhood friends still alive, and although he hated Smoke's new chosen profession, he couldn't see himself killing Smoke or Gabe.

He'd just never associate with them again. But things were definitely outta' control according to the information Smoke just relayed to him. He hadn't been in the hood in five years, and things were accurately still the same. *"Amsterdam probably made me soft,"* he silently conveyed to himself. And if so, survival in the hood would be that much more difficult. *"Oh well, fuck it, its whateva. Come what may."*

They went inside and Ray Ray took Love straight to the room and put her in bed. He gave her a gentle kiss on her forehead, then turned to walk out. But before he made it out the room, he heard a sudden scream from Sheila. He ran out the room and there Gabe was, standing with a gun in his hand.

"Whut up sucka." He spat with a grimacing expression.

Ray Ray instantly darted towards him at full speed, but the quick shot that Gabe released slowed him down. Ray Ray still managed to get a grip on Gabe, but the nine millimeter bullet that tore through his right bicep didn't allow him to do what he could've otherwise done. Sheila quickly instructed Myonly to go in the bedroom with her sister and lock the door as Ray Ray tussled with Gabe throughout the small space.

They knocked over lamps and slammed into walls vigorously during their fight. Suddenly, Ray Ray fortunately swiped the gun from Gabe's hand, knocking it close to Sheila. Gabe's mangled hand didn't permit him the benefit of gripping objects as firmly as he once did, so it was a disadvantage to him whenever somebody penetrated his space. Sheila was hysterical, and became more frantic when she saw the blood leaking from Ray Ray's arm.

Ray Ray was fighting hard, but was clearly losing the fight. Gabe took advantage of the wound and punched it several times.

"Sheila! Get the gun!" Ray Ray moaned as he continued to accept punishment from Gabe.

Sheila looked down at the gun and couldn't bring herself to pick it up. She hated guns, and was sick of all the drama that came with guns.

"Get da Goddamn gun Sheila! Uggh."

"Shut up nigga!" Plack!

"Uggh" Ray Ray moaned continuously as Gabe sat on top of him delivering blow after blow to his face.

"Yo bitch is scared just like you nigga, now shut up and take this ass-whoopin like a man main."

Sheila finally picked up the gun and nervously aimed it at Gabe.

"Don't hit him nomore Gabe, I mean it!"

Plack!

"Whutchu say bitch, don't what? Plack! Hit-plack! Him-plack! No-plack! Moe-plack!"

Sheila cried excessively as she watched the blood pour from Ray Ray's mouth. He was tired and out of breath as he struggled to get out a sentence.

"For God's sake Sheila, shoot this muthafucka."

"Main that bitch ain't got the heart to shoot, and when I get through beatin' yo ass, I'ma fuck the shit outta her then beat her ass too."

Boh! Boh! Boh! Boh! "You muthafucka!" Boh! Boh! Boh! Boh! "die!" Boh! "just-" Boh! Boh! "die!" Boh! Boh! Boh! Boh! Boh! Boh!- The chamber-ejector slapped back and white smoke seeped from the barrel of the gun as Gabe laid sprawled out in a puddle of blood, deceased with his eyes still open. Ray Ray slowly made his way over to Sheila as she stood there in shock with the gun still aimed and pressure on the trigger. He gently placed his hands upon hers and guided it toward the floor until the gun was lowered, then carefully peeled it from her firm grip. He suddenly stumbled, almost falling to the floor, but maintained his balance using Sheila's body for leverage. Sheila snapped out of her trance and focused on helping Ray Ray stay on his feet. His Sean John shirt and pants were soaked with blood, and more blood constantly oozed out rapidly from his wound.

"Ray Ray, stay on your feet baby. We 'bout to get you some help...Ray Ray!" Sheila yelled frantically as his eyes rolled to the back of his head.

"Ray Ray don't do this to me! Help me Goddamit! Stay up!" Ray Ray suddenly fell limp in her arms, and her limited strength only allowed her to lower him to the floor.

"Oh my God! No! Nooo!"

Three days later.

The heart monitor remained stable as Ray Ray slowly opened his eyes. His vision was hazy, he had a bad taste in his mouth, and the room smelled saturated with peroxide.

He was slightly confused, and he figured he was delusional when he saw the white square board with words seemingly inches away from his face. His focus was unclear, and it seemed like the voices that he heard consisted of a woman and two males. He instantly questioned his state of mind. *"Am I dead and Satan wants me to read my final instructions from a white board? Who the fuck is talkin? What the fuck is goin on?"*

He continued to search his mind for answers, then after a few minutes had passed, his focus became clearer and his hearing was improved.

He suddenly heard the female voice say,

"It may be another week before this individual comes out of his coma." Then he unexpectedly saw the white board with words again. He strained and finally re-focused his vision, and it was then that he realized it was actually a white piece of paper instead of a white board. He carefully read the words, "Close your eyes until I give you the okay to re-open them. Two detectives are here."

Ray Ray immediately obeyed the message and closed his eyes again to hopefully evade the detectives. He ended up falling asleep while waiting for a signal to let him know the coast was clear......

Ten hours later, he woke up again, only this time he didn't immediately open his eyes. He listened carefully for any sounds in the room, but there was none. He laid there and contemplated on how much longer he would play possum, then ten minutes later decided he would take a look to see whatever awaited him to see.

He slowly cracked his eyelids, trying to peep out the scene carefully, but couldn't really see anything with his eyelids so low. So he decided to open them a little wider. And just as they began to elevate,

"Open yo eyes nigga, I see you blinkin."

Ray Ray opened his eyes and there Smoke was, standing over him with a smile.

"Damn dawg, what took you so long to wake back up? I started to wake yo' ass up but my lady said it wasn't good to wake a gunshot victim up after losin the amount of blood you lost, so I had to wait. Anyway, let me run down what's what,-"

"Where is Sheila and my kids at dawg?" asked Ray Ray out of the blue.

Smoke suddenly displayed a disturbed expression, then just as quickly he uttered,

"They straight man, now let me put you up on how I'ma get you outta here."

"Where da' fuck they at Smoke!" Ray Ray snapped.

Smoke displayed that same annoyed expression, then cleared his throat before responding.

"Dawg, I'ma be straight up with you. The feds got Sheila, and yo' babies with my moms."

"Whut!" yelled Ray Ray, then he immediately started snatching the IV plugs from his body, enraged by what he'd just heard.

"Whoa! Whoa! Whoa!" said Smoke as he restricted Ray Ray from further movement. Ebony walked in just in time to witness the commotion.

"What is goin' on?" She asked in a voice filled with concern.

"Calm down Ray Ray, I know how you feel dawg, but you gotta' chill and listen to what's what or you gon' be locked up too, now chill dawg. Ebony, come over here and unhook this shit off him properly."

Ebony walked over and began to unhook the respiratory and intravenous plugs while Smoke explained the details of the recent events.

"Dawg, the night that Gabe got killed, Sheila called me cryin like crazy. She told me you had passed out and she thought you was dead,-"

"How she get yo' number?" Ray Ray interrupted.

"Man you know how female's is, they see damn near everything we don't want'em to see, and hear shit God can't even hear. Anyway, she gave me the location and I made it there in five minutes 'cause I was already in the area. The first thing I did was carry you to the car, then waited for Sheila and the kids to come out. But just as they came out the room, the damn police pulled up. The first muthafucka that pointed in Sheila's direction was a young bum-ass nigga who asked me for some pocket change soon as I pulled up. Sheila peeped him pointing at her so she told the babies to walk over to the snack machine and stay there until uncle Smoke comes over. Sheila didn't wanna put no heat on my car, that's why she didn't walk over to it. Anyway, the police walked over to her and asked her did she just come out that room. She flat out told them no, but that lil bum-ass nigga nodded his head "yes" when one of the four officers asked him again. They went in the room and saw that nigga Gabe stretched, then put Sheila in cuffs and put her in the back seat. They never noticed the babies, so I casually strolled over to the machine and got them and bounced. Now check this out, they know it was a male with her because that punk-ass bum told'em it was. But Sheila denied it to the fullest, and after they realized she was wanted by the feds for questioning, shit got deeper. And you already know they tryin to get her to tell'em where you at. Now whether she will or won't, I don't know. All I know is that she didn't so far, 'cause they woulda' had yo' ass chained to this bed when you woke up. Ya feel me? But check this out, it's two cops outside the door waitin' for you to wake up so they can talk to you about that bullet wound. It's routine for cops to do a small investigation whenever a gunshot victim is admitted, so it's really no big deal. But bein' the kinda' nigga that would rather be safe than sorry, I put together a plan for you to walk up out this muhfucka without being questioned. So hold tight for a minute while I make this quick phone call."

Smoke talked on the phone for a brief three minutes then hung up.

"Okay, put these clothes on playa, it'll be showtime in a few minutes."

Ebony helped Ray Ray put the shirt on over his arm sling, then Smoke helped him slip on the pants.

"Ay playa, check this out. You ain't gon' be gettin all this special attention from my woman." Smoke said jokingly.

"She already nursed you back to health while you was sweet dreamin, now the rest of that sweetness is goin' to me, you got it playa?"

Ray Ray tried to appreciate Smoke's humor by cracking a half-hearted smile, but the truth of the matter was, his mind was focused on nothin' but Sheila.

Five minutes after he was dressed, he suddenly heard a loud commotion outside the door.

"Bitch! Whatchu doin' comin to see my man? You know I don't play dat shit!" yelled the short dark-skinned girl with extensions and a big butt. She constantly pointed her finger at the light-skinned chick as she voiced her threats. Four other girls stood behind the aggressive girl ready for whatever. Suddenly a punch was thrown by one of the bystanders who felt there was too much talkin and not enough action. All the girls followed suit and began swinging wildly at the same time. Smoke cracked the door open and saw the two detectives trying to assist the hospital staff in breaking up the fight that erupted next door.

"Okay playa, that's our que, let's ride." He gave Ebony a peck on the lips, then slipped right pass the detectives with Ray Ray.

The first thing Ray Ray did was go see his babies. And they made the reunion more painful with the constant question of, "When is mommy gonna get here?" All Ray Ray could do was assure them that mommy would be home soon. Although he didn't know how soon, but he knew that he'd try everything in his power to get her back... Anything else was uncivilized....

CHAPTER 35

During the following weeks, the feds had been turning the city of Detroit upside down looking for Ray Ray. Sheila was officially charged for the murder of Gabe, and despite all the millions of dollars that Ray Ray offered attorney's to get Sheila some justice, it had no positive effect on her case. Money couldn't seem to penetrate a state legislation that had a federal influence in it. And the feds were pissed at Sheila's lack of co'operation, so they agreed to assist the state prosecutor on imposing the harshest murder sentence they could. They wanted her to regret withholding information, for a long long time.

****

The Barcardi 151 chased with a blunt took immediate effect on Ray Ray's system. He sat in one of his new safe-spots in the west 7 mile area and racked his brain trying to come up with ways to get his wife back. His children were still in the care of Yvonne, so he knew they were in good hands. He wanted to keep them away from him until things calmed down a bit, cause during times like these, anything was liable to happen. He took another sip of his drink, then pulled a few times from the blunt before putting it in the ashtray to burn out.

He began to clean the new weapons that Smoke got him as Phil Collins 80's hit, 'In the air Tonight' crept through the speakers in low volume. The melodic drum patterns and intensifying lyrics quickly became entangled in his emotions, and took on the role as theme music for his complicated predicament. Thoughts of his past and present encounters flashed through his mind as the song grew more intense. *"I can feel it, comin in the air tonight, oh lord."* He wiped the rag over the commando with more force as the song took effect. *"And I've been waiting for this moment, for all my life, oh Lord."* He placed bullets in the banana clip as if he was on the opposite side of a sandbag perimeter re-loading his weapon for another round with the enemy. He quickly grabbed the Mac-90 and performed the same duty. The song continuously pecked at his emotions, and just as it was about to end, his cell-phone rung. He didn't answer it right away, he gave himself a few seconds to get his thoughts in check, then picked up on the fourth ring.

"Hello."

"Ray Ray whussup baby, this Syann."

"Oh, whuddup Syann, what's poppin?"

"I need to talk to you about some real shit, so can I come over there?"

Ray Ray paused before answering.

"Naw girl, I don't think that would be a good idea. You know the heat is on blast right now, and I can't trust givin' you this address."

"Well meet me at a motel or somethin' because this is regarding your wife's freedom."

At the mention of Sheila's freedom, he quickly became more attentive and eager at the same time.

"Is you trippin' girl?" He asked skeptically.

"Dead serious Ray Ray."

"A'ight, I'll tell you what, meet me downtown at the

Renaissance in 30 minutes. And I'll come Scoop you from there, a'ight?"

"Okay Ray Ray, 30 minutes, holla."

Sheila laid in the cold overcrowded cell in the county and shed tears as she thought about her husband and children. She knew it was a possibility that she may never get to see Ray Ray or her babies again, and just the mere thought of it had her to the point of a nervous breakdown. She was a strong woman, and the physical side of incarceration was something she could deal with, but the mental side had started to wear on her fast......

Ray Ray and Syann sat in his safe-house and discussed her urgent message. She frowned after removing the glass of Bacardi from her lips, then proceeded to explain herself.

"Check this out Ray Ray, like I was sayin before, I can help you get Sheila back."

Ray Ray sat on the couch with a blank stare that said,

"Spit it out you dumb-ass broad" but instead, it came out in a calm tone. "How Syann, how can you get Sheila back?"

She took another swallow of the liquor before responding.

"I know a C/O who works at the county she's at, and he's a straight up dude. I can set it up to where he will walk her straight outta' there with no flack."

"How much?" asked Ray Ray, knowing a price came with everything.

"Twenty G's. ten for him, ten for me."

Ray Ray mashed the Newport in the ashtray before replying,

"A'ight, let's go for it. I'ma give you half upfront, and the other half when I see Sheila. Now how soon can you make this happen?"

"Two weeks from today." said Syann matter of factly.

"A'ight, that's straight, cause it will give me enough time to make some necessary arrangements."

"Arrangements as in gettin ghost huh?" Syann suggested.

"Yeah, something like that."

Syann got up and turned on the stereo. She pulled her Maxwell CD out of her purse and put it in the system.

"This the kinda' joint you ain't gotta' flip to every other joint, you can just let it ride." She said as she slipped out of her tangerine knee-high Stilleto boots. She reached back and pulled the small clip that held her hair in a pony-tail, allowing her jumbo curls to fall freely to the center of her back. Her French vanilla skin and slightly slanted eyes gave her the look of an Asian and black decent, but both of her parents were black. Her complexion and figure came from her mother. She had a small waist, with more than a mouthful of tits, and hips and ass that gave Jaylo a run for her money. Ray Ray couldn't help but notice how gorgeous she really was. When she smiled, her deep dimples almost instantly stole the hearts of her audience.

"I'll be right back." She said as she walked to the bathroom.

Ray Ray watched her ass jiggle and bounce with grace 'til she was out of his line of sight.

"It's time for that bitch to go." He said to himself as he noticed his semi-erection.

Syann came from the bathroom moments later, wearing nothin' but a tangerine bikini top, tangerine thongs, with her tangerine knee-high boots back on. She stood wide-legged with her hands on her hips with a slight grin.

"How do I look?" she asked with her hypnotic display of womanhood illuminating in the room. Ray Ray didn't bother to answer, He just casually looked off in another direction.

Syann strutted over and sat down on the couch beside him. She leaned toward his ear and gently clamped his earlobe between her thick pink lips. He pulled away and sighed,

"Cut it out girl."

Syann slid down in front of him between his legs, letting her knees rest in the thick carpet, then gently turned his face towards hers so they'd have eye contact.

"Ray Ray listen, it's like this baby. I feel that it would be immoral for a woman like myself, to not experience a man like you at least once during her lifetime. I know your heart is with your wife, and I can respect that. But I'm askin you to respect the fact that I'm not askin for forever, just one night, ya feel me Ray Ray?"

Her side of the debate was concluded in her most seductive tone of voice. And the only thing Ray Ray could think about was how he'd never been unfaithful to Sheila. Now it seemed that Sheila was the reason he was almost forced to enter the world of infidelity. He knew if he turned Syann down, there was a great possibility that she would renege on helping him get Sheila back. So with that thought in mind, he let the games begin. He reached in his pants and pulled out his semi-erect flesh, then gestured for her to do what she pleased with it. She slid her manicured fingers around it, and stroked it 'til it stood at full attention. She licked and teased it with her tongue to enhance the anticipation, then moments later, the warmth of her mouth caused his stomach to shift as if he was doing a Hawaiian belly dance. She bobbed her head up and down, taking more of him inside as she went on.

Ray Ray tilted his head back and closed his eyes, trying to force himself not to think about Sheila. She sucked on him for fifteen minutes before realizing he probably wouldn't cum like that, so she slid her thongs off, put a condom on him, and climbed on his pole facing the opposite direction. She gyrated her hips and rocked her body on him in tune with the slow Maxwell jam that graced the speakers. Ray Ray felt himself getting harder as he watched her fat ass shake like jelly and her curly hair bounce with her every move. He reached around and cuffed her soft titties with his good arm, toying with her nipples with his thumb. "SSS, Uhh"

She let out a soft moan as confirmation that she liked what he was doing. She found herself hot from his touch, and she worked her hips harder and harder in an effort to reach her climax. Ray Ray was well endowed, and the sex that he was giving was pleasing. But she could tell by the tenseness of his body that he was holding back, so she unexpectedly ceased all movement and climbed off of his still hard pole. She turned around facing him, then grabbed the base of his flesh and placed it back inside her. She slid down slowly 'til their pubic hairs were entwined, then made direct eye contact with him and spoke in a soft, but authoritative tone of voice.

"Ray Ray, I want you to know that I'm aware of you holdin' back on me. But I'm not mad because I understand baby. I know where your head is at right now, and I'd probably be the same way if I had a commitment as strong as your's and Sheila's."

Syann slowly grinded her hips in a circular motion as she continued to talk to Ray Ray.

"And speakin of Sheila, I envy her in a sense, because she got the kind of man that I've been dreamin about since my ado-sss,uhh-lescent years." Syann picked up her rhythm and looked at Ray Ray with her eyelids hung low.

She leaned her head down and used his shoulders as leverage to work her hips in a concentrated effort, then gazed back into his eyes to finish her statement.

"Ray Ray, I'm sure that a man of your character knows that understanding is the best thing in the world, SSS-mm, so I want you to please understand that if you scratch my back completely, I'll completely scratch yours."

She raised up and lowered herself, feeling the full length of his large dick before making her final statement.

"I know you can do it Ray Ray, especially if you really love Sheila."

Ray Ray suddenly felt his heart skip a beat and his anger shoot through the roof from the indirect threat Syann had just made. He knew she had the upper hand and that he couldn't afford to make a premature move now, especially with Sheila's freedom on the line. So he bit his tongue and restrained himself from slappin' the taste out her mouth like he badly wanted to, and came to the conclusion that playtime was over. He suddenly gripped her by the back of her head and pulled her lips to his. He kissed her hard and unmercifully, then gripped her waist and assisted her in her up and downward motion on his dick.

He slid his body about a half an inch down under her so he could penetrate every crevice of her pussy. Then he suddenly began to thrust upward with stiff, brute strokes.

"Ooh shit Ray Ray! That's what I'm talkin 'bout, Oh

fuck!"

Syann dropped her head and closed her eyes as she enjoyed the way he parted the outer lips of her kitty and gave her a full feeling in her belly. He rammed himself upward 'til she was crouched over with her face buried in his shoulder.

When he finally slowed down, he pulled himself out, then reached underneath her and inserted two fingers inside her. He worked his fingers momentarily for lubrication purposes, then put his pipe back inside her. He reached around and rubbed his wet fingers along the crease of her ass until he reached her hole, then pushed one inside until it disappeared. "Unnng." Syann moaned and received him eagerly as he finger-fucked her ass and thrusted inside her at the same time.

Ray Ray continued to work his finger in a circular motion as Syann moaned from the pleasure and formed several different fuck-faces. Ray Ray suddenly stood up, with her legs still wrapped around his waist, and his dick still buried inside her. He laid her on the floor and placed her legs over his shoulders. Then after making sure she was pinned down the way he liked it, he worked his hips vigorously.

"Unnggh! Unnggh!" Syann grunted and moaned as he pushed himself inside her with steady, deep strokes. He sexed her the way he did Sheila whenever he had somethin heavy on his mind. And he told himself that this was just the kind of fuck she needed. But unlike Sheila, she couldn't contract her pussy muscles enough to tame his dick when it was too much to bare, so she would have to withstand the punishment until he'd bust a nut.

Sweat dripped from Ray Ray and mixed with hers as he buried his face in her shoulder and humped like a savage.

His balls slapped against her ass and she screamed as if she was being tortured. But through it all, Ray Ray could tell that she wouldn't want it any other way, it was the nature of the bitch in her.

"Unnnnn! Shit! You makin me cum Ray Ray! Unnnggh! Yessss! Uhuh! SS-Uhu! Uhu! Ah, Ah, Oh God! Aaaaaaggh!" Her body shook violently as the hot cum leaped from her pussy. When it was finally over, she breathed a sigh of satisfaction and her body stilled. She opened her eyes and softly whispered, "I've decided to stay the entire night, is that alright with you?"

Syann was more than happy with the session, and she promised to go straight to the correctional officer in the morning to discuss the plan

Ray Ray spent the following two weeks making arrangements for the family to leave the country for good this time. He felt that the world was big enough for them to get lost forever, and he was determined to find out just how lost they could get.

****

The day had finally come for the plan to take form, and he paced the floor back and forth as he anxiously waited for the phone-call from Syann. He checked his watch for the umpteenth time to be sure he was on point.

"Damn, where this bitch at." He mumbled to himself as his patience grew thinner.

After waiting 30 minutes past the agreed time for the phone call, he grabbed his green Pelle and rushed out the door. He dialed Syann's cell and house number repeatedly, but still received no answer, which is when he went ahead and drove straight to the rendezvous point in hopes of them already being there. When he arrived, he cut off the headlights and killed the engine as he pulled behind the busy super-market. Then lit up a Newport and reluctantly played the waiting game all over again.

After putting out the twelfth cigarette, he angrily crunk the car back up and sped off fast. He drove straight to Syann's house and bammed on her door like the police do when they mean open the door now! He waited two minutes for someone to answer, then instinctively delivered two hard kicks, sending the door flying open from the force of the second kick. He carefully searched the house but no one was there. As his search continued, his worst fears were suddenly confirmed. All of her clothes, shoes, and most of her furniture was gone, right along with her.

Ray Ray pulled out his desert eagle and fired at the only picture left of her lying on satin sheets in a seductive pose. He demolished the picture and the coffee table that it sat on with all ten shots, then left.

When he finally made it back to his spot, he racked his brain trying to figure out why she would play him the way she did. He doubted if it was the money, cause under normal circumstances, ten G's was nothing to a woman like her. He couldn't put his finger on it, but all he knew was, she was a snake. And he vowed to kill her or have her killed whenever he found her whereabouts. Ray Ray found himself drinkin his second bottle of Bacardi. He kept drinkin and listening to Tupac's *'So Many Tears'* over and over. Just the thought of never seeing Sheila again sent his mind in a state of turmoil. It felt the same as when he lost his parents. His world felt empty. He suddenly slammed the almost empty bottle into the wall, then sunk into a deep state of depression.

CHAPTER 36

"Snzzzzzz, Snzzzzz,"

Syann raised her head up from the coffee table after snorting the two lines of cocaine. She sat in the motel room alone and thought about the latest turn of events. The world was sometimes awkward, and some people subconsciously found pleasure in conquering others. Syann was definitely one of those people. She would always step up to any challenge that her male counterpart would set forth, with no holds barred. She was the girl in high school who would walk around lookin' real pretty with a body language that said,

I know yall want this pussy, but yall ain't never getting this pussy."

And most of the dude's that were intimidated by her ways would never get the pussy... On the other hand, as soon as a confident thugged-out dude came on the scene, all he had to say was,

"I don't wanna' fuck you, cause I know you can't handle this dick." And he would end up sexin her the same night. She lived for challenges, and she always wanted to play at the top. She was fascinated with Ray Ray, because she never saw him compromise his character for nobody. She was sure he had sex with other women, but it never spilled in the streets who they were. In her eyes, he was the challenge of all challenges. And conquering him

would put her on a pedestal that separated the Divas from the Boss bitches. And that's just what she considered herself, 'A Boss Bitch.'

There was no room in her life for a weak man, and she knew that by having this fetish for such an emotional game, she was playin with fire at all times.

When she was just a little girl, her mother would say,

"No woman on the face of the earth can top what Eve did to Adam."

And Syann would always reply,

"Someday I'ma be better than Eve." And she's been strivin every since. She could've done Ray Ray a lot worse, but she didn't because she actually admired him. And even though she took it light on him, if fate allowed her more playtime, she would play again in a heartbeat, even though she knew he'd kill her on sight........

****

When Smoke walked in Ray Ray's spot, the first thing he noticed was Ray Ray passed out on the floor with several liquor bottles scattered throughout the house.

"Ray Ray! Get up dawg. What da' hell wrong with you man, get up."

Smoke shook him out of his deep sleep and helped him to his feet.

"Goddam Ray Ray, you smell like Sporty use to smell back in the day. And speakin' of Sporty, did you hear about him and his wife gettin' killed last week?"

Ray Ray didn't answer verbally, he raised his head up slowly and answered with his eyes, which said no.

Smoke continued.

"Yeah dawg, the word is, some Arabs paid a lil youngsta to put da' work in on them because Sporty's business was crankin harder than they shit. But don't even trip it, cause I had one of my fiend buddy's to go burn a few of they spots down and put a few slugs in they ass too, know whut I'm sayin? So that should fix them bastards. Anyway, back to you, whussup with you goin' out like a damn wino?"

Ray Ray didn't answer right away, he was mentally drained from the Syann situation. And now with the news of Sporty, his mental condition seemed to only get worse.

"Man you gotta' pull yo'self together for the sake of yo' kids, cause they need you more than ever now. And besides, don't forget you still a wanted man. We can't let da' hood take us under homie, we gotta bounce back and realize it's a deeper meaning behind the reason we still standin, know what I mean? We can still win dawg, fo'real."

Ray Ray looked at Smoke with exhausted eyes and balked.

"Man, I don't think I can ever win without Sheila by my side, I'm cursed man."

Smoke stepped a little closer to Ray Ray to make better eye contact before responding.

"Well let me ask you this dawg, can you win with Sheila in ya' heart? Because that's where she's been from jump, so the only thing left to do is face the reality of her being a casualty of a man-made war."

Ray Ray spoke up irritably.

"Dawg, don't start gettin' all philosophical on me, hittin me with them prison metaphors-n-shit. 'Cause all I know is I want my woman back nigga, flat out."

"I hear whatchu sayin Ray Ray, but don't start shittin on the things I learned in prison. 'Cause I learned some real shit when I was there. And speakin' of real shit, I read a book about a cat from Argentina named Che'Guevera. He was a freedom fighter who believed in fighting oppression through armed revolution. And the book opened my eyes to a lot of different things that jump off throughout our hoods and in our country. And even though it was based on South America, it still applies to us. It's simply like this, most of the war games that's bein' played is designed to basically benefit the muthafucka's that hold the most power, you dig. So you gotta understand that we ain't shit but live-stock to the top dawgs. And from time to time, they will even give you a cruel demonstration by checkmatin' yo' ass with a pawn. And to a chess player, how cruel is that?"

Ray Ray exhaled a deep breath as if he was exhausted from the conversation, then stated,

"Look at the big drug dealer suddenly get all self-righteous-n-shit. Since when did you join the mosque, nigga?"

"It ain't even about the mosque Ray Ray, it's about you layin up here actin like yous'a muhfuckin saint. And that you deserve the white picket fence with the brady bunch family status. When in all actuality, the shit that you was puttin' down in the streets don't warrant that kinda' ending. Nigga you thought you was a solution to a problem, but you was just a problem on top of a problem. And you don't seem to be gettin what I'm tryna drill in yo' big ass head. 'Cause you sittin here bein' real stubborn my G. You gotta realize that with or without Sheila, you still got off easy so far. So you betta' stop sittin here drownin in self-pity and recognize it. Now if you start slippin and let the feds catch you because of that rattin ass pig, that's where you fuck up at. And that's when you can say life's been a bitch, cause yo' babies gotta grow up without both of they parents. And that post-traumatic stress shit gon' get the priviledge of entertaining two fresh young victims. Now think about that bro." Tsssshhh!

The sound of the shattering glass suddenly caused Ray Ray and Smoke to jump to attention in panick mode.

"Whut da' fuck was tha- Ray Ray run!"

They both instantly darted toward the back door upon realizing a concussion grenade had been shot through the window.

Boom!!

The grenade ignited in the living room just as they made it to the kitchen.When they reached the back door, they stopped abruptly when they saw federal agents scrambling throughout the backyard. They bitched when they realized the house was completely surrounded, but Ray Ray had another plan in mind.

The primary reason he'd purchased that house was because of the adjoining yard with the house next door. He grabbed the commando from under the couch, while Smoke grabbed the AK-47draco.

"Come on dawg, we goin' out this way," yelled Ray Ray as they went toward the bathroom window. Smoke quickly understood why Ray Ray chose that route when he found himself landing in the neighbor's backyard after the short drop from the window. They ran in a low crouch with weapons gripped tight, then leaped a few fences and ducked behind a brothel of neatly trimmed bushes to try to determine how much distance they had on the law. After kneeling for a few seconds, they took off again because they could still hear the sound of walkie-talkies and verbal code exchanges close by.

They leaped a few more gates, then suddenly, two

German Warlock Doberman Pinchers came charging at them with sinister growls and trembling sharp teeth. Ray Ray quickly kneeled on one knee and let off two rapid shots, dropping them both within inches of impact, then took off running again. The agents aborted their current positions and went straight toward the shots.

The series of backyards ended, forcing Ray Ray and Smoke to walk down open streets. They knew they couldn't last long like this, so they agreed to jack the first car in the vicinity. And just as the thought was entertained, a black female turned the corner in a gray Honda Accord coming in their direction. They both ran toward the car simultaneously with guns trained on the driver. The scared girl came to a sudden stop, releasing both hands from the steering wheel.

"Please don't shoot!" she squawked over the classical Jay-Z Reasonable Doubt cd.

"Get out baby!" demanded Ray Ray.

The girl climbed out with no hesitation, but just as they were about to climb in, two agents showed up on foot.

"Freeze!" They yelled as they ran toward the car.

Boca! Boca! Boca! Boca! Boca! Boca!

Clow! Clow! Clow! Clow! Clow!

Ray Ray and Smoke immediately started blastin in their direction.

The agents ran for cover, and by the time they were able to return fire, the Honda was already out of range.

"Damn that was close dawg," confessed Smoke as he drove the Honda toward his house.

He glanced over at Ray Ray and bust out laughin when he noticed he didn't have on any shoes.

"What da' fuck so funny nigga?"

"You nigga, sittin there wit' them muddy ass socks on

and a wife beater. It's like old times baby!"

Ray Ray couldn't help but to join in on the laughter, cause he realized his appearance did look humorous. They finally made it to the house, and Myonly and Love were ecstatic to see their daddy. When Ray Ray held them in his arms, the realization of Smoke's lecture hit him, and he knew it was time to get outta dodge before he lost everything. The first thing he did was put a twenty thousand dollar contract on Syann. He wanted her head on a platter if he could get it like that. He figured she decided to get rid of him altogether and told the feds where he was at. And even if she wasn't the one who did it, he still wanted her punished as if she did.

Ray Ray accepted the fact that Sheila was gone, so he tied up all of his loose ends and said his goodbye's to Smoke and his family. Smoke vowed to get out the game after he flipped the last shipment, but little did he know it was too late because Gabe had already put the feds on him before Sheila killed him. And the feds had placed a tracking device on his Benz until they felt they had enough evidence to engage.

When they finally decided to arrest him, he just happened to be at Ray Ray's that day. So Syann actually wasn't the one who put the feds on Ray Ray's hideout afterall.

Scoop finally got out the hospital, and even though he was paralyzed from the waist down, he still sold drugs until a desperate fiend killed him one night for the six rocks he had left.

Smoke moved his family to the west coast. 'Cause despite his being wanted by the law, Ebony still married him and they still remain together.

Yvonne finally made all of her investments work for her, and became a wealthy woman. She is currently dating an ex gang member turned activist in the fight on gang-warfare and civil rights issues.

Brazil became home for Ray Ray, Myonly, and Love. And they adjusted to their new environment comfortably.

Two years later....

As Sheila finished her laundry, she placed her folded clothes neatly in her locker, then said her nightly prayers and got in bed. A few moments after she finally adjusted herself to a comfortable position, the sudden bright beam from a flashlight burned her eyes, as the clucking sound from the C/O's black boots came to a halt in front of her cell.

She irritably waited for the officer to move the light, but it stayed trained on her. She angrily threw her pillow over her face to give her eyes some relief, then attempted to fall asleep.

The officer pulled off his keys and opened the cell door. He walked over to her and forcefully snatched the pillow from her face. Sheila was use to the constant harassment from different C/O's, but she wasn't takin' no mess tonight.

Her cellmate was sound asleep, and the evidence was the sound of her snoring like a man. Sheila quickly jumped to her feet to confront the rude C/O, then suddenly, her facial expression changed into pure shock. She covered her mouth as the steady flow of tears streamed down her face.

"Oh my God! How did you-"

"Sshhhhhh, all that matters is I'm here, now let's go. Myonly and Love really miss you. They're waitin. And here, fire this up when we get to the car, it's that good purple, straight outta Amsterdam"....

****

Growin up in the hood is equivalent to being on the front line of any major war. The body count is staggering, and negative circumstances only create predicaments that are more hopeless than the one's that already exist. Economic uncertainty seems to overshadow prosperity. And at the end of the day, survival of the fittest is the last topic...

In the case of this crime story and so many others, I guess it's like the old sayin goes.

"You can take the boy out the hood, but you can't take the hood out the boy."

"Now tell me, how Hood is that?"

ABOUT THE AUTHOR:

D-Mack was raised by his grandmother on the eastside of Detroit Michigan. He is personally in tune with most of the harsh realities that jump from the pages of his urban crime novels, and is certified as being True to the Game by those who played in his circle.

D-Mack is an avid reader, and was inspired to pursue a writing career from authors such as, Iceberg Slim, Sister Souljah, and Charles Avery Harris. He is currently hard at work creating new material, and has a real passion for the literary world. He say's that he is most at peace whenever he's writing stories, sharing his craft with those who enjoy genuine creativity.

ACKNOWLEDGEMENTS

First and foremost I wanna thank the creator for allowing me to tap into my creative-energy and give the world the real from a real-life perspective. I definitely gotta thank all of my day-one people for the tons of support that yall gave me from the very beginning of this journey. Yall are the realist. R.I.P to all my homies and family-members that moved on to the other-side. As well as the many that died at the extremity of legislative abuse. Rest in power. I wanna thank my family and friends for the good times as well as the bad. Adversity is the building-block for resilient leadership. And to the youth, as well as the adults that write me letters from the penal-systems all across America, I thank yall for your recognition and appreciation of my gift to articulate my stories with expressive-naturalism. I accredit this skill to growin' up in a house-hold where my grandmother's raw-advice better prepared me for the challenges that inevitably propelled me pass the toxic clouds of energy that I found myself engulfed in, way too many times. And to my head-strong wife, partner in entrepreneurship. And partner in life, Shermane C Mack, I love you baby. And even though we clashed from time to time on this road to success, I thank you for remaining loyal and patient through all of my misfortunes. Especially when you bonded me out of the county without judgement because you knew I was innocent all along. But that's another story that I'll have to interpret for yall in another book. But I will say this, that incident left me extremely sucka-phobic. And reminded me of how fucked up police brutality is. So be careful who you ride with, 'cause it just might be a sucka. Whussup to my brother Suge on lock. Keep ya' spirit up bro, I pray that you will make it back to this side of the game soon. And despite all, remain optimistic nomatter what, love you dawg. I gotta say whassup to my fam Tav and Cork for keepin' my circle authentic, and doin' hella' good things for the community in a self-relient space, salute. Whuddup doe Shawn Ware, Black, Dutch, thanks for all the support my guys. Whuddup doe uncle Terry. Let's take boxing for the youngsta's to a whole nother level. Salute. Whuddup to my guy Otto, 039 4-life. Tell Ike we finally here... Antoine, whuddup lil bro. Don't give vegas too much hell. Whassup to my guy Voll Greene who I'm extremely proud of for droppin' his debut novel 'Dead Man Standing' Let's get it fam. Yall can grab that off amazon at any time too. And make sure yall support brother Willie D's youtube channel, along with brother Phil's advisory show on youtube as well. Blue Blood Sports tv, salute. And we can't forget about my guy Papaduck who also loves his people and wanna see growth in the hood. Whuddup doe Daminya, keep the faith my friend. Rip Karen. Salute to Dr. Boyce Watkins, who got some intellect for yall as well entitled IBM.com, a-k-a Intelligent Boss Moves.com. As well as his website entitled Blaggenuf.com It definitely can't hurt to learn how to be a boss. That's the path I find myself on these days, self-reliance homies. And at this very moment, I'm my own Boss, and the feeling is like no other... To all the entertainers who are takin' a pledge for criminal justice reform, and doin' righteous work for the better-ment of humanity, your sacrifice is greatly appreciated and I salute you whole-heartedly. I'm gonna conclude this by sayin' stay prayerful and know that every breath you take is equivalent to opportunity. I've been blessed to be involved in a conversation with some prospective individuals about taking this trilogy to another level. So I truly look forward to that possibility. In the meantime, yall make sure yall check-out the follow-up novels to this trilogy. And once again, I thank you humbly for all of your support. My gratitude is etched in stone... Hood Driven part 1, 2, and 3 is Available on Amazon. In paperback and Kendall. Once again, to all my day-one-people who I mentioned in the acknowledgements of my first printed edition, this continued focused-work is for yall. I love yall wholeheartedly... More to come soon. Holla atcha boy.

Hood Driven 2 "Last Breed of Gangsta's"

Hood Driven 3 "Loyalty Ain't Loyal Enough"

Hood Driven 4 "Every Betrayal Begins With Trust"